a September

Cold Fire

a September Weekes novel

Cold Fire

Peter R. Ellis

Elsewhen Press

Cold Fire
First published in Great Britain by Elsewhen Press, 2017
An imprint of Alnpete Limited

Elsewhen Press, PO Box 757, Dartford, Kent DA2 7TQ
www.elsewhen.co.uk

British Library Cataloguing in Publication Data.
A catalogue record for this book is available from the British Library.

ISBN 978-1-911409-06-9 Print edition
ISBN 978-1-911409-16-8 eBook edition

Printed and bound by CPI Group (UK) Ltd, Croydon, CR0 4YY

This book is a work of fiction. All names, characters, organisations, places, and
events are either a product of the author's fertile imagination or are used
fictitiously. Any resemblance to actual events, places, institutions, creatures
(mythical, semi-mythical, or extinct) or people (living or dead) is purely
coincidental.

Alison – my greatest support and love

Contents

Pronunciation guide

Many of the names and places that September encounters in Wales are in Welsh. General guidelines on pronunciation are as follows.

'll' does not occur in English, in the glossary it is written as 'LL'. The sound is made by partly opening the mouth, pressing the tongue against the roof of the mouth and blowing gently.

'dd', written as 'TH' in the glossary, is the hard th sound in 'this' and 'that' but not as in 'path'.

'a' is always as in 'cat' and not as in 'ape'.

'e' is always as in 'pet'.

'f' is the v in 'van' while 'ff' is the f in 'fan'.

'c' is always the hard 'k' sound in 'kid'.

'ch' is similar to ck and pronounced as in the Scottish 'loch' and not the English 'church'.

'g' is always hard as in 'God' and not as in 'german'.

'o' is like in 'on' but not 'open'.

'i' and 'u' are pronounced 'ee'.

'r's should be rolled.

'rh' should have an 'huh' sound after the r.

'si' is between the sh in 'shone' and the j of 'john'.

'w' is oo as in 'cool'.

'y' is sometimes the u sound in 'run', sometimes the i in 'bin' and occasionally the ee sound in 'been'.

'yw' is pronounced 'you'.

'ae', 'ai', 'au' and 'ei' are all pronounced 'eye'.

'eu' is the oy in 'boy'.

Glossary

Word	[Pronunciation] Meaning
Abaty Maesycymer	[a-bat-ee mice-u-cum-er] Abbey on the field at the meeting of two rivers
Adamant	[adam-ant] diamond
Aeddon Gruffudd	[aye-TH-on gree-fee-TH]
Caermarden	[keye-er-mar-den] Carmarthen
cawl	[ka-ool] broth
Cemegwr	[Kem-egg-oo-er] Creators, chemists
Cludydd o Maengolauseren	[clee-deeTH o mine-gol-eye-ser-en] bearer of the starstone
Cwm Dreigiau	[koom dry-gee-eye] Valley of the Dragons
cydymaith	[ku-dee-my-th] companion
Cyfaill	[kuv-eye-LL] friend
Emerallt	[em-er-aLLt] emerald
Eryri	[er-ur-ee] The mountain, Snowdon
Ffunel	[feen-el] a herb, Fennel
Gwawrwen	[Goo-a-oor-oo-en]
Gwlad	[goo-lard] The Land. The place September visited in her previous adventure.
Gwlyb Hoedl Gwyrthiol	[Goo-lib hoy-dil goo-er-thee-ol] the elixir or liquid of eternal life that allows September to exist in all times and places.
Llanllionio	[LLan-LLee-on-ee-o] village near Abaty Maesycymer
Llanymthefry	[LLan-um-thev-ree] Llandovery
Llelluched	[LLe-LLee-ked] valley in mid-Wales
Llyn y Fan Fach	[Llin er van vark] a lake in west Wales
Llysiau'r Hudol	[LLiss-ee-eye-er heed-ol] a herb, Vervain

Word	[Pronunciation] Meaning
Machynlleth	[Mak-un-LLeth] small town in mid-Wales
Meilyr	[My-lir]
Myddfai	[muTH- veye] village in Carmarthenshire
Rhiwallon	[rhew-aLL-on]
Rhuddem	[rh-ee-THem] ruby
symudiad	[see-mud-ee-ad] removal, a means of transportation
Trefycymer	[trev-u-cum-er] town at the meeting of two rivers
Twm Bach Watcyn	[toom bark oo-at-kin] little Tom Watkin
Ymadaelwch	[uma-die-look] be gone!
Ysgall Bendigaid	[us-gaLL ben-dee-guide] a herb, Blessed Thistle

Dramatis Personae

In the order that they appear or are mentioned

Name	Notes
Aeddon Gruffudd	14 years, apprentice
Ezekiel Soulbury	Master of Abaty Maesycymer, alchemist.
putti	cherub-like characters with bodies of infant boys and white feathered wings
Meilyr	middle-aged man, dyemaker and tanner of Llanllionio
Twm Bach Watcyn	moneylender in Trefycymer
Gwawrwen	late 30s, woman, herbalist
Adamant	a male unicorn
Emerallt	a female unicorn
Rhuddem	a female unicorn
September Weekes	16 year old schoolgirl
Cyfaill	a Brain
John Henshaw	gentleman, a Brain
Edward Tyson	gentleman, Fellow of the Royal Society
Robert Hooke	gentleman, Fellow of the Royal Society
Sir Thomas Maslyn	gentleman, Fellow of the Royal Society
George Wheler	gentleman, Fellow of the Royal Society
Sir Robert Boyle	gentleman, Fellow of the Royal Society
Ambrose Godfrey	assistant to Robert Boyle
Obsidian	a female dragon
Gabbro	a male dragon
Basalt	a male dragon
Rev. James Jones	Vicar of Myddfai

Name	Notes
David Jones	son of Rev. James Jones
Rhiwallon	son of the Lady of the Lake
The Lady of the Lake	
Mrs Gruffudd	Aeddon's mother
Mr Gruffudd	Aeddon's father
Mother	Mrs Weekes

Chapter 1

I am given a task by my Master

"Boy! Boy! Where are you? I have need of you!" My Master's voice came to me from below. He was in the crypt where he performed his manipulations. I was in the kitchen, searching through the sorry remains of our larder for something my Master would find acceptable for his table. There remained just a few parsnips, some herbs and a piece of mutton that the flies had settled on. My Master rarely troubled himself about the source of his food but relied on me to set it before him, unless of course he was too deeply involved in his work to think of food at all. How we would obtain new food supplies, I knew not.

I answered his call immediately as I did not wish to feel a stroke of the birch rod that he kept to punish my many misdemeanours, real or imagined. I hastened down the stone steps into the dimly illuminated crypt of the old abbey. The pale March sun slanted through the small windows at the top of the vaulted walls revealing a space cluttered with urns, jars, chests, furnaces and shelves filled with the Master's precious glass apparatus and other contrivances. The floor, which I had swept only the previous evening, was already covered in detritus from the Master's experimentation as well as the droppings of the mice and doves that he kept for testing his nostrums.

My Master, Ezekiel Soulbury, was sitting at his table which was covered in papers, vellum rolls and books but he held in his hand a letter, which I presumed to be that which he had received with great excitement earlier in the day. It had been sent by his cousin from the city of London and such epistles invariably stirred my Master into some kind of activity, although usually of the 'grumbling and muttered oaths variety'.

"Ah, there you are boy," he said at the sound of my feet on

the flagstones, "stoke the furnaces. We have much work to do. Stir the putti and set them tasks. Where are those mischievous cherubs? Come on, come on, don't be idle. I need heat."

This torrent of words poured out of my Master as he shook his head and beard of long grey hair. He waved his hand bearing the letter which stirred the dust floating in the air. It seemed that the letter had brought news of something that had inspired him to a new venture. I wondered what my part would be in it and how much more pain and suffering would be inflicted on me. My search for edible food was inevitably to be set aside as the Master embarked on this new enthusiasm.

I was unsure whether to follow the Master's first instruction and collect wood for the furnace or his second which was to find his other assistants, the putti. They at least could take some of the effort from the first task if they could be so persuaded, but where were they?

"Yes, milord," I replied, "I will set to immediately."

"That you must, while I assemble the necessary apparatus." The Master got up from his stool, momentarily catching his foot in the torn and threadbare robe which he wore over his rough woollen garb. Once he had had fine clothes of silk and satin but these had been scorched by fire, burned by acids or sold to raise funds for his endeavours.

The putti were obviously not down here in the cellar so I returned to the ground floor, whistling and calling for them. They had not come into the kitchen while I had left it nor were they in the cold dark hall. I climbed the wooden stairs to the upper floor and entered the Master's little used but grand bedroom. There they were, dancing in the sunlight that shone through the unshuttered, glazed window. Three small, naked, plump boys with feathered wings fluttering a few hands-widths above the floor, circling and weaving as if engaged in some galliard or other.

"Quickly. Come with me," I said, "The Master has tasks for you and me."

The putti stopped at the sound of my voice and hovered while looking at me with their heads cocked from side to side as if searching for further explanation in my face. They did not answer me but twittered to each other in their bird-like language then swept past me. I followed them back onto the landing and down the stairs and steps into the crypt. Without any further word from me they each brought kindling and firewood, one stick at a time, from the wood-store at the dark end of the space to the biggest of the furnaces and threw it into the firebox. I assembled the fuel to make a fire then went to my Master's bench to find his flint and striking iron. He was examining his pair of large, round-bottomed, glass flasks, evidently deciding which to use, while muttering in Latin and Arabic. He saw me pick up the fire-making tools.

"Ah, hurry, lad. Make the fire as hot as you can."

I struck a spark and ignited the kindling. Soon the flames were licking at the larger logs and some heat emerged from the furnace. The putti fluttered around, taking a close interest in what the Master was doing as well as dancing in the flickering flames of the furnace. It would be some time before the heat was great enough to perform whatever miracle of alchemy that my Master was determined upon.

The Master busied himself with collecting various other items of glass and stoneware.

"What is our purpose?" I had the temerity to ask.

"Ah, you seek the news the letter brought to me," Ezekiel replied. He was often secretive but used me as vessel to which to speak of his endeavours and the source of his inspirations. "Cousin Thomas reports on things he has learned at the gatherings of the society of noble philosophers and in particular the work of Mr. Boyle. He tells of a marvellous new substance which will no doubt assist our searches."

"What is it?" I asked, curiosity overcoming my rumbling stomach.

"The secrets of Cold Fire," the Master said, a grin spreading across his bewhiskered face.

"Cold Fire," I said, "what's that?"

"Indeed, what is it indeed? We shall seek it following the clues my cousin has gleaned. But, my lad, imagine. The Phosphorus, a substance that glows with a bright, white light yet gives out no warmth and is not consumed. What miraculous properties such a substance must have."

It did indeed sound a remarkable material.

"Where did Mr Boyle discover such a wonder?"

"Ah, my boy, that is the strangeness of my cousin's report." Ezekiel picked up again the letter from the table and peered at it through his spectacles. "He tells of an adept, one Hennig Brandt from the Germanic states, who obtained the substance. My cousin reports that Mr Boyle has discerned the source of Master Brandt's material. If my reading of my cousin's execrable hand is correct we must obtain a goodly quantity of urine."

"You want to collect piss?" I said, foreseeing that this would be my task, one that I was not looking forward to.

"Yes, my boy. And in quantities more than you or I can provide."

Around us the putti flapped their wings and screeched their high-pitched laughter.

Chapter 2

I set out to collect what
my Master needs

I trudged along the muddy track from the abbey bearing an old milkmaid's yoke on my shoulders, a pail hanging from each side. My Master had determined that this was the best means of collecting the quantity of urine that he desired. The pails were yet empty but I was not looking forward to my return journey. I had in my pocket a couple of pennies which my Master had given me as payment for the urine. Though a waste product of human activity, the liquid nevertheless has value to some so I hoped that the Master had given me sufficient. At least he had not foisted some of his alchemical gold on me. The pennies were true silver.

I could see my destination, the village of Llanllionio on the other side of the river, but I first had to walk the few hundred paces to the wooden bridge that would take me across. I plodded the same journey whenever provisions were required, although anything more than the simplest and most abundant fare had to be obtained from the town a mile in the opposite direction.

I was pleased to find that the waters weren't hammering at the bridge with as much force as a few days before. I crossed and climbed above the floodplain to the village. 'Village' may seem a grand term for a single street of poor hovels, some constructed from blocks of slate and others from such timbers that could be found. I passed the home I had shared with my mother and father, now fallen into disrepair but still with signs that someone had re-inhabited it. The small stone church with its squat square tower stood on a hillock set a little apart from the village. I walked on up the rough stony street flushed clean by the recent rain. A few faces peered out of doorways and heads nodded when they recognised me but their owners offered no conversation.

At the top end of the village I came to a somewhat larger, though hardly grand, building. It was in fact in a number of parts, a solidly constructed stone dwelling and timber framed barns and workplaces. I called a greeting and from one of the sheds came an answer. A moment later the owner of the voice emerged. He was just a finger or two taller than me, his dark hair and beard flecked with grey and his features grizzled. He stooped slightly and was clothed in a woollen smock with a leather apron. To my young eyes, he looked old but was probably not beyond forty years of age. What he lacked in height he made up for in girth. His arms and legs were twice the width of mine, as was his stomach.

"Aeddon! It is a pleasure to see you." He spoke in Welsh as all the locals did, my Master being the exception in being from the English-speaking class.

"You too, Meilyr," I replied, lowering the yoke from my shoulder and laying the empty buckets on the cobbled yard.

Meilyr watched me. "What brings you here bearing such a load?"

"My Master has need of urine and I thought you may have some spare."

There was a guffaw of laughter. "What is the old fool up to now that he has need for such an obnoxious material?"

"He has news from his cousin in London of a discovery that he wishes to emulate."

"London, eh. Those 'philosophers' that you have spoken of before, lad. Well that fool, Ezekiel Soulbury, has yet to reveal himself as their equal in ingenuity."

"My Master works hard at his studies," I said, though why I should be standing up for my Master I wasn't sure.

Meilyr examined me. "The least he could do is feed you, boy. You look as though you have hardly eaten for days." This was in fact true. "Come inside and let's get something inside you before I see to old Ezekiel's requirements."

He led me into the house. The interior was dark and sparsely furnished, but there was a table bearing bread and cheese.

"Help yourself, lad. Eat." He gestured for me to sit. I sat on a stool next to the large oak table and tore a handful of bread from the loaf. Meilyr went to the dresser set against the wall. He picked up a huge jug and poured liquid into a leather tankard.

"There, get that ale inside you," he said placing the tankard beside me. I mumbled thanks through a mouthful of crumbly cheese and moist bread.

Meilyr watched me for a few moments. "How is it with you really, Aeddon? Does that old wizard care for you as he promised?"

I cleared my mouth. "He is an alchemist, Meilyr, not a wizard. He does not deal in spells but in the great mysteries of our world. And yes, though he may be forgetful and careless of his own well-being he provides me with a place to rest and books to study."

Meilyr frowned. "You cannot eat books, lad. He promised to look after you and educate you, as he was bound, being somewhat responsible for your parents' demise."

The events that occurred some eight years ago, when I was a child of six, have a dreamlike quality for me. I recall the attack by the dragon and my father and mother dying but not the part played by Ezekiel Soulbury, Master of Abaty Maesycymer and adept in the ancient arts. However, I have been told many times, by others as well as Meilyr, that it was my Master's experiments that drew the dragon to Llanllionio on that fateful day. Since then his continued residence at the abbey has been the cause of some disquiet amongst the people of the area and the reason why it is me alone that is sent on such errands as today's.

"I am content," I said simply. Indeed, despite the multitude of tasks that my Master imposed on me and his threats of beatings, infrequently carried out, I was intrigued by his explorations and studied those books and scrolls that he permitted me with great interest.

"Does he still have those strange creatures in his power?" Meilyr asked.

"The putti? Yes. They still inhabit the abbey and answer to his wishes." I didn't add – 'some of the time'.

Meilyr shook his head, "Ungodly beings, soulless. I am sure he will regret conjuring them into existence."

The putti had been my companions throughout my time as

Ezekiel's apprentice. Annoying, unbiddable, incomprehensible, they were, but wicked? I did not think so. Their antics often amused me and diverted my Master's attention from my own activities.

At last my stomach was full and I sat back from the table.

"Thank you, Meilyr. I am satisfied."

"Good," he said, "I will let you have some more to take back with you, for yourself and the old fool. Having sent you on the errand for urine I presume he has not also thought to stock his larder." I grinned and thanked Meilyr for his generosity. I took the pennies from my purse and gave them to him.

"He gave me these to pay for the urine," I said. "Are they sufficient?"

"Enough. Come with me."

We went back across the yard to the wooden sheds. I picked up the two buckets.

"I'm not preparing dyes at the present, Aeddon, but the folk still keep me supplied with their piss," he said, "While it has many uses I currently have more than a sufficiency." He indicated a few barrels placed in a dark corner of the shed. I put down the buckets and held my arm to my face because the smell was quite overpowering. It wasn't just the stink of the stale piss but the odour from the tanning vats where hides were soaking.

Meilyr was as much a master of substances as Ezekiel Soulbury except that he devoted his talents to the preparation of hides and fleeces. He used all sorts of concoctions to clean and preserve and colour the materials. He picked up my buckets, went to the barrels and dipped them in, filling them to the brim with the noxious liquid.

I followed him as he carried the two buckets back into the yard. I put the yoke over my shoulders and he hung the buckets from the chains.

"Wait. Your supplies," he said and hurried back into the house. I stood with the weight on my shoulders not looking forward to my journey home. Meilyr returned in a few minutes with a bulging cloth bag on a cord. He looped the cord around my neck so that the bag hung down at my front.

"There you go, lad. Take care you do not stumble."

Soiling myself with my load was not something I wanted to contemplate. "Thank you, Meilyr," I said. I felt sadness at leaving his presence.

"Visit again soon. You know you are always welcome here even if your Master is not."

I smiled and began to walk away. The buckets swung from the yoke but did not spill while the parcel of food thumped against my full stomach. I set off back down the hillside to Abaty Maesycymer.

Chapter 3

I stoke the fires to do the Master's bidding

The heat in the crypt was immense. Since my return from the Llanllionio with the urine I had been employed in stoking the furnaces. Now the whole space was filled with the smoke from the fires which the flues were quite unable to convey to the outside. The smoke stank because, in addition to the wood, we were using coal from the Flintshire mines of my Master's cousin, Thomas Maslyn, the same who had initiated this endeavour with his letter.

My Master had filled his precious glass vessels with the urine and placed them on the furnaces. For hours now they had been boiling with flames licking around them. The acrid fumes had added to the smoke so that my eyes stung and I coughed repeatedly to clear my lungs of the stench. I had stripped almost naked because of the oppressive heat and my body dripped with sweat.

The putti seemed untroubled by either the heat or the stink. They were always naked of course but they fluttered around the crypt twittering in their strange language and occasionally flying close to the flames to examine the vessels. However, they played no useful part in the industry.

Ezekiel remained for the most part in the far corner of the crypt, as far away from the fumes as possible, examining his books and repeatedly reading the letter. From time to time he would approach the fires and check the progress of the vessels.

I had noticed little change. The volume had decreased substantially and the colour turned from yellow through orange to a murky brown, but I could see no sign of the mysterious substance that the Master sought, this 'Cold Fire'. Perhaps it would only make its appearance when the fires had cooled, but how long must the heating go on for?

It was already night when I received the answer. My Master had insisted that the heating continue while the liquid in the flasks had been reduced to a pasty residue. More fuel was required so I left the crypt to collect more wood from the woodpile in the cloisters. It was on my return with an armful of faggots that the mishap occurred.

I was coming down the stone steps to the crypt when I was thrown off my feet by the great force of an explosion and my ears rang with its roar. I spilled the faggots and tumbled down the steps stopping just short of the floor of the crypt. Dark brown smoke filled the room, thicker than before and I noticed tiny fragments of glass strewn across the stone floor. The furnaces still burned but some of the flaming brands and coals had spilled out.

Through my deadened hearing, I heard the Master coughing and spluttering at his desk.

"Are you alright, Master?" I called.

There was a grunt and more coughing in reply. I got to my feet and carefully made my way through the murk. Glass crunched under my sandals which I was grateful that I had kept on my feet. The putti circled below the arched ceiling, laughing as if the explosion had been a huge joke.

I found Ezekiel behind his desk, mostly protected from the blast by his thick gown and the book he had been reading. A few flecks of blood on his cheeks and forehead showed he had not escaped unscathed but his spectacles had protected his eyes.

"See what is left of the vessels," he ordered, "It may be that some of the phosphorus yet remains."

"What about the fires?" I asked.

"Close them up. We have no further need for fire this night."

I turned to the furnaces, damped down the flames and stamped out the embers that had been discharged onto the floor. The crypt became dark. Having determined that the abbey was not going to burn down, I lit a candle and looked for any sizeable remains of the flasks that had contained the urine. There were few pieces of glass bigger than a groat. Carefully I picked up such pieces as I could locate and laid them in the palm of my hand. They had cooled and were covered with a thin layer of brown grease. I took them to Ezekiel.

"Lay them on the desk, boy," he ordered. I did as I was told. The putti hovered above our heads. "Put out the light."

We each blew out the candles and were plunged into darkness. The pieces of glass glowed not at all.

"Success has not been our reward," Ezekiel said, "Quickly, restore the light. I must determine what error we made in the performance of the exercise." I relit the candles from the dying embers of the fires. The Master returned to reading his books and the letter while I began to sweep up the debris in order to return the crypt to some semblance of tidiness. The smoke and fumes had cleared leaving the ceiling a shade darker than before but that was only noticeable to me as the one who on rare occasions was tasked with cleaning it.

The temperature was now falling so I pulled on my clothes. With the remains of the glass vessels swept into a pile I went back to the kitchen and began to lay out some food, mainly that which Meilyr had provided. The putti kept me company.

I called down that I had prepared supper. It was some minutes before I was rewarded with a reply. My Master appeared with a candle in one hand and his cousin's letter in the other.

"The error was the result of my cousin's undecipherable hand. Look," he said holding out the sheet of paper for me to peer at. "The writing of an infirm spider and inkblots everywhere obscuring vital words and phrases." He settled himself at the table and without looking reached out for the bread. He carried on talking as if to himself alone. "It appears I initially misinterpreted Thomas' scribble. I thought he was referring to ordinary urine, the daily output of men and women, but as our experiment has shown that was a false assumption. His words must refer to some particular variety of that golden fluid, produced by some animal other than human perhaps. Surely it must be a special creature that disposes of a substance as mysterious and obviously of great value as the Phosphorus as if it is waste."

He pushed the letter across the table to me and stabbed at the blot which he considered was hindering his understanding of cousin Thomas' epistle.

"What do you think he means, Boy?"

I stared at the paper in the dim light. I too could see the words urine and heat and phosphorus but I could not discern any other details.

"A special creature's piss ..." Ezekiel mused, while chewing on a crust. He drew the letter back and peered at it again. "The light is described as being white. Surely the creature must be white also and one that glows in the night-time." He held the letter up to his face, removing his spectacles to examine it with his eyes directly. "Surely the word that is hidden is ... It must be."

He put the paper down and thumped the table.

"I have the answer, Boy," he cried. "We were mistaken to think that the piss of common people could produce something as wonderful as Cold Fire. I require the urine of the unicorn!"

I stopped chewing and my jaw sagged. What madness now was my Master embarked on? Even if we could locate a unicorn how could we persuade the magical creature to let us collect their piss?

"That can't be done," I said.

My Master glared at me. "What do you mean, Boy? There is nothing that is not possible with effort and ingenuity. We will learn where to locate the creatures and my books will inform me how to negotiate with them. You must prepare for our quest."

"But it is night, Sir."

Ezekiel looked out of the windows as if he had just noticed the time of day.

"Well, tomorrow. Be sure to be up at dawn. We must be away to seek a unicorn."

As I was normally up with the sun to commence my chores my Master's instruction made no difference, but it was late and I was tired. I begged to be allowed to go to my bed and with my Master's reluctant assent I trudged up the stairs to my room.

I awoke at first light and stretched wearily in my bed. I say bed but in fact it was just an old straw-filled mattress. Any furniture as valuable as a bed had long since been sold by my penniless Master. I remained wrapped in a threadbare woollen blanket for a few minutes trying to decide if Ezekiel's plan to find a unicorn was foolhardy, madness or simply impossible.

The putti continued to slumber by my side, curled up together, heads resting against stomachs to resemble a six-legged, six-winged creature. As I stretched and began to move they stirred and with fluttering wings they rose and followed me down below, hovering just above my head. I lit a fire and put some eggs that Meilyr had provided on a skillet. Then I went outside to collect water. I often gave thanks to the old monks who had built the abbey for they had ensured a steady supply of fresh, clean water within the Abbey walls, thus saving a trudge carrying heavy pails from the river

I returned to the kitchen, placed the cooked eggs on thick-cut hunks of bread and went in search of Ezekiel. My first thought of location was correct. He was asleep at his desk in the crypt. I gave him a shake and placed the plate of eggs and bread beside him. Then I went back to the kitchen to eat my breakfast in peace.

It wasn't long however before my Master called me. I hurried down the steps.

"Boy! There is much to do."

"There is?" I inquired, feigning poor memory for the quest he had outlined the previous evening.

"Yes, there is," he insisted, "We must make gold to purchase that which is required for our journey and to pay guides to lead us to the unicorn. Light the fires."

"Again, Sir?" I said reluctantly.

"Again!"

He called it gold. It looked like gold. It had the weight of gold. It wasn't gold. The Master's gold turned to black dust after a few weeks so if it was to be passed off as currency to purchase goods then we had to travel far to find merchants gullible enough to accept it. Mind you the effort required to make it and the cost of the ingredients was almost equivalent to the value of true gold, something my Master had so far failed to acquire or manufacture.

With a little assistance from the putti I soon had the furnaces alight while the Master crushed and stirred and mixed his powders.

"Come here, lad," my Master said, "continue stirring and grinding while I prepare the elixir." I took his place at the table, taking up the pestle to pound and mix the powders that contained grey and yellow and orange specks. The mixture was set on the flames to heat for some hours during which I had to watch the fires to ensure that the heat never failed.

During the time, my Master peered into the bubbling, fuming dish, occasionally smiling, sometimes groaning, often mumbling incantations in Latin, Arabic and other languages unknown to me. I did not know from where he had got his recipe for alchemical gold and he had never shown it to me in written form. He guarded his secrets even though the result was not the king of metals, the gold that never tarnishes or rots.

Eventually, around noon, the contents of the earthenware crucible were liquid and looked golden, although wisps of airs still rose from the surface. Ezekiel took a pair of iron tongs, lifted the container from the fire and poured the liquid into ingot-shaped moulds.

Ezekiel stood back and admired his handiwork.

"There, Boy, now you can go into town and purchase all that we need."

"What are our needs, Sir?"

"Provisions, sufficient for a journey of some days. Suitable clothing, shelter in times of inclement weather, weapons for our protection and containers to carry the unicorn piss. Ah, but I should have something here already for that; containers for ale or wine should suffice."

"And how are we to carry all these properties?" I asked.

"Horses of course, Boy."

"Horses, Sir? We have not one."

"Not one?" He held a finger to his chin as if pondering a difficult puzzle.

"You sold your last old nag to the knacker, last month," I explained.

"I did?" He nodded, "Ah, yes, I did."

"And there is another problem," I went on.

He looked at me as if I was being insolent. "There is?"

"No one in Trefycymmer will sell me anything in exchange for your 'gold'. They know it is not real gold."

"Not real gold! Of course it is," he blustered.

"It turns to dust in weeks," I insisted.

Ezekiel was silent. He sulked and pondered. He pondered and muttered.

"I must have the Cold Fire," he said, "Then I will regain my fortune. But to achieve the Phosphorus I must have the urine of unicorns. Therefore, we must go on the quest and I must have a steed, the purchase of which will require gold." Of a sudden he left me and strode up the steps into the house. I heard him on the wooden stairs and striding across the upper floor to his bedroom. There came sounds of chests and boxes being dragged and overturned. There was a cry of joy and then the sound of him returning.

"I have been keeping this for just such an occasion," he said, holding out for my examination a jewel encrusted, gold chalice. "The last abbot thought he had hidden it but Ezekiel Soulbury defeated his subterfuge."

I gazed at the glowing cup in awe. I knew of the rumour of the hidden treasure but had had no inkling that my Master had discovered it.

"Where did you find it?" I said.

"Never you mind, Boy. We will take it into town. I'm sure the good merchants will give us all that we need in return for such a fine object."

I thought of all the days I had gone hungry in the last winter while this valuable cup resided forgotten amongst Ezekiel's few remaining possessions. Its worth could have provided for Ezekiel, myself and even some of the inhabitants of Llanllionio who struggled in dire poverty. Over the years since my Master had inherited the abbey he had sold off anything and everything of value to pay for his experimentation. The place was just a shell steadily falling into ruin, exacerbated by the local peasants who stole the stone for their own hovels. Now he was prepared to sell his last treasure for a quest that seemed to me to be madness.

Chapter 4

We set out to buy supplies
for our quest

Ezekiel limped along beside me as we walked the main
thoroughfare of Trefycymer. He'd forgotten that the soles of
his shoes were worn through and was finding walking on the
rough ground painful. I think it was the first time he'd been
outside the old abbey since winter began and a much longer
time had elapsed since he had visited the town. Nevertheless,
the few townspeople on the street recognised him and gave
us a wide berth leaving us to make fresh footsteps in the
muddy, shit-strewn road.

Our first call was on the moneylender, for until my Master
had converted the chalice into coin we would not be able to
purchase provisions or horses. We came to the sign of the
three balls. Ezekiel pushed at the door and entered with me
behind him. Inside was a small dark room with an ancient
dwarf-like fellow crouched at a desk.

He looked up. "By the lord if it isn't Master Soulbury. It
must be three years or more since you honoured me with
your presence."

"Three years isn't long enough," my Master growled in
reply.

"Nevertheless, here you are, no doubt to do business. I
presumed you had already disposed of all your wealth in
pursuit of your pointless quests. Ah, but this is your boy.
Good day to you, Aeddon."

I had visited the moneylender on my Master's behalf on a
number of occasions, exchanging the few remaining items in
his possession with value for a few pieces of silver. I, at least,
was welcomed by the shopkeepers of Trefycymmer, even
though it was known that I was purchasing on behalf of
Ezekiel.

Ezekiel sniffed. "You have indeed cheated and robbed me of all that I possess of worldly value, but I have one item left which must impress even you." He dug into the canvas bag that he carried and pulled out a bundle of cloth. He placed it on the moneylender's desk and unwrapped the chalice. Even in the dim light of a late March afternoon, with the shutters closed and a single candle burning, the gold of the chalice glowed and the many-coloured jewels sparkled.

The moneylender did indeed let out a gasp. "As Christ was told at the wedding at Cana, you have kept the best to last, Soulbury! Surely this is the fabled Cup of Maesycymer?"

"It is," Ezekiel said, "Now how much will you give me for it?"

The little man stared with wide eyes at the object. I could see that he coveted it.

"But surely it is a possession of the Crown?" he said. "It belonged to the order and was forfeit when the Abbey was dissolved and the monks sent packing by King Henry. It belongs to good King Charles today."

Ezekiel thumped the desk with his fist. "Do not play games with me, Twm Bach. The last Abbot hid it so that the crown would never have it. I found it and it is mine. I am sure some of your more acquisitive customers would be interested in the Cup of Maesycymer, even if they can't brag about it."

Twm scratched at his hairy chin. I could see that he was weighing up the price he could offer against the worth of the chalice. In truth, it was priceless, not because of the gold and precious stones but because of its history. King Henry's men had searched the countryside for miles around the Abbey for the chalice which had resided in the Abbot's possession for centuries. It was once believed to have been made by a sorcerer, but few now thought that the works of men bore magic powers. Twm would not inform the King's men of the chalice's re-appearance if he could make a profit from its sale. The crucial question was how much profit he could make. Another was how desperate my Master was to have coin in his purse. I knew that his need for funds for his latest quest was great, but did Twm realise that? He was an experienced crook so I guessed he would.

"I might just be able to find a purchaser," Twm said with

what appeared to be deep reluctance.

"Of course you will," Ezekiel said thumping the desk, "so, what sum are you prepared to pay you snivelling little penny-pincher?"

Twm sat back and folded his arms. "Now, now, Ezekiel, there's no need to be impatient. Do you want to do a deal or not?"

Ezekiel shook with rage. I tugged on his tattered gown.

He turned. "What is it boy?"

"I think Master Watcyn will give you what you need if you listen to him, Sir." I said.

My Master breathed deeply, pulled himself erect and blew out through his tightly pursed lips.

Seconds passed before he spoke during which time Twm Watcyn smiled up at him.

"Of course. We have done business together for years haven't we Twm Bach," Ezekiel said. "What offer do you have to make, Twm?"

The little moneylender shifted his feet revealing a small chest used as a footstool, partially hidden from view under his desk. He slipped from his chair and bent down, taking a large iron key from his belt. He unlocked the casket, and took out a small cloth bag that jangled. He recovered his seat and placed the coin sack on the desk.

"There. Take it or leave it," he said. Ezekiel grabbed the bag, loosened the cord and tipped the coins into the palm of his hand. Gold glinted in the candle-light.

"You consider this sufficient payment for the Cup of Maesycymer?" he roared.

Twm smiled. "As I said, take it or leave it. You'll find no other buyer within three days' journey of Trefycymmer."

I watched Ezekiel's jaw moving but no words came out. He replaced the coins in the bag, pushed it up his sleeve and turned to the door.

"Come, boy. Let us leave this den of thievery." He strode out into the street with me at his heels leaving the chalice in the moneylender's possession. I shook my head. Surely my Master's urge to find this Cold Fire was the final descent into ruination? I wondered what would become of me, an orphan and pauper.

We parted then, my Master giving me a single gold coin to purchase all the provisions and equipment we would need for our journey while he went his own way in search of a steed for us both. We met again at the town cross as the sun, hidden behind clouds, set. I had hempen bags filled with supplies to feed us for a couple of weeks, along with oiled wool cloaks to keep the rain from us, leather hats and boots. I had also purchased a couple of short swords of undistinguished iron, relics from the war between the King and Parliament. In my pocket were silver and copper coins, the remainder from my gold piece. I was satisfied with my purchasing prowess.

My Master joined me leading a white horse and a donkey. The horse was sturdy enough but had obviously already seen the majority of its years. The donkey too was past its youth.

"They are companions," Ezekiel said by way of explanation. "I couldn't have the one without the other." I realised that the horse trader, like Twm, had rubbed his hands with glee when he saw my Master approach.

"So I am to ride the donkey?" I said, eyeing the creature somewhat nervously.

"No. You will walk. The donkey will carry our supplies," Ezekiel said. I wasn't sure whether to be pleased or annoyed. I didn't look forward to the long walk that I guessed was before us, but on the other hand the donkey did not appear to relish having a passenger, even one lacking weight such as myself.

"Now we must meet our guide." Ezekiel said taking hold of the reins and hauling himself into his horse's saddle. He settled himself unsteadily, betraying his lack of experience as a rider. I began to fasten my purchases to the back of the donkey.

"Who?" I asked.

"Gwawrwen," he said.

I stopped with a sack of parsnips in my arms. "The witch?" I said.

Ezekiel laughed. "You know that is popular hearsay. Just because she lives alone and seeks out herbs and fungi doesn't make her a sorceress."

I had to agree with my Master. There were no grounds for

believing Gwawrwen dealt in magic even if that was what the suspicious townsfolk and fanciful children liked to believe. Why she had not married and lived the life of a hermit I did not know, neither did I understand why my Master would seek her assistance.

"How can she help us?" I asked.

"Come along boy and you will be enlightened, but hurry. The light will be gone ere we reach her hovel."

I completed tying the goods to the donkey and took hold of its harness to tug it along. Ezekiel urged his horse into motion. In its own time it began to plod forwards. Thankfully, the donkey wasn't too reluctant to follow its comrade.

We took the road out of Trefycymmer along the north bank of the river, travelling further away from our home. After about half an hour walking in the growing dusk we turned onto a narrow track that rose up the hillside through woodland. We were soon out of sight of the road and river but a dim light came to us through the oak trees.

"This is her home," Ezekiel said dismounting. We walked, leading the animals between the trees till we came to the little clearing in which stood a small, roughly constructed timber dwelling.

"Gwawrwen! It is me, Ezekiel Soulbury. I have need of you," he called.

A door opened and a figure stepped out. Her most noticeable feature was her hair. It was as white as the snow on the mountain tops and long, reaching down to her waist. She was wearing a brown woollen dress, with bare feet and arms. She wasn't old. I had expected a bent, wrinkled old woman but she stood upright and her face was unlined.

She smiled and her blue eyes sparkled. "Well, the Lord of Abaty Maesycymer. To what do I owe this honour?"

"I have need of your knowledge, Gwawrwen."

"There can only be one matter of which I have knowledge that you might seek." The woman said with her smile broadening.

"Indeed," Ezekiel said.

"Unicorns?"

Ezekiel nodded. The lady looked beyond him to me,

holding the donkey.

"And this is your assistant, young Aeddon Gruffudd, his parents killed by the dragon?"

I was surprised that she knew so much about me.

"You know everything, Lady," Ezekiel.

Gwawrwen snorted. "Don't flatter me, Ezekiel. I have eyes and ears for what occurs in my vicinity despite living alone." Ezekiel produced a charming smile. "No flattery intended, but you are correct in both regards. This is Aeddon and we seek unicorns."

The lady beckoned us to enter her home. We tied up the horse and donkey and followed her. Inside was small but cosy. There was little furniture but many containers holding flowers and herbs and various fungi, and there were books. That surprised me. Ezekiel was the only person I knew who had books.

Gwawrwen indicated for Ezekiel to sit in her one chair, placed cosily beside her fire. I settled at his feet tucking my legs underneath me to avoid taking up too much of the limited space on her hearth. She brought us goblets and filled them from a pitcher. I sipped the drink. It was water with a hint of herbs that I could not name. It was fresh and revitalising.

She too sat on the floor, crossing her legs and folding her arms.

"So, unicorns. You want to observe one? Talk to one? Surely not kill one. That I would not permit."

Ezekiel shook his head. "I mean them no harm. I need their piss."

Gwawrwen looked startled and then she laughed. "You need what? Why?"

Ezekiel appeared shocked at her reaction. "It is an inquiry I am pursuing."

The lady shook her white hair. "Another of your quests."

"This is of great importance," Ezekiel said, "It is something new, not mentioned in the old texts."

Her eyebrows rose. "Not described by the ancients. What is it?"

My Master seemed to be struggling. Should he divulge the secret which he sought? After opening and closing his mouth a few times he spoke. "I seek the Phosphorus which produces Cold Fire. The philosophers of London have discussed it. It promises miraculous power."

Gwawrwen shrugged. "Perhaps it does, but you need the effusion of a unicorn to achieve your desire?"

"Yes, my Lady."

"Hmm," the woman contemplated. "Unicorns are rare in these modern times, Ezekiel. Although never prolific, once they roamed all the hills of Wales, but as men moved into their pastures, chopping down the trees and digging into the ground for its buried ores, so the unicorns retreated."

"I know all that, Gwawrwen," Ezekiel said, "Where can they be found now?"

She pondered Ezekiel's question but after a pause, spoke. "I know of just one place where they may yet be discovered in this vicinity."

I held my breath, waiting for her announcement.

"Yes, woman?" Ezekiel muttered.

"Cwm Dreigiau," she whispered.

I gasped. The name of the place was one I knew: Valley of Dragons. To the north, amongst the peaks of Eryri, the home of the beast that had killed my parents.

"Ah," my Master said, "You are sure? That is the only place where they may be found?"

The lady nodded. "Only the guardianship of the dragons prevents the unicorns being lost from our land entirely."

"The home of the dragons is a secret place," I blurted out. "No men have found it." I knew that after the death of my parents the dragon's lair had been sought by men seeking revenge and riches. None had succeeded.

"No men, it is true." Gwawrwen said softly.

"You know?" Ezekiel said.

"I don't know. I couldn't point to a spot on a map sketched on parchment, but I could take you there. The unicorns will guide me to them."

I didn't understand what Gwawrwen meant as I was unfamiliar with the fabled creatures, but she spoke with such confidence and authority that I knew she was right. My Master did too.

"You will accompany us then, my lady?" he said with none

of his usual certainty.

"I shall, Ezekiel Soulbury. It is a long time since I saw my friends, the unicorns, and I would like to again before they and I are gone from this world." She spoke as if both were soon to depart but she did not appear old or sick to me.

My Master made arrangements for Gwawrwen to join us the next day and then we were on our return journey. By this time of course it was dark, but the clouds had cleared and a gibbous Moon gave us sufficient light to find our way. We took the road back through the town where the buildings were dark but for one tavern from which merry voices emanated.

When we returned to the Abbey I had the task of tending for the horse and donkey, something I had not had to do since Ezekiel had sold the last of his previous mounts. He was in his bed, snoring, before I found my way to my own room. There the putti fluttered around me, gazing at me and muttering as if gaining knowledge of our expedition direct from my mind. I fell asleep on my mattress before they had settled.

Chapter 5

We begin our quest for the unicorns

It was noon by the time we set off. My Master rose late, presumably having made up for an almost sleepless night previously. I set his breakfast before him then began loading all that we would need for our journey onto the donkey. I decided to name the creature Cydy, short for "cydymaith" which means companion. He was the horse's companion and now looked to be mine for some considerable time. I left my Master to name the horse. Time after time Ezekiel rose from the crypt with extra packages to be carried. I had to tell him that the donkey couldn't carry everything, the horse would have to take some, but he would have nothing of it. Cydy looked somewhat unhappy when I at last completed his load.

Gwawrwen arrived carrying a light sack over her shoulder and still with her feet bare. Her mood reflected the bright sunny morning and made me look forward to accompanying her on the journey.

At last Ezekiel emerged bearing one of his large books.

"What need do we have for your books?" I asked, "We go in search of unicorns for their piss, nothing more."

"We will be traversing lands unseen by the eyes of men," my Master replied. "Who knows what wonders we may see and puzzles we may be set? My books may hold the answers so I must have them with me."

I made sure he kept his book with him once he had clambered into his saddle. We set off at a slow but steady pace, my Master on his horse in the lead with Gwawrwen by my side with Cydy.

Although apprehensive about the outcome of our quest I was excited at going on a journey. I had not been away from the Abbey for more than a day since I came into Ezekiel's care and service eight years ago. Neither had Ezekiel been absent for more than a day and a night. I wondered if the

Abbey and our habitation would still be standing when we returned or whether the people who lived in the area would carry off all the stones. Perhaps the putti would defend my Master's holding, although I doubted it somehow. They had become agitated when they came to understand the purpose of my preparations and hovered forlornly when I made to depart. They wouldn't or couldn't leave the confines of the abbey, I'm not sure which, and I wondered what they would do in our absence. Would they be there to greet us when we returned or would they disappear back to wherever Ezekiel had summoned them from? Since he wasn't really aware of their place of origin I would have to wait to find the answer.

First, we walked to the bridge, crossed the river and proceeded up the track through Llanllionio. Some villagers peered out at us from their doors but none came out to greet us or hail us with best wishes. In fact, I noticed that most of the expressions on their faces were of fear or anger when they saw who was on the horse and who was accompanying me.

We came to Meilyr's homestead and he was standing at the entrance, his hands on his hips and his feet planted apart.

He ignored Ezekiel and spoke directly to me while his eyes flicked to and from Gwawrwen. "You are going on a journey, Aeddon?" he said. I nodded. Ezekiel hadn't instructed his horse to stop and was already plodding further up the track.

"That experiment with the urine not successful then?" he asked

"No," I replied, "apparently, the urine was not suitable for the purpose so we are searching for an alternative."

"You don't have to tell me the source you seek," Meilyr nodded at Gwawrwen who treated him to a smile. "Take care lad, your travelling companions have a reputation for attracting trouble."

I took heed of Meilyr's warning and thanked him.

"I hope your search is, um, fruitful, Aeddon, and your Master satisfied. Here take this for your journey." He handed me a large leather bottle. I pulled the cork and sniffed. It was strong ale.

"Thank you, Meilyr."

"Drink it sparingly," he warned. He waved and turned his

back on us. I added the bottle to Cydy's load and urged the animal on. We increased our pace to catch up with Ezekiel.

Above the village, we joined a path that turned to follow the course of the river some distance below us. The path hugged the side of the valley above a steep scarp. At least the way was relatively level for now so I had breath for speech. While Ezekiel rode on ahead I fell into conversation with Gwawrwen.

"You have seen unicorns?" I asked.

"It was many years ago," Gwawrwen replied convivially, "twenty or more, and I was a mere child."

"Where were they?"

She looked around, and reached out with her arm to point at the surrounding hills. "All around. They were never many but they roamed all the hills and valleys of Wales in times past."

"But not everyone saw them," I said. I had heard others speak of unicorns. My parents told me tales of the creatures when I was small, and Ezekiel had mentioned them in passing before they became part of his current interest, but I had the impression that few people had ever really been close to the creatures.

"That is true," Gwawrwen said, "They avoid contact with men, and women, but for the few that they call."

"They called you?"

She tapped her head. "Yes. I felt their summons here and they lead me to them."

"What did they want you for?"

"I don't know really. Perhaps just to make my acquaintance. They allowed me to approach them, to touch them and they sniffed my body and snickered."

"Is that all. But why?"

She shrugged. "Who knows. My Mother said they chose me because of my talent with herbs. My father said perhaps they instilled the talent in me. Certainly, after my first meeting with a unicorn I was filled with certainty that I would study the lore of plants, and subsequent meetings reinforced my desire."

"Your mother and father ..."

"Died when I was young. I was left to fend for myself from

the age of ten. But I was happy on my own, tending the flowers and trees."

"What happened to the unicorns?"

"They went away. It is said that as the number of people inhabiting the hills increased so the unicorns retreated. I don't think it is a recent occurrence but the rate of their disappearance has increased since the monarchy was restored and the peace has encouraged industry."

I wanted to know more about these fabled animals. "Why do people speak of unicorns as if they are magical creatures? Surely they are no different to cattle or horses?"

Gwawrwen thought for a moment before answering. "I suppose in many respects they are as other animals. They breathe, they eat, they piss." She laughed, "which is as well for your Master's project." She paused, "But there is something special about them and it is not just their shyness of human contact. They have an influence on the land which can only be described as magical."

"But is there such a thing as magic?" I asked.

She looked at me with sadness in her eyes. "Oh, Aeddon, what a strange question. Surely your Master wields magic."

"He is a philosopher, an alchemist," I said, "he handles the forces of nature and manipulates substances."

"Mishandles, so I hear," Gwawrwen laughed, then became serious again. "Do you not see any magic in his work?"

I thought of the putti, conjured, I heard, from a ball of clay, I knew not how. They resembled no other beings I had met in my short life. They certainly seemed magical.

"But surely someone wielding magic would not be penniless and starving as Ezekiel is," I observed.

"Wizards do not desire riches. Ezekiel may not yet have full control over his powers, but magic he certainly wields. He summoned the dragon." She raised her hand to her mouth. "Oh, I'm sorry, Aeddon, I forgot."

"It's alright, Gwawrwen. I have little memory of the events that took my parents. I didn't see the dragon and Ezekiel has been reluctant to talk about it."

Gwawrwen frowned. "I'm not surprised but he bears a responsibility for the death of your mother and father. He is supposed to be caring for you but he seems to treat you like no more than a servant."

I shrugged. It was all that I had known. My early childhood with my parents living in Llanllionio was but a hazy memory. All I knew was my life with Ezekiel, which was indeed one of Master and Servant or Apprentice.

"You seem to know Ezekiel well," I said, "Yet you have not visited us at the abbey, and until yesterday I knew little of you except for the gossip of the townsfolk."

Gwawrwen looked ahead at the horse and its rider and to my inexperienced eyes she seemed to be sad. "We grew up close," she said, "He is only a year or two older than me." I gasped because Ezekiel's bent figure, dark eyes and ragged hair made him look far older than the upright, smooth-skinned woman who strode by my side. "It's true," she insisted. "Of course he didn't live all the year round at the Abbey then. His father was wealthy and had many estates. Ezekiel was not the first son, and he was lucky to receive the Abbey as an inheritance. Anyway, whenever the family was lodged at the Abbey, Ezekiel and I would play together. He was very interested when I recounted my meetings with the unicorns and hoped that they would summon him too, but they never did. Nevertheless, it was that desire that I think set off his urge to study the mysteries of the world."

"You remained friends?"

"Yes, when he became the owner of the Abbey and he employed your parents I visited often. But he became more and more withdrawn, a recluse, desiring only his own company as he worked on his secret endeavours. From time to time he would show me results he was proud of – his alchemical gold for example."

I laughed. "The gold that crumbles to dust after a few weeks."

Gwawrwen chuckled, "The very same. And he desired my presence when he said he was going to summon and tame a dragon." She was thoughtful for a few breaths. "I attended him at his bidding but I should have done more to stop him. I knew how dangerous dragons are and doubted his ability to control one. My doubts proved only too true."

"What happened? Please tell me," I appealed.

She looked at me, obviously trying to decide whether it

was right to leave me in ignorance or to appraise me of the event that made me an orphan. She made a decision.

"You are fourteen years old now aren't you, Aeddon? A young man. You should know your past." She took a deep breath, "Ezekiel said he had found an ancient text which detailed how to summon creatures such as putti and dragons. He made up the material to the formula the text described and ignited it in the nave of the abbey. I watched from a distance. It produced fire and a plume of coloured smoke which had a most detestable odour. Ezekiel read out an incantation from the text. I don't know what language it was, it certainly was not Welsh. We waited as the smoke filled the air above the Abbey and sure enough a dragon was summoned."

I gasped even though I knew that a dragon had appeared.

"It appeared from the dark cloud over our heads. It was huge, red, with broad wings, and when it roared it breathed fire. It circled the Abbey, singeing the crops with its fiery breath. Ezekiel stood in the Abbey shouting commands which it ignored. I hid behind the fallen stones."

"How did my parents die?"

"They were in the kitchen garden, digging parsnips. When they saw the dragon they ran and that was the death of them. The dragon saw their movement and descended on them, grasping them both in its talons. It dashed them against the walls of the Abbey and flew away. Their bodies were never found, presumably because the dragon took them back to its lair."

"So the dragon went and was not seen again?" I said, the image of my mother's and my father's deaths repeating over and over again in my head. I had been in the village playing with other children of my age. We had been scooped up by the villagers and shut away in the house so didn't observe the events as they unfolded. By the time I had extricated myself from the house and run all the way back to the abbey it was over and the dragon gone.

"That's true. The people accused Ezekiel of foolhardiness and made him vow to look after you but he retreated further into his books and experiments. I was angry with him for having attempted such a dangerous task and he was too proud to admit his error so we parted and have not spoken until yesterday."

"But you agreed to join us, readily."

"I did ..." We walked on for a few steps. "I suppose I am both intrigued and worried by this latest enthusiasm. Perhaps if I am by his side I can prevent another disaster. This time I will not hide myself away for my own safety. There again, the chance to see unicorns once more ... Well, we shall see, shan't we?"

We fell into silence, both thinking our own thoughts as we walked further and further from the land that I knew well.

Apart from brief halts to recover, we continued on our way until the sun was low in the western sky. We had followed a well-trodden path but had seen no other travellers. Ezekiel called a halt when we approached a sizeable lake. We camped in woodland beside a stream which fell gurgling down the hillside to the dark waters. I unloaded Cydy so that he could have some rest, while Gwawrwen went off amongst the trees. Ezekiel sat with his back to an oak and fell asleep.

Gwawrwen returned with a bag of mushrooms and some firewood. "It is not as dry as I would like but you may have success in igniting a fire," she said.

I arranged the smaller pieces of kindling and took out the flint and steel that I had brought. Sparks I produced aplenty but fire not at all. I persisted but was beginning to tire when I felt the presence of my Master looming over me.

"Stop, that incessant scraping," he grumbled.

"But Master, we need fire to cook our supper," I replied.

"Let me show you how to command a flame," he said. He pulled a small metal box from one of his many voluminous pockets. He opened it and tipped a small amount of a grey powder onto the kindling. "Now strike a spark."

I did as I was commanded, crouched over. A spark leapt from the flint onto the powder. At once there was a burst of flame and smoke and a strong sulphurous stench. I was blown backwards and felt the heat on my face. Indeed, my eyebrows and fringe were singed.

"There's your fire," Ezekiel said. He returned to his resting place. The kindling was, as he said aflame and being consumed at a great rate. I added small sticks and larger ones and despite their dampness they quickly caught in the ferocity of the flame. Very soon we had a blazing fire on which we could put our pot filled with water from the stream. Gwawrwen dropped in mushrooms and herbs and I added turnips and a little meat.

"Having an alchemist with us has some advantages then," Gwawrwen quipped, nodding to the fire and the sleeping form of Ezekiel. I knew my Master had some talent in his chosen field but I had not experienced his ignition powder before.

"He has secrets I know nothing of," I said.

"I'm sure he does," Gwawrwen agreed.

"And what of you?" I asked as we settled to watch the pot simmering.

"Do I have secrets?"

"Yes. At least the people seem wary of you as if you do have powers of which they are unsure."

Gwawrwen sighed and shook her head slowly. "Most people are afraid of that which they don't understand. My parents spoke of how I was blessed by the unicorns, but others didn't see them so became suspicious of me. When I was left on my own and spent my time in the woods people wondered what mysterious deeds I was engaged in. In fact, I was collecting fungi and herbs and flowers and learning their uses, but people thought of spells and curses rather than cures and perfumes. I became an oddity, a loner, someone to be wary of."

"Did you mind?"

"Not really. I enjoy my life in the woods and some people have come to value the oils I extract and the infusions that I make. But what of you, Aeddon? Are you not alone, despite having Ezekiel to order you around?"

I thought about what Gwawrwen had said. Did I feel alone? I missed my mother and father but I rarely felt lonely.

"Ezekiel's not so bad," I said, "bad-tempered, selfish, demanding, yes, all of those, but he means me no harm and he does give me some instruction. And there are the putti too, of course."

"Ah, yes, those imps. What do they do?"

I laughed. "Not a lot. They fly around all day, getting in the way, occasionally doing a little to help such as carrying sticks

to the fire, but most often they just chatter and tease me. They make me laugh."

"Hmm. I do wonder what nature of creature they are. They seem without intent of harm but I worry. While Ezekiel only has desire to learn about the world, and make gold, he is dabbling in dark arts."

I didn't understand what Gwawrwen was referring to. All I saw was my Master mixing powders and liquids and heating them on the furnace or in an alembic and then usually throwing the resulting mess on the hearth. I saw little evidence of him exercising powers of good or ill. Perhaps this latest project would be different, particularly as he had engaged the assistance of Gwawrwen.

As the sun sank behind the trees and the hilltop, our cawl was ready and we ate hungrily. I passed around Meilyr's leathern bottle and we each had a swig of his strong ale. That was sufficient to make my eyelids heavy. Ezekiel settled himself to sleep so Gwawrwen volunteered to take the first watch. I wrapped myself in my cloak and was soon lost in sleep.

Chapter 6

We approach the home of the unicorns

It was nearly noon next day when we descended into the valley and entered a small town. I was unaware of its name but Ezekiel seemed familiar with the place. The buildings were largely hovels with few if any offering wares or provisions for sale. We reached a crossroads at the centre and there stopped. There were no other travellers or bystanders although I felt that we were being watched from behind doors and shutters.

"My familiarity with our route has brought us this far," Ezekiel said from atop his horse, "but now we need your guidance, Gwawrwen, to lead us to Cwm Dreigiau."

Gwawrwen stepped up on the steps at the base of the old stone cross that formed the meeting point of the four ways. She looked to the left and right but then pointed in the direction we had been travelling.

"I feel no call from the unicorns but I know that the place we seek is in the high mountains. We continue on," she said. She stepped down as Ezekiel spurred his horse onward. I followed with Cydy. So we left the town without conversing with a single one of the inhabitants, but they watched us, I am sure, till we were well out of sight.

Soon we were climbing again, this time in steeper, more rugged country. My legs felt heavy and my breath came in short pants. Cydy laboured with his full load, occasionally pausing and refusing to move until he too had recovered his energy. Ezekiel rode on, his horse finding its own footsteps. Gwawrwen seemed untroubled by the exertion and lead the way.

We emerged above the trees onto a ridge. Down below us in the valley was a river and lake and beyond, another line of ragged hills. I stood puffing but Gwawrwen held her head up and stared to the north.

"I feel them," she said in a soft voice, "They call to me."

"The unicorns?" Ezekiel asked, still seated on his horse.

"Yes. They recognise me and welcome me to their fastness."

"Where?" Ezekiel demanded.

Gwawrwen pointed ahead. "There beyond those hills and the next. You cannot see where they reside, no one can. We will not know we are there until we are."

"Hmm. Is that some kind of riddle?" Ezekiel mumbled.

"No," Gwawrwen said, "The home of the unicorns and the dragons is hidden from the view of men. The unicorns will let me, let us, enter, though we shall not be aware of the barrier. They will guide me the rest of our journey."

"Good. Well, let us get on," Ezekiel said, "I do not want to be exposed when the rain falls on us." He looked to the west and I followed his gaze. Heavy clouds were building and a growing breeze was sending them in our direction. I too was eager to get down into the valley and under shelter.

We made our camp again beneath the canopy of leaves beside a small river that fed the lake. It was well-timed as the sky darkened and the rain began to fall. The wind blew between the trees and the water dripped from the branches but for the most part we were kept dry. Once again, I found that it fell to me to make camp. Ezekiel dismounted stiffly and settled in a dry patch beneath a large oak tree. Gwawrwen went foraging again to supplement the rations that we carried.

When it came time to light a fire the rain still fell and the ground was wet. I approached Ezekiel.

"Master," I said, "May we have some of your powder that produces fire?"

He muttered and grumbled. I insisted that there would not be a hot supper unless there was the means to get wet wood alight. He accepted my arguments and made as if to rise then sighed and fell back.

"Why should I do all the work?" he said, reaching into his pocket. "Here boy, use it yourself. Mind you use just a pinch, unless you want to make a roman candle of yourself." He reached out his hand holding the metal box.

I took it. "Are there no incantations I should speak?"

"What? No, boy, it's just a powder that accelerates burning. Now leave me to rest. All the bones in my body ache from riding that infernal horse." He leant back and was immediately asleep.

I returned to my hearth. Gwawrwen was standing nearby, watching. I opened the box, took out as Ezekiel had instructed, a pinch of powder between my forefinger and thumb, and sprinkled it on the little heap of twigs and kindling. Then I took up my flint and steel and struck a spark. I was more wary this time and kept my head back. There was a very gratifying puff of smoke and flames leapt an arm's reach above the fire but it soon settled down to a steady flame.

"You'll be an alchemist yet," Gwawrwen said, joining me to feed the flames and set our pot to boiling.

By the time the food was ready, the rain had eased but a chill was on the air. We were pleased to huddle around the fire and eat a hot meal although Ezekiel grumbled at missing his chair and bed, just about the only remaining pieces of furniture he still possessed. After passing around Meilyr's ale, Ezekiel again settled down to sleep. I offered to take the first watch on this occasion. I was surprised that I felt less fatigued than the previous night despite the greater effort required on this day's journey. Perhaps I was becoming accustomed to exercise. Gwawrwen accepted my offer and settled beside the fire, which I stoked up to keep the cold at bay.

The sky, seen through the small gaps in the canopy, had cleared and the stars shone through like tiny beacons. I tried to remain alert, straining to hear any sound, but there was none: no bird calls, no rustling of small animals, no fluttering of bats or swishing of owls. My eyes were beginning to close despite my determination to remain awake when all at once there came a great roar. It went on and on, louder by far than the baying of any large dog that I had previously heard. The deafening howl seemed to come from close by. The branches of the trees themselves seemed to tremble with fear.

I shivered and wrapped my arms around myself but Gwawrwen stirred and rose to her feet. Even Ezekiel opened his eyes.

"What is it?" I shouted in order to be heard over the din.

"That is the call of a dragon," Gwawrwen replied, turning her head to fix the direction the sound came from. The roaring ceased and the silence seemed quieter than before, a total absence of noise. "Do not be afraid," Gwawrwen went on, "It is not close, although it may sound to us as though it is almost upon us. Sounds carry great distances at night. We approach the dragon's lair but we have some distance to travel yet, perhaps a whole day's travel."

"There will be dragons with the unicorns?" I asked, still trembling.

Gwawrwen nodded. "They inhabit the same land, as they share some characteristics."

"Magic?"

"Perhaps."

"Shh, sleep," Ezekiel growled. "No dragon will trouble us this night." His snoring resumed.

"He's right," Gwawrwen said, "We have a considerable journey before we come into the dragon's range of sense."

"But we will?" I guessed.

"Oh yes, but I am sure the unicorns will give us protection. Sleep now, Aeddon. I will take the next watch."

I was grateful to be allowed to let sleep take away the terrors of the dragon's roar.

The following day was difficult and long. All three of us, even Ezekiel, had arisen before the sun rose, eager to be on our way, although I was apprehensive about what lay ahead of us. We tramped up zig-zag paths to the next ridge, down into the valley beyond and up an even steeper path. Even Ezekiel was forced to dismount for fear that his horse may lose its footing but Gwawrwen strode forward, increasingly eager to meet the creatures that called to her. The day was cold and the wind strong, particularly when we emerged above the trees. Rain squalls blew over us, soaking our clothing even under the waxed cloaks that we had purchased so that we shivered and our teeth chattered.

The top of the ridge was clothed in mist and we clambered up the last stretch barely able to see our hands grasping the rocks in front of us. We reached level ground and I took a few steps further into the thick fog.

"No, Aeddon! Stop!" Gwawrwen called. I stopped and turned to look at her. I couldn't see her but then a shadowy figure approached me and she was by my side.

"What's the matter?" I asked.

"You don't know where you are going," she said, "Look down."

I did as she said and I saw that I was standing on the edge of a sheer drop. One pace more and I would have fallen to certain death. I stepped back, shaking.

"You knew?" I asked. "You have been here before?"

"No," she replied. "I have not been to this place but I felt that you were in danger. The unicorns warned me."

"They know all of us are here?"

Gwawrwen shrugged. "They know I have companions, but they welcome us."

"Where?" I said.

Gwawrwen pointed downwards. "We must descend through the mist."

I knelt down to peer at the edge. "I can see no path here."

"Follow," she said. She turned back into the fog and I followed her, tugging Cydy. We found Ezekiel leaning against the horse. He joined us as we went on into the mist.

I heard running water and soon a stream crossed our path. We turned to follow it and in a few paces it disappeared over the edge and there was the roar of falling water hitting rocks somewhere below.

"Here!" Gwawrwen called, "There is a path down beside the waterfall."

She was correct, although a steeper, more precarious route would have been hard to find. We scrambled down with the animals picking their own way, four feet perhaps more sure than two. One moment we were surrounded by cloud, the next we emerged into glorious sunshine and a view which I am sure I will remember as long as I live.

There below us was the whole valley with golden pastures and trees of brilliant green. A stream fed by the waterfall ran into a lake whose water was the deep blue of the twilight sky. The sides of the valley curved upwards becoming steadily steeper until the grass was replaced by scree and then vertical cliffs pock-marked with caves. There seemed to be no exit from the valley, it was really an oval bowl. The sun shone above us with a warmth I had not felt since last summer and the scent of innumerable flowers filled the air

"This is the home of the unicorns," I said, stating a fact rather than a question.

From just below me, Gwawrwen replied. "Yes, it is. They are down there among the trees."

"And dragons sleep in the caves in the cliffs," growled my Master from behind me. I looked again at those foreboding crags afraid that a dragon might appear at that moment, but it did not.

We continued down, our way becoming easier as it grew more horizontal. The waterfall descended into a circular pool besides which stood a boulder at least three times my height. Its shape was quite memorable as it resembled the fruit of an oak tree in its cup. After exchanging comments about the extraordinary rock, we went on and soon stood on the meadow beside the stream. The grass was soft beneath my feet and the green was sprinkled with blues and reds and whites and yellows of wild flowers. We did not stop however. Gwawrwen continued towards the wood beside the lake. When we approached the trees, I saw that they were spaced apart giving each the opportunity to spread its canopy. They were ancient trees, clothed with moss, with boughs twisted into weird shapes. Despite the shade the leaves provided and the gentle breeze that blew, I felt warm and content.

"We'll camp here," Ezekiel said, dismounting from the horse, "and then find these creatures that have lead us here."

Gwawrwen appeared torn. I thought she might urge us on to meet the unicorns but she turned and faced us.

"Yes, if you wish. It is as well that we do not intrude on the unicorns with all our baggage."

I shrugged and started to unload Cydy. Then I heard a sound something between a horse's bray and a cow's moo.

"They are letting us know that they are aware of our presence," Gwawrwen said.

"Well, if they are close, let us make their acquaintance," Ezekiel said striding forward, "Bring the bucket boy!"

Despite my Master's haste, I completed the unloading and made sure that Cydy and the horse were settled before searching for the bucket which we had brought specially to collect the unicorn urine. Ezekiel, hopping from one foot to the other, could hardly contain his urgency to find the creatures and complete our quest. Gwawrwen was calm and serene, as if in a trance caused by the proximity of the fabled animals.

With the bucket in my arms, I signalled that I was ready. Both Ezekiel and I looked to Gwawrwen to lead us the final few yards to our destination. She appeared to awaken and smiled at us.

"Come. This way. They are not far." She led us to where the trees grew closer together, nearer to the lake. By now the sun was low, barely above the ridge, and the light beneath the branches of the trees was as at dusk, but while in other circumstances I might have felt wary of meeting night creatures here I felt secure and relaxed. In a few minutes we came to another clearing. My eyes had adjusted to the dim light and stepping into the open I was dazzled. The grass itself appeared to glow and the air sparkle. In the middle of the clearing was a huge oak tree, its trunk a man's height across, and standing near it, with their heads lowered cropping the grass, were three of the creatures we had come to meet.

For many years I had had an image of a unicorn in my head, perhaps drawn there by tales of the animals. I had imagined an animal like a white horse with a horn stuck on its head. These beasts bore some resemblance to my imagination but there were striking differences. They were more cow in shape than horse, but bigger than any bull I had met, and the horn curved upwards from the end of their long broad faces. They were indeed white but their fur was short and lay flat against the well-muscled bodies.

One unicorn looked up and, seeing us, plodded towards us. If I hadn't been with Gwawrwen I would have been frightened, I am sure, by the sight of this huge animal with its fearsome horn advancing towards me. It stopped however when it reached Gwawrwen and lowered its head. The woman laid both her hands at the base of the horn and closed her eyes. They remained in this pose for some minutes and I could sense Ezekiel becoming agitated beside me.

At last Gwawrwen removed her hands and turned to us.

"The unicorns welcome us and have given their consent," she said.

"We can collect their piss?" Ezekiel said stepping forward eagerly.

"Yes, but not until the morning," Gwawrwen replied.

I took courage and stepped forward, approaching to within an arm's reach of the unicorn that had communicated with Gwawrwen.

"May I touch it?" I asked, almost not believing my audacity.

"It is he," Gwawrwen said, "and his name is Adamant, the jewel, the diamond, but yes, you may stroke him."

I touched my fingers to the unicorn's body in the middle of his broad back which came up to my head height. The fur was thin but I felt a great heat coming from the creature's body. I rested my hand flat against his flank and smoothed the hair. For such a large and strong animal, the fur was remarkably fine and soft. The unicorn snickered as if he was enjoying my action. A feeling of contentment filled me. Gwawrwen smiled and urged me to continue. I continued to caress the magnificent beast.

"So we must sleep a night in this place?" Ezekiel said as if any delay in his project was to be avoided.

"We could not retrace our steps in the dark," Gwawrwen said.

Ezekiel looked up into the darkening sky as if noticing for the first time that night was falling.

"Hmm, I suppose we must settle for the night," he agreed. "I hunger. If we cannot collect the piss now, then let us prepare our meal before we lose all light."

"The unicorns would appreciate us not lighting a fire to cook our cawl," Gwawrwen said.

"What then are we to eat?" Ezekiel roared. Adamant stepped back at the noise and I withdrew my hand

"Hush, Ezekiel. You'll annoy the unicorns. They will provide for us this night," Gwawrwen said.

"How?" Ezekiel said, "will their magic summon a banquet for us?"

Gwawrwen chuckled. "Nothing so fancy, Ezekiel, but a food like which you will never have tasted before." Ezekiel looked bemused. Gwawrwen continued, "Aeddon, take your bucket and milk one of the female unicorns. They are called Emerallt and Rhuddem. They will allow you to do so."

"You propose to obtain unicorn milk for our meal?" Ezekiel said, "I haven't drunk milk since I supped at my wet nurse's breast. Milk from animals is peasants' food!"

Gwawrwen laughed, "That may be true Ezekiel but you have eaten or drunk nothing that satisfies like unicorn milk. You'll see."

I looked at the two other unicorns grazing beneath the huge oak. Would they really let me collect their milk? Reluctantly I took my hand off Adamant's flank and picked up the bucket. Although intended for the urine, I had cleaned it before we left Maesycymer. I approached the nearest of the unicorns warily. The animal raised its head and though it could not speak or make an expression I felt its acceptance of me. It stood still as I placed the bucket beneath its udder and I knelt down. The unicorn was bigger than any cow that I had seen but it stood patiently. It had been some years since I had milked a cow or sheep and I was no expert but when I gave the teat an experimental squeeze the milk squirted into the bucket.

"That's right, Aeddon," Gwawrwen said. She had joined me and rested her hand on the unicorn's long head. "Rhuddem appreciates your gentle touch and your young hands."

Gwawrwen's words encouraged me and I got stuck into my task. The feel of the teat in my hand was in some way comforting and the smell of the rich, creamy fluid that poured into my bucket made me long to drink it. It did not take long till my bucket was close to full.

"I think that will be sufficient for us," Gwawrwen said, "You do not know how filling unicorn milk can be."

I released the teat and stood up. I caressed the side of the animal and mouthed my thanks. The unicorn snickered and gently tossed its massive head.

Gwawrwen took her hands from the horn. "Let us return to our camp site. We will meet the unicorns again in the morning."

I picked up the bucket and backed away from the creatures not wanting to turn and lose sight of them. All three looked at us with their small eyes.

We retraced our steps to where we had left Cydy, the horse and our luggage. We quickly made ourselves comfortable for the night as the sun disappeared behind the ridge and we were cast into darkness. The only light seemed to come from the bucket I had carried. The unicorn milk glowed with a pale white light. Gwawrwen took her cup, dipped it into the milk and raised it to her lips. She sipped and sighed.

"Ah, it is as I remember. Come, Ezekiel, Aeddon, drink. You will never taste anything as wonderful as unicorn milk." She drank again. Ezekiel took up his tankard and filled it and I followed with my own.

Ezekiel let out a long, satisfied sigh as I raised the cup to my lips. The milk was still warm from the animal and its taste so far surpassed that of cow or sheep or goat, or even the unrecalled milk from my mother's breast, that I marvelled at its qualities. Creamier, yes, sweeter, definitely, more so even than honey. As it fell into my stomach it filled me with a joy and pleasure unmatched by the hard bread and maggot-ridden meat that was my usual fodder.

Ezekiel returned for a second cupful but when I had finished mine I felt as full and replete as if I had eaten a ten-course banquet.

"The remainder will suffice to break our fast," Gwawrwen said, laying down her cup. I felt sleepy.

"Should we keep watch?" I asked.

My Master had already lain down and was snoring quietly.

"I am sure that we are safe in the unicorns' company," Gwawrwen said, "but I will stay awake. I will stir you when it is time for you to watch."

I was grateful for her words and lay down on my blanket. My eyes quickly closed.

I was awakened suddenly from a previously peaceful slumber, by what I was not sure. Had it been a noise, a roar perhaps? It was almost too dark to see anything but I could just make out the bundle at my side that was Ezekiel. I could not see Gwawrwen close by. I peered into the surrounding darkness trying to make anything out. The trees were dark on dark but as my eyes acclimatised I saw the equally dark forms of the donkey and horse and a subtly paler outline of Gwawrwen and a unicorn standing close together. I presumed from its bulk that it was Adamant with which Gwawrwen was in conversation.

I was about to rise and join them when there came a great howl that was deep in tone and unlike a bird or other animal. So loud and uncanny, it made my teeth grind and my bones shiver. It must have been the same noise that had awakened me. Now I let out an involuntary cry.

"Aeddon! Do not fear," Gwawrwen called and ran towards me, the unicorn lumbering behind her.

"What is it?" I said, the noise still echoing in my ears.

"A dragon. That's what it was. The same that disturbed us last night," said Ezekiel stirring at my side.

"Is it coming for us?" I cried, trembling.

Gwawrwen knelt beside me and put her arms around me. "No. The unicorns protect us, but the dragons roost in the caves above the scree. One called to its mate a short while ago and that was the answer."

"Nevertheless, they are stirring," Ezekiel said. "We will have to beware on our return in the morn."

Despite the gloom, I saw Gwawrwen nod. "Yes. The unicorns will not be able to give us protection from dragons when we climb out of their pastures."

I felt the warm, sweet breath of Adamant on my neck and turned to see the great head of the creature lowered, its curved horn arching over my head. The animal was immense and yet I felt safety in its proximity.

"Return to your sleep you two," Gwawrwen said. "Adamant will be our guardian while we rest." I settled back down, still a little fearful lest a dragon let out its terrible cry again but soothed by the presence of the unicorn.

Chapter 7

I carry out the task for which we came to the unicorns

It was a bright, sunny morning when I awoke. The terror of the dragon's call was a distant memory and I was full of joy to see that all three of the unicorns were grazing near our camp. Gwawrwen was moving from one to the other, stroking each in turn and bending to converse silently with them. I rose and greeted her then took myself away to see to my toilet and wash in a small stream. When I returned Ezekiel was stirring.

Gwawrwen poured some of the remaining unicorn milk into my cup. She picked it up and held it out to me.

"Drink. It has not turned over night. You will be filled with strength for the day."

I took the cup and held it to my lips. The milk had cooled but still tasted as fresh as it had done the previous evening and still had its exquisite taste. One cupful was sufficient to make me feel I could take on whatever exertions the day would bring. Ezekiel too drank his fill then he spoke to me.

"Boy, the unicorns await us. Now you can carry out the task we came for. Collect their piss."

Gwawrwen agreed that the unicorns were ready to comply with our request, but first I went to the stream to wash the dregs of the milk from the bucket. I returned and placed it on the ground between Adamant's stout rear legs. A torrent of golden yellow urine poured from him quickly filling the bucket to the brim.

"Let us fill the wineskins that we brought, then you can collect from the others," Ezekiel said, rummaging in his baggage and bringing out half a dozen leather skins that he must have kept from the days when he could afford to buy Spanish wine. Thankfully Ezekiel had kept the skins moist and supple so that when we transferred the urine from the bucket it didn't leak from the seams. I went to the other two unicorns in turn, repeating the process. Collecting the surprisingly pleasant smelling liquid from each animal did not take long but transferring it to the wineskins did, so the sun was well up in the sky when our task was complete. Now I had to burden Cydy with the weight, but our stock of food had diminished considerably on our journey so there was some leeway in his load.

At last we were ready to commence our return journey. The unicorns stood patiently watching us and I was reluctant to leave their presence. So too was Gwawrwen who leaned against Adamant, her hands and arms pressed against his side.

"Come on woman. It's time we left," Ezekiel grumbled. He mounted the horse and turned it towards our route homewards.

Gwawrwen pulled herself away from the creature and blew kisses and waved to the three unicorns who watched us as we set off. Our path joined the course of the small river that flowed from the waterfall and we walked easily over the soft pasture. Even Cydy with his heavy load did not complain. As before, Gwawrwen walked by my side.

"Well, Aeddon, what do you think of them? Aren't they magnificent creatures?" she said.

"They are," I replied, finding it difficult to express my feelings about the unicorns. In truth I was in awe of their stature, their soft fur, their nobility. "I am surprised how easily they complied with our request although I suppose even for a unicorn, piss is but waste."

"They are not always so compliant," Gwawrwen replied.

"Do they expect something from us in return?" I asked as only Gwawrwen had conversed with the creatures, although how she had done so I knew not.

"Only our promise to cherish them and keep them from such harm as man can cause."

"Did we make such a promise?" I said.

"I promised on our behalf and I will make sure that Ezekiel abides by it."

"How can unicorns be harmed by us?"

"In the past, men have driven them from their pastures in order to plough the soil and grow crops or to dig up the minerals that lie beneath. Also, men have killed unicorns to cut off their horns."

I was horrified at this revelation. "What can be done with the horn of a unicorn?"

Gwawrwen looked sad, "Some people think it holds strong magic for curing illnesses or exciting passion."

"That's bad wizardry," I said thinking that to use the unicorns in this was truly dreadful. "But surely animals as big as Adamant can defend themselves?"

Gwawrwen sighed. "You would indeed think that Adamant would have the power to see off attackers but men are resourceful and have learnt how to capture and kill even the noblest of creatures."

I had to agree as lions and bears had been driven from our land and even dragons occupied but few sites now. Thinking of the dragons brought a recollection of the terrible noise they had made in the night. I trembled at the thought that they might be waiting in their lairs for us as we climbed out of the realm of the unicorns.

Our path started to rise. It became narrow and rocky and twisted back and forth. The morning was still bright and the sky clear so, unlike our descent through cloud, we had a clear view of the valley below and cliff above us. This was both pleasant as I could look back at the home of the unicorns and fearful because, as the path became precipitous, every step brought the terror of a fall. Even Ezekiel had become afraid and dismounted from the horse. Now he picked his own footsteps while leading the horse by its bridle and allowing it to find its own footing. Gwawrwen led the way and I brought up the rear leading Cydy, who had the worst of it, being loaded down with all our baggage. He snorted with complaint frequently and took his paces at lengthening intervals.

Slow indeed was our progress and the ridge hardly seemed to grow closer. We had long before cleared the tops of the trees in the valley and now we had climbed above where even stunted trees grew. There were just small patches of vegetation beside the waterfall that splashed beside us continuously. The path was narrow, steep and composed of loose stone that shifted underfoot and then was sent skittering down the side of the cliff.

I was bent over, taking extra care with each step, when I was jerked erect by a deafening squawk similar to that I had heard in the night. I looked up into the blue, cloudless sky and saw what I first thought was a large bird such as an eagle. Then it turned towards us and I saw that it was actually more distant than it had appeared and was a huge creature.

"A dragon!" Ezekiel cried, "Today we are not protected by the mist. It can see us. Hurry! We must reach the top and find shelter." He endeavoured to hurry up the path but the stones slipped beneath his feet. Only the taut bridle and the horse's sure footing kept him from falling. He recovered and took more care to hasten upwards.

I found myself frozen, trapped by the sight of another creature of legend. The dragon was swooping down at us from a great height, its wings outstretched. As it grew I could see that it had similarities to both a bird and a lizard but much larger than common versions of either. Its head and tail were lizard-like, black and scaly but its body and wings were that of a great bird covered with feathers of blood red.

"Come, Aeddon!" Gwawrwen called, "It isn't far."

Her words alerted me to the danger we were in. I urged my legs into motion and I tugged on Cydy's bridle. I climbed as fast as I could, using my spare hand to steady myself, but as much as we hastened the dragon was approaching at far greater speed. I could not stop myself from turning to watch it every moment or two. Its form grew until I could see that it was immense. Its body from nose to the tip off its tail was almost as long as the nave of Maesycymer abbey. The reach of its wing was a similar great distance and its body the size of a small house. As it drew closer its call became a bone-juddering howl.

We were still yards from the clifftop when it was upon us. Its shadow obscured the sun and half the sky but before it dashed us and itself against the cliff it cupped one wing, turned, and soared up again into the sky. As it passed mere feet from me the gale it had created nearly blew me from my feet and I felt the breath from its mouth. The stench surpassed even the foulest cesspit. I gagged and almost choked but marvelled at the ability of such a huge creature to fly and manoeuvre with such finesse.

"Now!" Gwawrwen shouted, "Before it returns. We can reach the top."

The dragon was still rising as we stumbled onto the almost flat plain between the two summits which guarded the end of the valley. Our climb was over but where could we hide?

"There!" Gwawrwen pointed to an outcrop of rock which had an overhang that offered a little protection. Yet it was fifty yards from our position. We ran. I tugged on Cydy but in truth he needed no persuasion to gallop away from the marauding dragon. Ezekiel too, ran alongside the horse.

The dragon was once again filling the sky as it stooped to attack us. The three of us and Cydy crowded under the lip of the rock but the horse was exposed. The dragon descended, its mighty legs lowered and the talons, each the size of a soldier's pike, stretched out. At the nadir of its dive the dragon's claws pierced the flanks of the horse and then with one beat of its great wings it rose again, effortlessly carrying the horse with it. The poor creature never uttered a whinny as it was taken from us. The dragon rose and dwindled in the distance bearing its prize.

"My books!" Ezekiel cried, running from our hide and waving frantically at the departing dragon.

"Is that all you can think of?" Gwawrwen called after him, "Think of the fate of the poor beast to be torn to pieces by the monster!"

Ezekiel stopped, turned and returned forlornly to us. "But what am I to do now? Do I have to walk?"

"Cydy can't take any more weight," I said, "unless you want to dispose of the unicorns' urine."

The reminder of the piss-filled bags seemed to cheer Ezekiel. "Of course. We have succeeded in our quest. The dragon will be satisfied for long enough for us to complete our escape. We are safe. What need do I have for books? Soon I will be the bearer of Cold Fire and others will read of my success." He turned and strode off in the direction of our return.

I looked up into the sky. "What if there is another dragon hungry for flesh?" I said.

"No doubt there are others in their lairs," Gwawrwen replied, her eyes also on the sky, "but it seems that they prefer sleep to hunting. Let us move on quickly and put as much distance between us and them as we can." We followed Ezekiel and soon came to the path that descended into the next valley, one altogether more familiar and less magical than the home of the unicorns, Cwm Dreigiau.

Chapter 8

September finds herself in darkness and filth

September's feet slipped on the wet cobbles and she felt herself falling. She put her hand down to save herself and it touched something cold and greasy and squelchy. The shock made her recoil and she recovered her balance. The spinning lights faded from her eyes and she looked around. It was dark. Well, not quite. The light was very dim, twilight perhaps, and there were a few small, yellow glows in the buildings that surrounded her. Buildings? They seemed to press her close, all angles and beams. So, she was outside. Somewhere.

She took a breath, perhaps the first since her arrival, and coughed. Stinking air filled her lungs and she wanted to get rid of it but couldn't. After a few more involuntary breaths the reaction lessened and she was able to acknowledge the odours and not just be revolted by them. There was the stench of raw sewage, of decay, of smoke from fires burning some fuel she had no experience of. She raised the hand that had touched the ground to her nose, fearing the worst. She was correct. She had put her hand in something disgusting. How could she get it off? She couldn't wipe her hand on her skirt. Her skirt? She looked down and in the dim light saw that she was still in her school uniform: blazer, shirt, skirt, tights, and sensible black shoes.

September forgot her soiled hand. What had happened to her? Normally, and it had become normal for her, when she transported from home she transformed into a version of herself with a svelte body and long hair, clothed in blue light. Yet here she was still the somewhat plump (despite her recent fitness regime) schoolgirl with the cropped white hair. She was disappointed.

The smell returned to her and she felt in the pockets of her blazer with her clean hand. There was a tissue, probably used, but better than nothing. She wiped the dirty hand compulsively until she was fairly sure she'd got the muck off. She wished she carried one of those little bottles of handwash with her but she didn't. September resolved not to put her hand anywhere close to her face or any other part of her body.

What to do with the tissue? She looked around herself. In the semi-darkness it was difficult to see anything clearly but there didn't seem to be any typical town litter - bottles, cans, plastic bags, that sort of thing - just muck, everywhere. The stink didn't suggest a clean place so she casually dropped the tissue at her feet. Now she could return to the main questions; where was she and what was she doing here? Cyfaill had suggested a need for her special powers, but where was he?

"Mistress September?"

September spun around. A man stood in the shadows. He stepped towards her. His appearance was odd.

"Cyfaill?"

"No, my lady, but I have connections with the person you are thinking of."

"You're a Cemegwr, a manifestation of the Brains?"

The man bowed and September noted that he wore breeches and tights and a fitted coat that came down to his knees. He also had a wide-brimmed hat on his head, with a feather.

"You look like you're in a pantomime," September said.

"Pardon ma'am?" the man said. "Ah, you are not familiar with this period. It is 1680, my lady."

"1680?" September was surprised but not shocked. In recent weeks she had been to so many different places and times she was past being shocked by the act of transport. "Where are we?"

"London."

September had only been to London once, on a school trip, but it hadn't looked or smelt like this place. Then again, it hadn't been 1680 on that visit.

"Why have I been brought here?"

"We sense a stirring in the Malevolence. Something is

about to happen that could allow the evil to enter this universe."

September was confused. "But that can't have happened because I was born more than four hundred years after this time and the world was sort of okay."

"This is not your universe, Mistress."

"Oh, I see. I think." September vaguely remembered Cyfaill's attempts at explanation.

The man nodded, "You understand that that there are many universes similar to yours that make up just part of the Omniverse. This is not far removed from your own so you share many aspects of history up to this point."

"But it's still 1680, a long time ago?"

"You are forgetting that time is just another coordinate in the fabric of the Omniverse. To us all the times in all the universes are simultaneous."

"But because you're not omnipotent you can't tell what is happening everywhere and everywhen," September reeled the sentence off as if she had heard it before, which she had, sort of.

"That is correct, my lady."

"So my universe is not in danger?"

"Not directly, but if the Malevolence gets a foothold in part of your multiverse it could spread and endanger all the universes within it."

"Hmm, we'd better get to sorting it out then." September felt confident after her previous success over the Malevolence. "What's going to happen?"

"I don't know."

"Er, you don't know! What are we doing here, then?"

Even in the shadows, September could see that the man was embarrassed.

"There is some hint that we might find clues here, Mistress."

"A hint of a clue! What does that mean?"

"There may be someone or something that will help us nearby."

September looked around at the candlelit windows of the buildings around them.

"Well, you'd better take me somewhere then to start looking

for them or it. No, hold it, I've got a few questions first."

"Yes, my lady?"

"What shall I call you, if you're not Cyfaill?"

"I will be known as John Henshaw, gentleman."

"I guess that the clothes you're wearing are what any "gentleman" would wear in 1680?"

"Yes, my lady."

"Then why am I still in my school clothes?"

"Because you are not of this universe. You are uniquely able to move between universes and times, as you know. You are September, Cludydd o Maengolauseren and possessor of the Gwylyb Hoedl Gwyrthiol."

September recalled the words but they didn't answer her question. "But I don't look like when I was the Cludydd in that other world."

"This isn't the universe in which you had that presence."

"Oh," September was disappointed, "so I'm stuck with this body am I?"

"It is your form."

"But won't I look out of place wearing twenty-first century school gear?"

"The people in this universe will see you as they expect to see you. Here, as my companion, you will be my lady, a woman of considerable social standing."

"I wish I had the clothes to match."

"I think you would feel more comfortable as you are, Mistress September. The clothes of women of the aristocratic class in this period were not designed for ease of movement."

September shrugged, "Oh well, let's get going. I'd like to wash my hands if I can."

"There is a tavern just down the alley, my lady, and I think some people are gathering there." He pointed with a gloved hand and September made out some movement in the gloom, a door opening, and she heard voices.

"Come on then."

Henshaw lead the way and September followed, looking down at her feet to see where she was stepping. She didn't fancy putting her feet in more of the smelly muck. Thoughts followed each other through her head. What was expected of her? Was she in danger? What was special about 1680s

London? She trembled. It was almost as disorientating and confusing as her arrival in Gwlad and while she might have developed some powers she had no idea whether they were available to her here.

They passed under a sign that showed a crescent Moon on one side and a full Moon on the other. The door to the tavern opened and two men in rough clothes staggered out and, ignoring September and her companion, lurched off down the alleyway. Henshaw held the wooden door, entered, and waited for September to join him.

It wasn't a large room but warm due to the fire that burned on a hearth sending copious amounts of stinking smoke up the chimney. There were also candles around the walls that added to the smoky atmosphere and mixed with the general odour of unwashed bodies and stale beer. There were four boards on trestles with benches alongside, occupied by men of various ages and dress. One table held four men of a somewhat more refined style. Their clothes looked relatively clean and had more embellishments in silk and lace. Like the men at the other tables they drank from pewter tankards. One, with a round clean-shaven face of about thirty, looked up and rose to his feet.

"Ah, Sir John. How pleasant to see you." He beckoned to Henshaw, "Join us. Tell us, who, pray, is your companion?"

"This is my niece, September Weekes." Henshaw turned to September, "This gentleman is Edward Tyson, physician and recently made Fellow of the Royal Society of London for Improving Natural Knowledge."

"You embarrass me, Sir John," Tyson said, waving his arm at the gathering around the table, "We are all Fellows here. Come and join us." The conversation at the table stopped as the other gentlemen looked up. On seeing September they struggled to their feet with various nods and bows and mutterings of 'My Lady'. Tyson hailed a portly man in grubby brown clothes talking to the drinkers at another table.

"Bring a chair for the lady, Landlord, and good wine. And an ale for Sir John."

The man scuttled off to another room. He returned almost immediately bearing a chair and held it while September settled into it. A young woman emerged from the same room carrying a wooden tray bearing a tankard slopping foam, a goblet and a jug. September almost chuckled as the girl approached. Though she wore a scruffy reddish-brown skirt down to her ankles, her cream blouse, spattered with stains, barely covered her breasts. She placed the tray on the table in front of September.

"There you are my lady." The last words were said in a manner that suggested she did not consider September much of a lady to be seen in such an establishment frequented just by men. Nevertheless, she poured wine from the flagon into the goblet then left to answer hails and lewd requests from another table.

"Let me introduce you, Miss Weekes," Tyson said. "Here we have the great Mister Robert Hooke, the designer, with Sir Christopher Wren, of the new London and a most expert practitioner of the art of discovery."

September looked at the man to whom Tyson pointed. He was small and seemed somewhat bent and was decades older than his companions. He nodded in acknowledgement of Tyson's comments although gave a little grimace at the mention of Wren's name. September knew the name of Wren (hadn't he designed St Paul's cathedral?) but that of Hooke was new to her. She wondered if the rebuilding Tyson referred to was the aftermath of the Great Fire of London. Now when did that happen?

"On my right here is Thomas Maslyn. His father owns estates in Flintshire from which coal is mined, much of which is burned in the fireplaces of London such as is warming us this even, so Thomas will soon be very rich indeed."

"That is true, if we continue to put up with the stink from the infernal stuff," Hooke growled.

"It is cheaper than firewood which grows scarce," Maslyn replied good-naturedly to Hooke and offered a smile to September.

"And lastly, we have George Wheler, who is still engaged in writing about his visit to the antiquities of Greece from which he returned four years ago."

Wheler nodded to September and said, "I have been involved in other matters but my account will shortly be published."

"And what is keeping you busy Tyson?" Henshaw said, "still chopping up that porpoise?"

"Ah, that investigation is complete," Tyson said with an eager glint in his eyes, "Now I have another task which is taking all my daylight hours."

"Pray what is that?" Henshaw asked while September tried to follow the conversation.

Before Tyson could answer Thomas Maslyn butted in. "He is dissecting a mermaid."

September's eyes shot to Maslyn. "But mermaids don't exist."

"So some people have said," Tyson replied, "But I have the body of one washed up dead on the Isle of Wight just three days ago."

"A real mermaid?" September said still not believing what she was hearing.

"Indeed, my lady," Tyson insisted, "The head and torso of a woman and the lower parts of a fish. Well, not a fish, it more resembles the rear part of a porpoise which, as Henshaw noted, I dissected a short while ago. Why do you look surprised my lady? Surely if creatures such as porpoise and dolphins and whales inhabit the seas and yet have the form of land creatures such as dogs and cattle and sheep, as my dissections have confirmed, then there can be a type of sea creature that shares the qualities of mankind? My porpoise showed very similar bone structure to those land animals I mentioned and like them it suckles its young with milk from mammary glands so the comparison is proved I say."

Henshaw spoke, "If this obviously most interesting exploration is calling on your time, Edward, what are you doing here at this hour? Has not the Royal Society met for today?"

"Yes indeed, John, but we await a carriage to take us to the home of Sir Robert Boyle. He is putting on an evening soiree to demonstrate the phosphorus."

"Phosphorus?" September said recognising the word.

"We hope to experience the Cold Fire," Wheler said. Hooke and Maslyn nodded agreement.

Henshaw exchanged a glance with September then said.

"This sounds most interesting. Do you think Sir Robert would allow Miss Weekes and I to attend too?"

"I'm sure he will," Tyson said, "It will be an honour to have the company of the lady. In truth, it is probably time that we commenced our journey to Pall Mall. Our conveyance will be nearby." Tyson stood, called the landlord and threw him some coins. The other men raised their tankards and drained them, then also stood. September realised that she had not even tasted the wine provided for her and raised the goblet to her lips. She took a sip. She had drunk wine at home on a number of occasions, particularly when her older sisters were celebrating birthdays. The taste made her screw up her nose. The wine was acidic and had a strong flavour completely unlike the wines her father purchased. She put the goblet down and stood in order to follow the Fellows from the tavern.

The sky was now completely dark outside the inn with only the smallest glimmer of candlelight from a scattering of cracks in shutters. September and Henshaw groped along behind the four gentlemen who turned from the alleyway into a street which was hardly wider. Looming in the blackness was what appeared to September to be a cart with two horses and a shadowy figure of a driver. The men clambered aboard hauling the bent figure of Hooke up beside them. Someone, September wasn't sure which of the men it was, reached down and helped her aboard the vehicle. Henshaw climbed up beside her.

As September seated herself on a rough wood bench, the driver spoke and the cart lurched forward. Although they moved at barely more than walking pace, the cold breeze made September shiver. Henshaw put his arm around her shoulder and drew her to him. The four Fellows were already in deep conversation.

September whispered to Henshaw, "Do you think this Cold Fire has something to do with the Malevolence?"

"I do not know, but the fact that we met up with these four gentlemen seems to be a considerable coincidence."

"But what does it mean? I've heard of phosphorus. I think it's an element, but how can fire be cold?"

"I do not have answers to those questions, my lady.

Perhaps this Robert Boyle will provide them."

"I think I've heard of him. I'm sure his name was mentioned in Physics lessons, something to do with gases."

"I am sure we will learn more when we arrive at his residence."

"And what was all that about mermaids? Surely they aren't real?"

"Tyson's description suggested that they are. Do not forget September that this is not the reality you are familiar with. You are not in the past times of your own universe."

"You mean there may be things which are real here which would seem impossible at home?"

"Yes, my lady."

They were travelling along a wider road now, lined by some grand and obviously new buildings. Despite the lack of street lighting there appeared to be a considerable number of people out in the night, walking, on horseback or in carts and carriages. Flaming torches showed the way.

"Where are we?" September said loud enough to be heard by the other passengers.

"This is Threadneedle Street, my lady," Edward Tyson said turning to speak to her. "You are not familiar with it?"

"No, I haven't been in London long," September replied.

"Your uncle is entertaining you by showing you the city by night?"

"That's right."

"Not a common pursuit, but I am sure Sir John has your safety in mind," Tyson noted.

September turned back to Henshaw and whispered. "The men seem to know you, especially Tyson. Have you spent a while here in this form?"

Henshaw bent his head close to September's. "No, September. I arrived with you, but in the same way that people will see in you what they expect to see so they have a knowledge of me drawn from memories that I have planted within them."

"You can read people's minds?"

"No September. Their thoughts are a complex jumble that is impossible to interpret. I can just insert fragments of images and conversations in their memories that give the semblance of a former meeting."

"Oh," September muttered still not understanding. They continued to trundle through the streets. September listened to the conversations between the gentlemen and looked at the buildings as they passed, dimly illuminated by candles and oil lamps. There were many gaps which Henshaw informed her were still awaiting new buildings following the Great Fire fourteen years before. They circled around one area which seemed to be a huge construction site. There were great blocks of stone and wooden scaffolding reaching up into the night sky.

"Where are we?" September asked.

"The site of St Paul's cathedral," Henshaw answered. "Mr Hooke here is much involved with the design of the new building with Wren, as he is with the reconstruction of much of London."

Shortly they crossed a narrow river hemmed in by buildings.

"The River Fleet," Henshaw informed September, "and now we are entering Fleet Street."

Soon the buildings became grander and on their left September could just make out gardens. She asked which street they were in and Henshaw replied with The Strand. This historical tour of London excited September but she could not forget that she was here in order to face evil. Again.

Chapter 9

September arrives at the home of Sir Robert Boyle

"Do you see the figure of King Charles astride his horse, my lady?" Edward Tyson said leaning towards September. She looked in the direction of his outstretched arm and saw the dark figure he described on top of a tall stone plinth. They were at a triangular junction of thoroughfares with grand buildings on each side.

"What is this place?" she asked.

"Charing Cross," Tyson replied, "The statue was erected just five years ago to commemorate the murdered king. The parliamentarians tore down the cross that previously occupied the spot during the war."

September had a vague idea that he was referring to the English Civil War and the subsequent restoration to the monarchy of King Charles II but a full understanding eluded her. Their journey in the dark passed by grey buildings poorly lit by torches and candles, with raucous shouts emerging from what must have been pubs and hints of figures lurking in the dark shadows, of which there were many. She felt confused. Drawn from her own time and place she didn't even know what season of the year it was although the cold air and dark evening suggested it was not summer. Her purpose here was to defeat the Malevolence once more, but what form her opponent took in this universe, she had no idea. She just felt cold.

"How much longer will we be?" she asked Tyson.

"It is not far now, my lady. We are about to enter Pall Mall."

"Good. Perhaps Mr Tyson, you would tell me about the mermaid you are studying. How are you sure it is a mermaid and not another animal that lives in the sea?" Perhaps if she found out more about what people like Tyson did she would get a better sense of where she was.

"Ah, but that is exactly what the mermaid is, my lady. She did indeed live in the sea but she has the appearance of a female, not unlike yourself but with hair the colour of straw, a face with nose and eyes and mouth, two arms, and being female she had two breasts."

"Perhaps she was a woman who drowned?"

"That could not be because her lower half had the form of the porpoise I mentioned earlier, a muscular tail with fins. Like the porpoise, she could swim with ease but would have to come to the surface to breathe the air."

September could barely believe Tyson's description, "And you think there are more of these um, people, living in the sea?"

"Of course. They are a secretive people that avoid contact with us inhabitants of the land but nevertheless the sightings of them by sailors and by coastal dwellers suggests that there are many of them living in the oceans. Perhaps, in unexplored parts of the globe, in shallow waters, there may be whole communities of the mer-creatures with a civilisation that approaches our own."

Thinking aloud, September said, "If mermaids exist I wonder if other fairytale creatures do too. What about fairies and goblins and unicorns and dragons?"

"Certainly they exist, my lady, though you will not come across such creatures here in London. This is man's domain. But in the wild places, you will find these magical beings. Ah, here we are."

September looked ahead and saw that instead of darkness there was a beacon of light. Hundreds of torches marked the entrance and driveway into a great house.

"This is Robert Boyle's house?" September asked.

Tyson answered, "Well, in truth it is his sister, Katherine, the Viscountess Ranelagh who owns the house. Her husband died some years ago. Mr Hooke here can tell you more about the house as he designed the recent alterations."

The carriage came to a halt and the men stepped down. Henshaw helped September to the ground treating her as the lady that the others addressed her as. Servants guided them into the house and at length into a large room. Numerous candles illuminated the space well enough for September to realise that it was an unusual place to find in a smart house. Although there were rows of plush chairs they were obviously placed there just for the evening's entertainment. The room's fixed furnishings seemed more workmanlike and exciting. There were furnaces set against the wall and sturdy tables on which stood objects of glass and pottery, the purpose of which September could not guess. On the walls there were shelves and racks holding many other oddly shaped glass objects. It was apparently a laboratory although one unlike those at the school she attended.

Most of the chairs were already occupied by gentlemen and ladies in clothes which September guessed were the current fashion. Large balloon-like dresses for the ladies and tights and tight-fitting jackets for the men. September and her companions were shown to vacant seats. September, Henshaw and Thomas Maslyn at the rear while Hooke and the other two were seated in the front row. Servants started to put out the candles until just a single candelabra of six candles remained lit on the table set before the audience.

The expectant crowd hushed as they waited for the arrival of the host of the evening's event. They did not have long to wait. The door opened and, through the gloom, walked two men. The leading one wore a flowing wig and a richly embellished frock coat while his companion seemed to be dressed in more workaday clothes.

The finely dressed gentleman who September guessed was Robert Boyle, stood behind the table and faced the audience, blinking and looking a little self-conscious.

"Greetings, my ladies and gentlemen" he said in a soft, nervous voice, "It is my pleasure this evening to demonstrate to you the qualities of the Phosphorus. I have no doubt that many of you, ladies of letters as well as gentlemen, have already learned about this substance from the pages of the Philosophical Transactions of the Royal Society of London. I do not intend to bore you or disturb the sensibilities of the ladies with a description of how the material is obtained. Instead I wish to display the miraculous properties of what I have called aerial nocticula and some have referred to as

Cold Fire and indeed it is this that explains the late hour of this entertainment."

Boyle paused and turned to his assistant who from the shadows at the back of the room had taken a glass jar from a cupboard. Boyle took the jar and the assistant placed a cover over the candles. September was astonished to find that rather than being lost in the darkness, Boyle was now illuminated by a pale yellow glow emanating from the jar.

"The jar contains a liquid form of the material," Boyle said while holding the jar up for all to see, "which will continue to glow for many hours." He gave the bottle a gentle shake, swirling the liquid, and it immediately gave out a brighter glow. The audience gave out a collective "ooh".

Boyle placed the jar on the table in front of him and picked up an artist's brush that had been set there. He loosened the cork that sealed the jar, removed it and dipped the brush into the liquid. When he withdrew it, the brush glowed brightly.

"As you see, the brush coated with the material appears like a burning taper, but," here he held his hand close to it. The audience gasped with fear that Boyle would burn himself but he did not even flinch. He spoke almost with a chuckle "no heat comes from it."

"Now Mr Godfrey, the next demonstration if you please," he continued. The assistant lifted up a picture frame and held it beside Boyle. In the dim light cast by the jar of phosphorus the canvas appeared dark and blank. Boyle dipped the brush into the liquid phosphorus and then made brush strokes on the surface. When he stepped aside his glowing initials could be seen. The men and women around September gasped.

"I am sure I am not alone in contemplating applications for this luminescent material," Boyle went on, "as a source of light onboard ship or in other locations where fire is a considerable hazard, or indeed to paint the figures on the face of a clock so that the time may be read at night. The phosphorus causes no harm as in my next revelation. Perhaps a gentleman or even a lady would come and stand at my side."

There was muttering, and various men made as if to move but the lady sitting next to Hooke in the front row stood up and moved to stand next to Boyle. Once again he removed the cork from the jar but this time dipped his fingers into the liquid. When he drew it out and raised it, all could see his finger glowing brightly but obviously causing him no discomfort.

"Please my lady, proffer me your bare hand," he said. The lady removed her glove and held out her hand. Boyle rubbed his glowing finger over the palm of her hand. She looked at it, her expression showing amazement. "Hold your hand up for all to see."

September, like all the other watchers could clearly see a circle of light on the woman's palm. Boyle bowed his head, "Thank you Ma'am. You may return to your seat." He then went along the front row dabbing his phosphorescent finger on each gentleman's coat and leaving a glowing patch on each.

"There. You are marked by the aerial nocticula," he said, "but have no fear. It will slowly fade and leave no mark."

Boyle returned to the table where Godfrey had, by the light of the jar, been setting up some other apparatus. One was a small glass phial that shone with a light almost as bright as the much larger jar of liquid phosphorus. Boyle picked it up and waved it to the audience

"In this small container a miniscule quantity of the Phosphorus is mixed with oil of cloves and yet it produces enough light to see one to one's bed without the fear of setting one's night dress alight with a candle," he said with considerable pride in his voice. The gathering clapped eagerly.

"To continue, I have revealed the liquid nocticula to you, now for the icy nocticula which I have so named because it is both solid and resembles ice in its appearance." He took up a pair of tongs from the table and reached into a trough of water, drawing out a tiny chip of material which was almost impossible to see in the gloom. Godfrey lifted the cover from the candles. September found the burst of light almost dazzling. Boyle held the piece of phosphorus in the flame for a few moments until it began to spit and spark. He withdrew it and Godfrey quickly covered the candles again. Now, Boyle plunged the tongs and the burning phosphorus into a round flask almost a foot in diameter. The Phosphorus burned with a bright yellow light and gave off clouds of glowing smoke which first filled the flask and then billowed out of the top neck. The men and women cheered and clapped with glee although some stirred in their seats as if ready to make a dash for the door.

Boyle spoke some more about the marvellous properties of phosphorus using words that September struggled to understand. As Boyle talked Godfrey placed a small pile of black powder on the table in full view of the audience. Nonchalantly, and while continuing to talk, Boyle transferred a tiny piece of the solid phosphorus onto the heap. He carried on speaking, casually describing the powder as that used in cannons and once was planned to blow up the seat of parliament in the time of King James. He reminded his listeners that a flame was needed to fire gunpowder. Just as he finished the sentence there was a bright flash and a roar. A cloud of smoke from the table hid Boyle and Godfrey from view. Many in the audience cried out, some in the front row pushed back in their seats. The smoke slowly cleared and the light grew as servants moved around the edge of the room lighting the candles. Robert Boyle emerged from behind the table, somewhat smudged by soot, and looking a little sheepish.

"Thank you. That is the end of my exposition." He bowed. His admiring audience clapped and roared their approval of his demonstrations. September joined in but leaned towards Henshaw.

"I don't see any sign of the Malevolence in all that. It was just like a show I went to see with school where a scientist did lots of wild things with chemicals."

Henshaw nodded, "You are correct, September. I cannot comprehend what this excitement has to do with the evil. Perhaps some of the learned gentlemen present may help us more."

People were already leaving, no doubt to get away from the smoke that still filled the room. Thomas Maslyn offered September his arm to escort her outside with Henshaw following. The atmosphere outside the house was cold and now smelled cleaner than before. September breathed in the air with some relief.

"You have no conveyance, Sir John," Maslyn said, "At this hour it is not wise to be afoot in London. Perhaps you will accompany me to my residence which is but a few paces from this point?"

Henshaw bowed. "That is very kind of you Maslyn. We will be honoured to accompany you."

Maslyn apprehended a passing manservant carrying a burning torch and having handed over a coin beckoned September and Henshaw to accompany them. The servant set off with the torch held aloft. They left Boyle's residence and re-joined Pall Mall which was still busy with pedestrians and carriages. They turned up a narrower side street but soon emerged into a square.

"You do not know this area of London, my Lady?" Maslyn enquired of September.

"Uh, no." she replied.

"It is Saint James' Square. My house is nearby."

They crossed the dark square and walked up another side street guided by the torch carrier. They turned a corner and then stopped at a tall row of brick built terraced houses. Maslyn mounted some steps and thumped on the door. It was opened quickly by a maid. Maslyn thanked the torch bearer and handed him another coin.

"Now my friends, please enter my home." Maslyn stood in the hallway and invited September and Henshaw past him. The hallway was lit by a single candle but the maid led them into the front room which had a dozen or more candles burning.

"Elizabeth, bring wine and victuals," Maslyn ordered. The maid hurried out as Maslyn spread his arms indicating the easy chairs arranged around the fireplace. "Please sit my lady and you too Sir John. Rest yourselves."

September sat, feeling her body gradually warmed by the burning coals that provided a welcome sight in the hearth. Maslyn saw her looking at the flames.

"Coal fires are quite the fashion in the city now that firewood is becoming scarce," he said, "which is much to my father's satisfaction."

"Ah, yes, you said your father owns coal mines," September nodded, "in North Wales?"

"That's correct. I have some business in overseeing the sale of the material here in London. Some people complain that the smoke from the coals is polluting the atmosphere of the city, but I say it is no worse than wood, the traditional fuel. I am quite sure that coal will soon become the choice of all as forests are protected to provide wood for the navy."

"Your father is going to make a fortune," September commented.

"Indeed, my lady, he already has."

The maid arrived with a tray bearing a flagon, delicate glass goblets and a plate of bread and meats. She laid it on a low table placed between the three, poured wine into the glasses, bowed and withdrew.

September did not need much encouragement to attack the food. She was surprised at how hungry she was. In her previous experience as the Cludydd she had not felt hunger, thirst or fatigue. This adventure was obviously different.

When all three had food and drink, Maslyn addressed them. "Well, what did you think of Boyle's extravaganza?"

"Quite remarkable," Henshaw muttered through a mouth full of bread. "This Phosphorus is certainly a unique substance."

"Yes. Mysterious is it not that it burns without heat and gives out light without being consumed?" Maslyn said.

September sipped the wine and found the taste more pleasant than that provided by the tavern.

"How is it made?" she asked.

Maslyn drew a breath. "Ah, that was a secret which Boyle revealed a short while ago in his letter to the Philosophical Transactions, although his details of the process were few. He has entrusted the task of making the phosphorus to Ambrose Godfrey."

"He was the assistant this evening?" September said.

"That is correct. Godfrey has been Boyle's handyman for some time. It is said that he is now starting to manufacture the Phosphorus for those who may wish to investigate its wonders further, and even to utilise its properties in the manners that Boyle hinted at."

"But where does it come from?" September asked again.

"Boyle did reveal that although as he said this evening it may perturb ladies."

"I'm not bothered. I want to know more about phosphorus," September said.

"You are indeed a woman who has an uncommon interest in natural philosophy," Maslyn said grinning broadly at her. "Boyle revealed that the source of the phosphorus is none other than urine."

"Urine?" September exclaimed.

"Yes, my lady, simple everyday piss. Apparently, Godfrey collects it from the Viscountess' household every day in order to get sufficient to make the small quantity of phosphorus demonstrated to us this evening. If Godfrey intends to produce a greater amount he will have to call on the emanations of the population of London."

"It's just pee," September said again feeling let down and confused.

"Well, it does have to go through a long process with considerable heating, so I understand," Maslyn said.

"I just don't see what that has got to do with the Malevolence," September muttered.

Maslyn looked mystified. "I beg your pardon, my Lady. What is the Malevolence?"

"My lady was just musing," Henshaw intervened. "Tell me Maslyn, has anyone else endeavoured to make the Phosphorus following Boyle's partly divulged recipe?"

Maslyn frowned, "I know of none although no doubt there will be other alchemists in the city who will endeavour to emulate Sir Robert."

"But news of the discovery will have spread beyond the city?" Henshaw queried

"Indeed," Maslyn nodded. "I myself sent word by letter to my cousin who counts himself a philosopher."

September's interest was aroused. "Your cousin?"

"One Ezekiel Soulbury of Maesycymer Abbey."

"Where is that?" September asked.

"It is in a remote part of Wales, somewhat to the north and west. He inherited the house and lands but has frittered most of the fortune on his alchemical searches."

"He's an alchemist too, like you said Boyle is?" September was becoming interested in this Soulbury.

"He is and has devoted his life as well as his former wealth to the endeavour, futile though it may be."

"Futile?"

"Yes, my lady. Most philosophers now think the search for the Philosopher's Stone that will turn base metals to gold, is an idle pursuit with no chance of success."

"That is what your cousin has been trying to do?"

"Indeed it is and he has claimed some success."

"He's made gold?"

"Well, he claimed it was gold but it crumbled to dust after but a few weeks so it was not apparently true gold."

"And that's all?"

Maslyn shrugged. "Just about. Oh, he did manage to summon a dragon once which almost destroyed him."

"A dragon!" September was excited.

Maslyn looked surprised. "Yes, my Lady."

"They exist?" September was wide-eyed and open mouthed.

"Of course," Maslyn said, "few in number they may now be and secretive, but it is well known that the wilds of Wales hide a number of the beasts."

"You said the dragon nearly destroyed him?" September said.

"Indeed I did," Maslyn said. "Two of the peasants that laboured for him were killed and he was lucky the abbey was not burned to the ground. Dragons are dangerous and vindictive creatures."

"Evil?" September whispered.

"There is no doubt they are capable of evil," Maslyn said nodding his head.

"And you think your cousin will try to make phosphorus?" September asked beginning to become fearful as well as intrigued.

"I sent word to him because I was quite sure that Boyle's work would provoke his interest. Although with the details so sparse I do not know how successful he might be, or indeed whether he can locate sufficient supplies of the, um, raw material."

September turned to face Henshaw. "Can we talk, Henshaw?" Henshaw raised his hand. September noticed Maslyn's face freeze as if in a trance.

"Sir Thomas will have no true recollection of our conversation, my Lady. Our conversation will be as clouded in subterfuge in the same way that your dress appears to him that of a lady of the present time. You may speak as you wish."

September glanced again at the blank expression on their host's face. "I don't feel that we are close to the Malevolence here, but this story of an alchemist in Wales with dragons, well don't you think it's worth a look?"

Henshaw nodded, "I think you're right, September. It does appear more hopeful, if that is the right word in connection with the Evil, than what we have seen here in London."

"How do we get there? There are no trains, I suppose?"

"Not in this period, September."

"I don't fancy going all that way in a cart like we were on earlier."

"No, my Lady, but you do have the means to travel anywhere."

"I do?"

"I believe it was called Symudiad on your previous excursions."

"Oh, you mean just go there?"

"Yes, September."

"But I need to know where I'm going, a picture or description." She looked around the room. The dim light barely illuminated the dark wood panelling but she could see paintings hanging on the walls and vague impressions of portraits. "Perhaps Sir Thomas has a picture I could look at. Can we find out, Henshaw?"

Henshaw again waved his hand in front of Maslyn. "Ask, my Lady."

September addressed her question to Maslyn. "Do you have a picture of the place?"

He flinched as he regained consciousness. "I beg your pardon my Lady. What did you request?"

"Do you have a painting of this Abbey where your cousin lives?"

Maslyn looked confused, "Do you mean a representation of the Abbey itself and the land around it?"

"Yes, a landscape I suppose it's called."

"It is an enthusiasm of the wealthy in the Netherlands for such paintings, but the Dutch fashion has not yet arrived in England."

"No one paints landscapes here?"

"Not to my knowledge, my Lady, but, ah, now that you have raised the matter, I wonder?" Maslyn rose from his seat and left the room.

"Where has he gone?" September asked.

"Hopefully, to find something that will give you an image of your destination, September," Henshaw replied. "While we wait I think I shall avail myself of some more of these fine meats." Henshaw tucked into the food on the table while September sipped on her wine.

Maslyn re-appeared soon, grasping a sheet of yellowish paper.

"Perhaps this will be of help to you," he said placing the sheet into September's hand. She looked at it. The paper was rough and thick but it had on it a drawing done in charcoal. It showed mountains, a river and the ruins of a church.

"This is it, the abbey where your cousin lives?" she asked.

"It is a fair representation, my lady. I had almost forgotten that I possessed it. It was done by an acquaintance who had travelled in the Netherlands and became amused by the Dutch fascination with the formations of the land and the constructions of the inhabitants. He came with me on a visit to my father's holdings in North Wales and we travelled to Maesycymer to be entertained by my cousin. My friend passed the time during our stay by making these, ah, landscapes."

"It is an accurate picture?" September asked while staring at the outline of the hills.

"It seems familiar to me although it is some years since it was drawn. I am sure there has been no change to the surroundings and while my cousin's home may have become more dilapidated, I doubt whether there has been significant change."

"Thanks," September said looking intently at the picture. She knew from previous experience that she didn't need to recall every detail of the appearance of a place she wanted to go to. Regardless of how Symudiad worked, and she had no ideas on that, it seemed to draw on her buried memories of a place rather than a conscious visualisation of every landmark. She stood up and handed the picture back to Maslyn. "Shall we go?" she said to Henshaw.

"You are not leaving now are you my lady?" Maslyn said with a hint of horror in his voice, "It is night, and the streets are dark. You will find no honest people abroad at this hour and no transport."

"I don't need transport," she said.

Henshaw also rose, but took September's hand. "Maslyn has a point September. It is night here and it is also in Wales. It would perhaps be wise to arrive in daylight."

September considered, "Hmm, maybe you're right."

"It would be an honour to accommodate you for the night," Maslyn said, "I have a bed for you my lady, with tight cords and a mattress free of bed bugs."

"Oh, thank you," September replied not sure whether to be grateful for his offer.

"Let me guide you," Maslyn said.

"I'll stay here," Henshaw said, "and rouse you at dawn."

"Mmm, thanks." September followed Maslyn from the room and up a dark flight of bare wooden stairs. Maslyn took a lit candle from a wall holder and pushed a door open. The faint light revealed a large bed with a small table beside it. The only other furniture was a trunk beneath the window. Maslyn placed the candle in a holder on the table.

"There is a chamber pot beneath the bed," Maslyn said, "May you have a pleasant night my lady." He backed out of the door leaving September alone.

She went to the bed and sat on the mattress which was covered by a woollen blanket. It felt rather hard but had some give in it. She swung her feet up on to the bed and lay her head on the pillow. She wasn't going to get undressed, definitely not, but she felt tired. Her eyes drooped.

September was roused by a sharp knocking. She opened her eyes to see the door of the bedroom open and Henshaw step through. He looked exactly as he had done the previous evening. A grey light came through the small lattice window with crinkled glass that distorted the view of the building opposite and the clouds. September pushed herself into a sitting position. Her eyes felt sticky and her back stiff but she had apparently slept soundly.

"Come in Henshaw. Is it early?"

"The sun, what you can see of it, has risen but it is early spring so the hour is about seven."

"Time to go then."

"Yes, September, although Maslyn has provided food for you to break your fast."

September didn't feel hungry and she was eager to meet this alchemist cousin of Thomas Maslyn. "Would he miss me if I just went now?"

"I don't think so, September. As I said, you have no existence here. In the same way that your appearance and conversation fits in with his expectations, so your departure would not leave a question in his mind. He will forget you were ever here."

"Oh, well that's alright then." September wasn't sure that she liked being so forgettable. If she didn't really exist here where was she really? Was she even real? "I might as well go then."

"Yes, September. Good luck."

September was surprised. "Why do you say that? You're coming too. Aren't you?"

"No, September. This manifestation is localised here in London. If the Brains feel that you need further assistance then they will create a new entity to join you."

"Oh."

"Perhaps you will return to London and then I will meet you again."

"So I'm left on my own to find this link to the Malevolence and stop it letting the evil through?"

"Yes, September. That is your destiny and the destiny of the Omniverse."

September knew from past experience that simply hoping she could go home and be a normal teenager would not help. She had been given a task and some powers with which to perform it although she had no idea how those powers worked in this universe. She felt a lump in her throat and tears welling in her eyes.

"I don't know what I'm doing here!" she sobbed.

"Yes, you do," Henshaw said gently but firmly, "You will oppose the Malevolence when you find it. You have the unique knowledge of the Malevolence that enables you to understand and defeat the evil. You have the skills gained through your previous challenges to aid you and the power of Brains to support you. The task is difficult and you are our chief hope of turning back the Malevolence but we have confidence in your abilities."

September sniffed. "Well thanks, that's a fat lot of help. It's still me on my own in somewhere I've never been before. Somewhere which has dragons." She had just recalled that detail and she shivered.

Henshaw placed his large hands on her shoulders. "You have the strength to succeed, September. Believe in yourself. You are the Cludydd o Maengolauseren." His words recalled her previous triumph along with all the heartbreak and effort that had involved, but they cheered her a little. Energy seemed to flow into her from him.

"Alright. I don't suppose there's any other way out of this."

"That's it girl." Henshaw removed his hands and stepped away from her. September stood up, walked to the window and looked out. It was drizzling.

"I hope the weather is better in Wales," she said. The picture of Maesycymer came into her mind. It wasn't just the rough charcoal drawing Thomas Maslyn had shown her but was filled with detail and the colours of grass and trees, the flowing river, the peaks and the grey stonework of the abbey. Her view of London became obscured by swirling, violet light. It grew in intensity until all sight of the room with its dark walls, ceiling and floor were lost. She felt the floorboards disappear from beneath her feet.

Chapter 10

We travel back to Maesycymer
lacking a horse

Our return to Maesycymer was not a happy journey. Ezekiel moaned the whole way, not about the fate of his horse, no doubt eaten to the last morsel of hair and bone by the dragon, but about having to walk and the loss of the few items that he had deigned to carry with him. Gwawrwen largely ignored him except to urge him on when he lagged behind us. I just walked alongside the plodding Cydy, the poor creature weighed down with bags of unicorn piss as well as what remained of our supplies. My thoughts were mainly with the unicorns in their magical valley and I am sure Gwawrwen's were too. We didn't converse much except to say a few words when we set up camp for the night beside a stream.

Once again, Ezekiel allowed me to use his powder to light the fire and Gwawrwen cooked us a tasty stew from the limited stock of vegetables and meat we had remaining. We were scared to let the fire grow large in case the dragon was still prowling and fancied the donkey as a dessert to the horse, or possibly one of us as a tasty snack. So we sat close together to keep warm but did not speak.

We settled down soon after eating. It was already dark, and we each took a turn on watch. I presume that Ezekiel remained awake for his period. He relieved me during the first part of the night and Gwawrwen did not comment when we arose in the morning. It had thankfully been a quiet night and we had each slept but still a pall of gloom hung over us despite having succeeded in our quest.

It was late in the afternoon when we walked down the track to the village at the crossroads. Again, there was no welcome for us from the village folk but I was sure we were being watched from behind doors and shutters. I wondered if

Gwawrwen might suggest that we stop there overnight but Ezekiel seemed eager to continue, that is, if eager is the word for someone who groaned with every step. We eventually camped a mile or two further on in a dip on the hillside. There was no water nearby to fill our cauldron so we ate the dry strips of meat that we had left for our supper and once again curled up together to keep warm.

The following day dawned dull and wet. Although I knew that unless we met some mishap on our way we should reach home by nightfall, nevertheless the rain soaking my jerkin still added to my miserable state.

At last we topped the final ridge and there below us was the river that lead to the abbey. My spirit lifted a little, partly because the rain had ceased but mainly because I looked forward to sleeping in my own mattress. The light was fading in the west as we trudged down the hill through Llanllionio and across the river. We reached the Abbey as the final light disappeared from the sky.

Ezekiel had regained some good spirits on the final few yards and as he passed through the gate of his property. He hurried to fit the iron key into the main door of the house.

"Come, hurry boy," he cried to me. "Get that animal unpacked and bring the unicorn piss to me in the crypt." He disappeared inside without any thought of assisting. I sighed and lead Cydy to the stable he had left five days before.

"Don't worry. I'll help you, Aeddon," Gwawrwen said, following me.

"Don't you want to get back to your home?" I asked.

"No. I think I'll stay a day or two. I am interested to see whether the old fool has any success."

I felt my spirits lift. It would be pleasant to have her company, especially as I expected my Master to be issuing frequent commands as he got down to his task.

We unloaded the donkey and carried everything inside. It was Gwawrwen who delivered the urine to Ezekiel while I made sure that Cydy had water and food. When I eventually entered the house it was a hotbed of activity. Ezekiel had lit candles in the hallway, kitchen and his workplace in the crypt. He was hurrying back and forth, aided by Gwawrwen. Adding to the commotion were the putti who fluttered overhead, chattering in their incomprehensible language and pointing at Ezekiel, Gwawrwen and the objects they carried. When they saw me, all three came to me and hovered around my head. I wasn't sure whether they were pleased to see me or had forgotten who I was and were merely surprised at my presence. I brushed them aside and made my way to the steps down to the crypt.

"Ah, boy, at last! Where have you been?" my Master said.

"Tending the donkey who has served us so well," I said, somewhat annoyed by Ezekiel's attitude.

"Well, I have need of you now. We must start the distillation of the unicorn piss. We need heat, a great deal of it." He spoke as if heat was a material to be released from the fuel like water from a tank. Reluctantly, because I could easily have fallen into a sleep immediately, I trudged down the steps to my Master's workplace. Gwawrwen was there arranging firewood in the main furnace.

"I'll assist you Aeddon," she said.

"Why are you helping him?" I said, "He'll have us labouring for him all night."

"I don't think anything will stop him this eve," she said, "Now he has the material he sought he is driven to complete the task."

"But this material, this Phosphorus, does not interest you, does it?" I said.

"I suppose I am a little intrigued to see how my friends, the unicorns, can affect the outcome of Ezekiel's experiments."

I sighed. It was indeed going to be a tiring night. "Alright," I said, "Let us do his bidding."

I didn't feel even the little comfort my mattress offered that night although I did achieve a few hours of sleep curled up on a blanket like a dog in the Master's workshop. At least once we had the fires burning the crypt became warm and my clothes completed their drying. Ezekiel required such a great quantity of heat that the furnaces had to be kept supplied with wood frequently throughout the night. I wondered whether we would have sufficient supplies to achieve a conclusion to the task but we kept the fires roaring all the night long and into the following day.

Gwawrwen was as good as her word and assisted me so we took turns to doze on the floor. Ezekiel, I am certain, did not sleep for a moment. Throughout the night he tended his alembics, adding more of the unicorn piss as the levels fell in the vessels. All the time the putti hovered and skittered around the crypt sometimes flying so close to the furnaces that it was a wonder that they did not get singed, but they seemed unconcerned by the heat. They were however extremely curious about what was happening in the vessels and chattered and pointed with their fingers incessantly.

By morning the crypt was full of smoke and fumes and Gwawrwen and I were driven to seek fresh air outside the Abbey. More firewood had to be brought from the rapidly decreasing log pile. The sun was up and the sky clear but for a few small white clouds. I paused to look around at the hills, remembering that beyond them, just a couple of days' journey away, was the valley of the unicorns and dragons, the former so peaceful and kind and the latter fierce and murderous. Both were imbued with the mysteries of magic but were there two kinds of that hidden power or was it but one, with the ability to support both good and evil? I could come to no opinion myself and resolved to ask Gwawrwen when the opportunity arose, but at that time I was too tired.

Throughout the day, the work continued although to be fair the demand for firewood fell as the volume of the urine decreased. By nightfall the liquid had been reduced so that one flask was sufficient to hold it all and one furnace alone could provide the fire, although Ezekiel kept it at a tremendous heat such that I feared that the vessel would shatter at any moment.

I did not see it, but from Ezekiel's cries and mutterings it seemed that the great volume of liquid was now a sludge which emitted airs of a most disgusting odour. Gwawrwen and I kept our distance, sitting on the steps to the crypt for hour after hour while Ezekiel's behaviour became more and more bizarre. He raved like a madman urging the material to transform into the Phosphorus and called on the masters of his art to assist him. I feared for his sanity and felt sure that he would harm himself. I wanted to pull him away from the furnaces but Gwawrwen held me back.

"He is in such a mood that calling on him to desist from his task could drive him into a rage," she said, "and then it would be you who could sustain injury. We'll watch him and ensure he does himself no harm."

I did as she said but my muscles were tense as I prepared to leap to save him if he should lose all sensibility. He worked on into the night, all the time the putti circling above him, their incoherent cackle apparently urging him on.

I awoke as a dim grey light filtered into the crypt through the small high windows. My head was resting on Gwawrwen's shoulder but my legs were stiff from the unusual position on the steps. The roar of the furnace had ceased and the heat from the fires had died.

"What's happened?" I asked through my sleep-caked mouth.

"I think it is finished," Gwawrwen said. "Ezekiel is examining the contents of the final flask." Indeed, he was scraping inside it with a wooden spatula. The putti circled lower, at shoulder level, as if endeavouring to peer into the flask and see what my Master had made.

Ezekiel was silent, his tongue poking out between his lips as he carefully dragged the material from the neck of the vessel. The end of the spatula emerged and Ezekiel froze.

My muscles locked too, with my mouth hanging open in amazement. Beside me Gwawrwen became rigid. All three of us stared at the lump of material on the end of the rod. No bigger than a pea or perhaps a bean, it nevertheless grabbed hold of our attention. It was the whitest substance I had ever seen: whiter by far than the plumage of a swan or the petals of a lily, whiter even than the purest snow. It wasn't just that it was white; it glowed with a whiteness that no candle could match. The putti hovered over it, cooing like doves, their naked bodies and feathered wings reflecting the pale white light.

After a few moments, the light grew brighter yet and the source appeared to grow. It gave off wisps, not of smoke or vapour but of incandescence itself also a brilliant white.

"Cold fire!" Ezekiel exclaimed.

"Does it not feel hot?" Gwawrwen cried and pushed herself to her feet.

Ezekiel remained like a statue, his eyes fixed on the torch that he held.

"No heat," he muttered, "but cold. It feels colder than the hardest frost. It draws heat from me. My hand is numb. I cannot feel it."

As he spoke the sphere of white grew until it engulfed his hand. Still he did not move.

"Put it down, Ezekiel!" Gwawrwen called. I was on my feet too and about to step towards him. Gwawrwen grabbed my arm.

"No, don't go near that light! It has him in its cold embrace."

The source of the light continued to grow at a greater rate, the intensity growing as the volume increased, filling the room with light. It grew so bright that it hurt the eyes to look at it. I lost sight of Ezekiel in the fiery whiteness and of the putti too. Why they hadn't fled I didn't know, instead they seemed to welcome the enveloping light.

Now I could feel the cold emanating from the light. My skin was goose-bumped and I shivered. The air I breathed felt colder than on the coldest day of winter.

"We must save him!" I said and pulled at Gwawrwen's restraining arm.

"No, Aeddon. We must save ourselves. He has been consumed by the Cold Fire." Indeed, as she said the words, the light expanded to envelop the whole of Ezekiel's workbench and reached up to the ceiling. Gwawrwen backed up the steps pulling me with her. I struggled. My Master needed me but my will faltered as my limbs burned with the cold. I relented and let Gwawrwen tug me up into the kitchen and out of the Abbey.

I stood on the cobbles looking around. The morning air felt strangely warm on my skin although the sun was barely above the eastern ridge. The Abbey looked as it always had done, the stones grey, but as we watched, the fierce white glow emerged from the doorway accompanied by an icy breeze.

Hand in hand, Gwawrwen and I backed away. When would this cold fire cease its growth? When it had consumed all the heat in the world? We could not take our eyes away from the sight. Now white light shone from the windows of the upper rooms as well as from the ground floor. It seemed that in but a few minutes the whole Abbey would be obliterated by the white sphere.

"What's happening?" The voice of a girl said from behind me. I turned, as Gwawrwen did, and saw a young woman standing there. She had white hair just like Gwawrwen but looked little older than myself and she was dressed in a simple dress of blue silk.

"Who ...?" I began.

"What is happening?" she repeated.

"We don't understand," Gwawrwen said, "The Cold Fire ..."

"Phosphorus? This is phosphorus?" the girl said.

"That is what my Master was endeavouring for," I said. I glanced back at the Abbey. The white light now appeared to be shining through the walls and the roof.

"How much did he make?" the girl asked.

"A piece no bigger than the tip of my smallest finger," I replied.

"No!" the girl exclaimed, "That can't be right. It wouldn't make this much light and anyway it's even brighter and whiter than Mr Boyle's Cold Fire. And the cold. Do you feel it?"

"Yes," Gwawrwen said, "It is emanating cold as a normal fire radiates heat."

"But it's not possible," the girl shook her head as if trying to dismiss the sight of what was happening. "Where did it come from?"

"The Phosphorus?" I asked.

"Yes," she said.

"Unicorn's urine," I said.

Her mouth fell open and her eyes widened. "Unicorns. But they ..."

"Are magic," Gwawrwen said. "Come, we must retreat or we will be swallowed up and frozen to an icicle." She grabbed my hand and pulled me towards the gateway. The girl in blue followed, looking over her shoulder as the brilliant white sphere emerged and engulfed the Abbey.

We broke into a run and didn't stop till we were a hundred

paces from the Abbey. We stopped and turned, the three of us in a line, panting. I was between the two white haired women. They looked almost identical except for their dress and that the newcomer was younger. My eyes were drawn back to the Abbey by a crash of thunder.

Even the outer walls had now been swallowed up by the light that was too bright to stare at directly. Overhead dark clouds had formed and lightning arced down. The lightning looked pale in comparison with the incandescent sphere. As we stared, snow started to fall but just in a column about twice the diameter of the white ball. Frost covered the grass outside the Abbey and was spreading towards us as we watched, like white cracks propagating through glass.

"I think it's stopped growing." Gwawrwen said. Although it was impossible to look straight into the light I did feel that I agreed with her. The monstrous globe before us was no longer expanding at the extraordinary pace with which the luminescence had grown from the tiny piece on the end of Ezekiel's spatula.

"I don't think what's happening has finished, though," the blue-gowned girl said. "Perhaps we should get further away?"

The frost on the grass was nearly at our feet so I wasn't reluctant to follow the girl's advice. We retreated further along the track, not running but walking quickly and frequently turning to check that the cold fire was not overtaking us.

We reached the bridge and paused. Still, the light that had replaced the Abbey was the brightest thing to be seen, brighter even than the sun that was now rising into a clear sky but for the dark clouds above where the Abbey had stood. The clouds were growing however, and even at our considerable distance there was a growing chill in the air.

"Who are you?" I asked of the girl.

"My name is September," she replied. It was a strange name for a girl I thought but I recalled the months being used in other names, Saint Augustine for example.

"We have a resemblance in our appearance," Gwawrwen said, fingering her white hair, "but I do not know you."

"I'm not from round here," September said. "In fact I'm

not sure where *here* is exactly."

"This is Maesycymer," I said, "and that is the Abbey."

"Not any more, I think." September said. "Oh, god, I think this is it."

"This is what?" Gwawrwen queried.

"The Malevolence. It's found a way to enter this world."

"Malevolence? What's that?" I asked.

Before the girl could give me an answer there was a cacophony of noise from the white ball. Three flying creatures emerged from the light, and rose, circling over the phenomenon. Though we were a good distance away I could see that they had arms and legs and heads as well as wings.

"Are they the putti?" Gwawrwen asked squinting into the brightness to make out their form.

"What are putti?" September asked.

"Wingéd cherubs," I replied, "My Master summoned them some years ago to be his servants but they provided little service."

"Winged cherubs?" September repeated, "They can't be real, surely?"

"They had the form of infant boys but with feathered wings and they refused all offers of clothing."

September shook her head as if trying to understand something incomprehensible. I suppose it was. Who else knew of putti, save in tales? But I had become used to their presence.

"They may have had the appearance of innocent children at one time," Gwawrwen said, "but no longer. Look!"

The three flying creatures had expanded the circle of their flight so that now they were approaching us. Like Gwawrwen I now looked at them more closely and suspiciously. Though bathed in the white light of the luminescent globe their skin was not the smooth white of a child but dark and leathery. Their wings were parchment stretched over thin bones, like those of bats. The faces, which took on features as they came nearer, were more like that of an old crone. They had hooked noses and mouths that were twisted into a horrible grimace with forked tongues of blood red flickering between their lips.

"If once they were the putti," Gwawrwen cried, "Then now

they are demons!"

The creatures had seen us and were now diving from the sky towards us. Gwawrwen and I flung ourselves onto the ground, cowering, but September remained standing. I heard her muttering.

"How do I save us? I cannot feel the powers within me that I had before"

I had covered my head with my arms and curled up into as small a ball as possible but from the corner of my eye I saw what happened. The three demons swooped towards us while the girl in blue stood defiant. But she did nothing. The creatures were almost upon us when September was engulfed in violet light and then she was gone. I felt a powerful gust of air rush into the space where she had stood just as the demons got there. The wind buffeted them sending them spinning and floundering. One crashed into the ground and lay there stunned but the other two recovered and circled up into the air again as if looking for their quarry. And then I saw September standing about a hundred paces from us on the bank of the river downstream from the bridge. I wondered how she had got there.

She was waving and shouting. Obviously, her purpose was to attract the attention of the demons again. The two in the air saw her and dived towards her. I struggled to my feet and grabbed Gwawrwen's arm.

"We must find somewhere to hide," I said tugging her to her feet. "September has drawn the demons from us."

Gwawrwen looked shaken and fearful. "Beneath the bridge," she said. "That is the only cover." We ran side by side the few yards to the bridge and scrambled down the bank. The river was still high so we had to enter the water. It was cold, very cold, but not as cold as that which I had experienced close to the Cold Fire. As we waded through the water under the bridge I kept watching what happened to September.

The demons swooped like a falcon on a pigeon but as they seemed about to rake her with their claw-like fingers she was again enveloped by indigo light and disappeared. Again, a blast of air took hold of the creatures and threw them into the river. They struggled in the water trying to free their wings but were washed away from us.

"Come on. I think it's safe for a while," September's voice came from behind me. I turned and she was peering under the bridge from the bank. Gwawrwen and I waded back and clambered out. We both shivered uncontrollably.

"We need to get somewhere out of sight, I think," September said.

"The village," I cried, "Meilyr will take us in." I ran around the buttress of the bridge and set off across it with Gwawrwen and September close behind. As we ran up the village street there was no sign of any people. I guessed they had taken refuge in their homes. We reached Meilyr's door and I hammered on it and shouted my name.

I heard the wooden bolts being drawn back and then the door opened. Meilyr stood there brandishing an axe.

"It is you, Aeddon. What has Soulbury been up to now?"

"Let us in please, Meilyr, and I will explain as much as I know." I said.

Meilyr stood back. "Of course, come in." The three of us hurried inside. Meilyr closed the door and shut the bolts with a crash. He turned and faced us. His eyes fixed on September.

"I know Gwawrwen but who is this other who bears a likeness?"

I replied excitedly before the girl could herself. "She says her name is September and she can move without walking."

Meilyr looked confused. "What do you mean?"

"It's called 'Symudiad'," September said.

"That just means 'removal'," Meilyr commented with no loss of bemusement on his face.

"That's it," September went on, "I can remove myself from one place and go to another."

"You are a sorceress?" Meilyr said, wonder now replacing confusion.

"Um, I don't know." It was the girl's turn to look uncertain.

"I think before we can answer more questions we need a moment of recovery," Gwawrwen said, "We have just observed wonders and had a narrow escape from attack by three horrors."

Meilyr was stirred into action, "Of course. I am not being a good host. Sit, please and I will get refreshment." The three of us took stools around the large oak table. I leaned on the board feeling lifeless. The sight of the Abbey and all inside it, including Ezekiel, consumed by the Cold Fire, the attack by the demons, the cold of the river and our race to find cover had left me exhausted and drained of emotion. The two women seemed to be in a similar state. We each remained staring at nothing until Meilyr returned with a large jug which he set down in front of us. From the dresser he took four tankards and placed them beside the jug then filled each from it with foaming ale.

"Drink! The ale will recover your spirits."

Gwawrwen and I drank deeply, but September only sipped at her vessel tentatively.

"Now tell me what has been going on," Meilyr said when he had drained his tankard. "I and other villagers were going about our business when we saw a bright light blot out the Abbey across the river. Then there came great crashes of thunder and screams loud enough to wake the dead. At that everyone ran to their homes expecting another appearance by a dragon."

"That would be a welcome substitute," Gwawrwen said.

"What has Ezekiel done this time to produce such a dramatic effect?" Meilyr said.

"It is a result of the Phosphorus. It gives out Cold Fire," I said.

Meilyr nodded, "Ah, the Phosphorus. That for which he sought unicorns' piss."

"That was his purpose," Gwawrwen nodded in agreement.

"But he didn't make ordinary phosphorus," September said, "He made something special."

"Something magic?" Meilyr asked.

"I don't know what magic is," September said shaking her head, "but it's opened up the universe to the Malevolence."

"The Malevolence?" the three of us said together.

"You used that title before," Gwawrwen added. "What is it? Some evil power?"

September nodded, "All the evil there is. Usually it is kept away, outside, beyond. I don't know where. Just a little evil seeps in normally. But this special phosphorus that your friend at the Abbey made has done something to the structure of the universe and let the Malevolence through."

"What will it do?" Meilyr asked in a voice no more than a whisper.

"Destroy everything," September said. The three of us gasped with dismay.

"How can we stop it?" Gwawrwen said.

"That's my job," September said, "except I don't know how."

Chapter 11

September wonders what the appearance of the Cold Fire means

September looked at the three people gazing at her in fear and awe. The old bearded man who had given them shelter, the resourceful boy who seemed a little younger than herself, and the woman who resembled her, well at least a slim version of her white-haired self. They were no doubt scared by her words about the Malevolence but they had no idea of the terror that awaited them. Of course, they would have some experience of evil, what time had not seen sickness and war and people behaving ruthlessly, but nothing was like the total, unrelenting hate of the Malevolence and its desire to destroy all living creatures.

From what she had seen it appeared that this was what the Brains had sent her here to prevent, a break in the fabric of the universe that allowed the Malevolence access. She was too late to stop it so now it was her task to push the evil back from where it came and seal the rent in the cosmos. But how? This was not somewhere she was familiar with. On Gwlad she had learned how to wield the Maengolauseren that had summoned her and the seven metals that the people used which had their miraculous powers. That knowledge was no use to her here. The laws that governed this universe were different. The world seemed like her own, at least a past version of it. The London of 1680 that she had observed looked a bit like historical dramas from TV and she even recognised the names of some of the people mentioned in conversation. Nevertheless, it wasn't her universe. Here people talked of mermaids, and unicorns and dragons as if they were real and not fabled creatures. Today she had seen demons flying in the Welsh sky. Here, therefore, magic must have a true presence.

The Brains, Cyfaill and Henshaw, had suggested that she would have powers which she could call on, but apart from the ability to move instantly from place to place she could think of nothing she could use to oppose the Malevolence and no way of utilising the character and memories of Malice, her dead twin sister, that she carried within her.

She realised that the three of them were expecting her to say more.

"I'm not from here," she added.

"We can see that, my girl," the man that the boy called Meilyr said, recovering some normality in his voice, "A young woman with the looks of Gwawrwen would be well known."

Aeddon added, "And I haven't seen anyone here able to move from one spot to another in the blink of an eye."

"I'm sure I would know that there was someone who could be my sister, or child, residing near me," Gwawrwen added.

September shook her head, "No, you don't understand. When I said "here" I don't mean here, this place. I mean this universe, this time."

Now all three of them stared at her in a mixture of disbelief and incomprehension.

"You are from heaven? An angel?" Meilyr said.

"No, Meilyr," Aeddon interrupted, "she doesn't mean that. Does she look like an angel? No, you mean you are not from Earth. Is that right September? Perhaps one of the other planets that circles the Sun?"

"Ah, you know how the planets are arranged?" September said. So people at this time and place had some understanding of the universe.

"My Master had the works of Galileo Galilei in his library. At least until he sold them."

September nodded. She'd heard of Galileo. "Right, but I'm not from another planet. I'm from Earth but not this one."

The three of them looked at her not understanding. "My home is like yours," September went on, "but it's slightly different."

"Ah, a world in the shadows," Gwawrwen said, "hidden from view and set apart from us like an image in a mirror."

"Something like that," September replied, not sure if

Gwawrwen had the right idea or not."

Meilyr frowned. "What is different in your world to ours?"

"Well," September was unsure how much to reveal. It was pointless trying to explain all the changes that three hundred and thirty years or so had brought. "We don't have magic," she decided on. "At least, some people believed in it but it doesn't exist."

"But you have magic," Aeddon said, "You have come to us from your world and you can, what did you call it, Symudiad."

"I'm special," September said, then regretted it, "I mean, for some reason I was selected to fight the Malevolence. Me and members of my family."

"You have been given a task which you must see through," Meilyr said, nodding as if he understood.

Gwawrwen looked thoughtful. "Your family you say. We share a likeness, perhaps our families are related across the worlds. Where does your family live?"

It was no point naming her home town. It didn't exist in the seventeenth century, but September knew where her ancestors came from. "They're from a place called Llelluched, near Machynlleth."

Gwawrwen smiled. "I know it. It is two day's walk to the south. I have family there as well. They are miners."

"That's right, my family were too," September suddenly felt a sense of belonging to this white-haired woman. "But you can't be the seventh child?" She had met all the white-haired seventh children of her ancestors when fighting the Malevolence on Gwlad and retained all their memories.

"No," Gwawrwen said shaking her head, "but I had an aunt, Dilwen, who was the seventh child of her mother and she had white hair. Her daughter does not though."

"Dilwen! Yes," September exclaimed. She was the second of her six predecessors. "Perhaps if we met she could help me."

Gwawrwen's expression became sad. "I'm sorry, Dilwen died in childbirth twenty years ago."

September's head dropped. She had no idea when most of her ancestors died as she had only met them as young women when they had been drawn to Gwlad. She knew nothing of their subsequent lives.

"This talk of white-haired women is not dealing with this Malevolence," Meilyr said. As if to back him up there was a piercing screech. The four of them rushed to the windows and looked out of the cottage. The three demons were circling overhead.

"Close the shutters!" Gwawrwen ordered. "We must not let those creatures see us again."

Meilyr and Aeddon closed the hinged shitters plunging the room into darkness. Meilyr lit a pair of candles on the table and the four resumed their seats. September looked at her three companions in the flickering illumination.

"What wickedness can those beings of the devil perform?" Meilyr asked, glaring at September.

"Plenty, I'm sure," she replied, "but they are only the start. Soon the spirits of the Malevolence will arrive and spread across the world. In fact, I'm not sure why they haven't started already."

"Spirits?" Aeddon asked.

"Yes. Spirits of the dead and unborn," September explained, "All they feel is hate and they will destroy everything."

"Everything?" Gwawrwen asked.

"Everything that is alive – plants, animals, people," September said.

"How do they have such power?" Aeddon asked.

"I'm not sure," September replied, "On the other world they took the form of monsters, and infected people making them turn bad."

"Monsters like the demons?" Aeddon said, eyes wide.

"Sort of," September said.

"But it hasn't happened yet," Gwawrwen said, "These spirits of hate have not entered our world."

September considered. "The spirits come from the dark, a dark so black you can't imagine it."

"Where is there a place so dark?" Aeddon asked, "since beyond the planets the stars go on for ever."

September struggled to answer. "Um, they come from somewhere else, not in the universe."

"But surely the universe is all there is or can be," Aeddon said, "That is what the books say."

"I'm sorry, Aeddon, I can't explain it any other way," September said, "but I've been there and it is empty."

Gwawrwen was scratching her cheek, "But the Abbey has been engulfed in light. How can light bring forth darkness?"

"They are opposites," Meilyr said, "like the shell of an egg and the chick that grows inside. The shell is dead but it gives forth life."

"The globe of light is an egg!" Aeddon said jumping to his feet.

"That's right, or something like," September exclaimed, "and it hasn't cracked yet."

Gwawrwen was thoughtful. "Then perhaps we have time to do something?"

"But what?" September said. She felt useless and afraid.

"The unicorns," Gwawrwen said. "The cold fire came from their piss. Perhaps they have knowledge of this Malevolence?"

"The vale of the unicorns is more than two day's walk away," Aeddon said.

"Yes, but September can take us there in an instant," Gwawrwen said.

September nodded. "If you can give me a picture of it. I can take you. All of you perhaps."

Gwawrwen shook her head. "I think Aeddon and Meilyr should stay here and warn the people of Llanllionio to stay inside, out of the reach of the demons, and also to keep a watch on what is happening at the Abbey."

Aeddon and Meilyr nodded agreement although Aeddon appeared disappointed.

"I dearly wish to meet the unicorns again but I don't want to go from here and leave my Master trapped in what has become of the Abbey."

"I'm sorry Aeddon, but I think he is either dead or converted to one of the Malevolence's servants," September said.

Aeddon's face drooped but then he stiffened and held his head up. "That as may be," he said, "I shall wait here and hope to find out his fate."

September nodded agreement. "We must go and meet these unicorns, then" she said wondering at her own acceptance that the fabled creatures lived. "Describe the place to me."

Gwawrwen spoke of the meandering river in the hidden valley with its towering cliffs, the grove of trees and the grassy meadow filled with wild flowers. September took her hand and saw a picture of the place in her mind. "Hold on to me, Gwawrwen," she said. Gwawrwen gripped her waist as September willed their movement. Falling shafts of violet light surrounded them, obscuring the dark cottage. They moved.

Chapter 12

September carries Gwawrwen to the valley of the unicorns

September's feet found uneven rock. She toppled and fell, loosening Gwawrwen's grip on her. She sprawled across the rough ground as the light dispersed and she could see. It wasn't what she had pictured. Gwawrwen lay by her side on the jagged stone at the edge of a precipice. Not far away a stream rushed over a waterfall with a roar. She sat up and looked around at the ragged ridge and seeing below a lush valley with trees and meadows and a winding river – her intended destination.

Gwawrwen stood and offered a hand to tug September on to her feet.

"I hope your journeys do not always end so uncomfortably," Gwawrwen said, smiling.

September shook her head. "I don't know what has happened. I've done Symudiad many times and never failed to go to exactly where I was meant to be. Why aren't we down there?" She pointed down into the valley. She felt shaken, unsure why her powers had failed her, the powers that stopped her feeling like a lonely, lost schoolgirl.

"It is the realm of the unicorns," Gwawrwen said, "Perhaps they do not allow visitors to arrive so abruptly. We must make our way down the trail."

"Unicorns have the magic to block my power?" The thought troubled September. Only Malice had been able to stand up to her and even she had been overcome with the help of the Cemegwr. "They must be very powerful indeed."

"Follow me. You will soon meet them and learn the extent of their powers."

"How do we get down? It's a sheer drop."

Gwawrwen chuckled. "For those the unicorns allow to

enter, there is a path, steep it is true, but negotiable. We followed it a few days ago. Come on. We may not have much time and it will take us a while to reach the unicorns." She set off towards the edge of the cliff and began the descent. September followed warily picking her footsteps on the narrow, indistinct path. The dizzying drop into the valley made her move slowly and frequently she put a hand out to steady herself.

Gwawrwen stopped and looked back seeing that September had fallen behind. Over the noise of the waterfall she called out, "What is the matter, September?"

September looked up from her feet, and swayed as she took in the panorama.

"I'm scared," she replied, "I'm not used to this."

Gwawrwen called back. "It gets easier soon, but we must hurry."

"I know," September answered, resuming her scramble resting on her hands while she chose her next footstep. She was relieved when Gwawrwen's predictions proved true and the path became less steep. Below her she could see the pool that received the water from the waterfall and beside it, like a guardian, a great round rock looking a bit like an egg in a shallow egg cup. She grew in confidence, striding out faster and catching up the older woman as the path turned from bare rock to soft grass.

They strode on following the river. Now, despite their speed and the resulting shortness of breath that September felt, she was struck by the beauty of the hidden valley, the long grass packed with wild flowers of all colours and scents, the tinkling water as it sped along its channel and the increasing number of trees.

Gwawrwen stopped and signalled September to pause. She was grateful as it allowed her to catch her breath and cool down a little.

"The unicorns are in that copse," Gwawrwen said.

"You know where they are?" September gasped.

"I feel their presence as they sense ours, but we must approach slowly and not rush up to them."

They walked on under the trees, September searching with her eyes and ears for signs of the fabled animals but detecting none. Then they stepped into a small clearing with the sunlight streaming through the foliage and there they were, three creatures that paused in their grazing and looked up at them through large, pink eyes.

"They're woolly rhinoceroses!" September said, almost bursting into giggles.

Gwawrwen turned to her and spoke firmly, "They are unicorns."

"But all the pictures I've seen show unicorns as white horses with horns on the top of their heads," September said. "These have horns on the end of their nose like a rhino and their bodies look like rhinos too except for the white fur."

"Horses do not have horns. These are unicorns," Gwawrwen repeated, "Now we must approach them slowly. Copy what I do."

Gwawrwen moved towards the largest of the unicorns with September at her side. Although the difference to what she had expected was a surprise and September was annoyed with herself for giggling, the animals impressed her. They were much more heavily built than horses and their horns looked more business-like than the decorative attachments on the fairy-tale creatures. Gwawrwen reached the animal and placed a hand gently on its horn which was about half a metre long and more than ten centimetres across at its base. September placed her hand alongside Gwawrwen's. The horn was warm and throbbed with life. She felt a presence in her head.

<Welcome, bearer of the Maengolauseren,> she heard soundlessly.

"You know who I am?" she said aloud.

"You don't have to speak to them," Gwawrwen said.

<No, of course not,> September thought.

<We know of you and your exploits,> the unicorn said. In her head the voice had a deep but gentle and kind tone. September found she knew that his name was Adamant and that it was the Welsh for Diamond.

<How?>

<We have connection with the beings you have known as Cemegwr.>

<So you know of the Malevolence then.>

<Yes, but our knowledge is incomplete. We did not realise that the substance that Ezekiel Soulbury wanted to extract from our waste would disrupt the fabric of our world and allow the Evil to come upon us all.>

September was relieved that the unicorns understood the problem, but did they have a solution? <What can we do to stop the Malevolence from coming?>

<We fear it may be too late to prevent the spirits' arrival.>

<But we must be able to close the rift!> September felt her fear grip her.

<Perhaps there is a way but you are the one to do it, not us.>

<How?>

<That we do not know.>

September was aghast. <But if you can't tell me, I can't do it. The spirits will pour through and destroy everything.>

<We have some powers to resist their hate, as do our allies.>

<Allies? Who?>

<Dragons.>

September felt Gwawrwen's mind explode beside her <Dragons! But they are our enemies too. They attack us and our homes. Just two days ago, after we left you, a dragon took the horse that Ezekiel rode. Surely dragons won't help us against this Malevolence?>

The unicorn calmed Gwawrwen. *<It is true that dragons dislike your people and your habit of claiming the land for yourselves. They are protectors of the Earth and will oppose any that seek to destroy it.>*

<So they will help us?> September thought.

<Yes, and they approach now. Come, we must meet them in the open.> The unicorn began to move causing September's and Gwawrwen's hands to fall from its horn. The other unicorns followed. Although they moved at a slow gait September and Gwawrwen had to run to keep up. Soon they emerged from the trees onto a wide meadow. Diamond and the other unicorns stopped. September and Gwawrwen caught up and replaced their hands on the male creature's horn.

Its head lifted up. *<Look, they come.>*

September looked up into the clear blue sky. There were

dots that looked like birds launching into flight from the top of the ridges on both sides of the valley. Some were already circling high above them. As they descended in lazy loops she amended her opinion – they were like birds but huge, bigger than any eagle. Lower still they came and now September could make out details.

"They're flying dinosaurs!" she cried out, "Pterodactyls."

"I don't recognise your words," Gwawrwen said, also looking up into the sky.

"But they're extinct! They lived millions of years ago," September insisted.

"Dragons have always lived," Gwawrwen said, "and we have always feared them."

Now September had a clear view of the leading dragon as it prepared to land. She noticed that it was unlike the flying dinosaurs she had seen in books as a child. These creatures had blood-coloured feathers covering their bodies and wings, but their heads and tails and talons were those of the fierce reptiles of pre-history. Neither did they resemble the dragons of tales as they had just two legs and wings like birds.

<I didn't know there were so many> Gwawrwen said through her contact with the unicorn.

<We provide protection for them here,> Adamant replied <A safe home away from people like yourselves who would destroy them.>

<They have been hunted because they take our sheep and cattle, as well as horses and even people.> Gwawrwen said.

<All creatures have to eat,> Adamant said, <Dragons need meat and you have disposed of their usual prey – wild grazing animals, wolves and bears.>

The lead dragon touched down on the grass twenty metres from them and others landed behind forming an arrow shaped phalanx allowing each to see the unicorns and women. September thought they looked ungainly standing on the flat grass. The air and the ragged peaks were their environment. She was scared but also impressed. The creature was thirty metres long from the tip of its beak to the end of its tail with a wingspan a similar distance until it folded its wings to its side. It stood on two legs the size of sturdy tree trunks with clawed feet two metres across. It lowered its head and stretched out its neck towards them. Its beak-like mouth opened and September saw rows of teeth and smelt a foul sulphurous odour. The dragon let out a piercing howl. The pain in her ears made September take her hand away from Adamant's horn so that she could cover them. Seconds passed and the echo rebounded from the distant mountains. September remained trembling, staring at the gigantic beast, too scared to move, wondering if she was about to be gobbled up in one mouthful. She felt something soft and leathery nudge her arm. She flinched and turned. It was Adamant's broad muzzle. She realised he was trying to get her to put her hand on his horn again so they could communicate.

<The dragon offers his greetings,> September heard in her head.

<Is that what that noise was?> September thought.

<Yes, although he also asks why we are consorting with people.>

<Gwawrwen and me?>

<Yes.>

<Have you told him about the Malevolence?>

<The dragons are aware of the dangers the Earth faces.>

<Can you ask him to help us?>

<I have.>

<What does he, she, it … I don't know what it is. Does it have a name?>

<In your language she is called Obsidian.>

<That's a rock.>

<Yes, one of the foundations of the Earth, like the dragons.>

<Oh, yes. I see. Can I speak to Obsidian?>

<Just think. Your feet are on the ground. Your thoughts will carry to her. She may not reply. Dragons are not accustomed to conversing with people.>

<Why is that?>

<Because people are usually trying to kill them.>

<Oh.>

September looked up at the huge head of the dragon which had lowered so that it was only a few metres above her. The large red eyes stared at her from the black reptilian face, as if examining her closely. She wondered how people managed to kill such large and powerful creatures. September took a deep breath, closed her eyes and composed her thoughts.

<Obsidian, I am September.>

The reply crashed into her head. <I KNOW WHO YOU ARE. THE UNICORN HAS INFORMED US.>

<Oh, good. Then you know that I was sent here to fight the Malevolence and stop it destroying everything.>

<YOU DO NOT SEEM TO BE SUCCEEDING.> There seemed to be a chuckle in the dragon's thoughts.

<No. You're right, because although I was brought here I don't know what I must do and the Malevolence is about to spread over the Earth, if it hasn't started already.>

<YOUR PEOPLE MEDDLED WITH THE STRUCTURE OF REALITY.>

<Um, yes, well, it seems Ezekiel did something he didn't really understand.>

<AND BROUGHT EVIL ON US ALL.>

<Yes, but will you help us fight the Malevolence?> There was silence in September's head. Some seconds passed before Obsidian replied.

<WE WILL OPPOSE THE EVIL OF WHICH YOU SPEAK. IT IS OUR DUTY TO THE EARTH, NOT TO THE PEOPLE WHO SEEK TO DESTROY MY CHILDREN AND MY BROTHERS AND SISTERS.>

<No, I see. I don't think people here realise what you are. But perhaps you'll help me. The Brains sent me to defeat the Malevolence and I need all the help I can get.>

<HOW CAN WE HELP YOU WHO BORE THE MAENGOLAUSEREN, THE PROTEGÈ OF THE CEMEGWR?>

September was surprised again at how her past exploits were known to these magical creatures.

<Because this place, this universe, is unfamiliar to me. I don't know how to push the Malevolence out.>

The dragon bowed its head as if showing that it understood the problem.

<YOU WILL NEED POWERFUL MAGIC.>

<Yes, I think I realise that, but how do I learn it?>

<YOU ARE BORN TO MAGIC ALTHOUGH

LEARNING HOW TO USE IT IS IMPORTANT. YOU WERE CREATED BY THE CEMEGWR TO WIELD THE MAGIC OF THEIR LITTLE UNIVERSE. PERHAPS YOU WILL BE ADEPT AT THE MAGIC OF THIS UNIVERSE.>

September felt that they were going around in circles.

<Maybe I do have the ability but I don't know where to start. What do I have to do to wield this magic?>

<WE CAN NOT HELP YOU, ONLY THE MAGICIANS OF YOUR OWN PEOPLE CAN REVEAL THE SPELLS THAT WILL WORK FOR YOU.>

September was lost for a reply. If she couldn't be helped by unicorns and dragons, magical creatures if ever there were any, even if they didn't look like the pictures in the fairy stories she'd grown up with, who could help her?

The dragon cocked its head, listening to something. Then it lifted its head and unfurled its wings. It let out another long roar, that threatened to burst her ear drums.

<THE SPIRITS OF HATE ARE IN THIS UNIVERSE. THEY APPROACH.>

The dragon flapped its wings in long, slow actions. The wind it created blew September and Gwawrwen off their feet and they tumbled over the grass to land at the feet of the unicorn. The dragon lifted off the ground followed by its fellows. They quickly gained height, circling and climbing into the sky over the valley. September scrambled to her feet, in awe of the sight. She watched as the dragons gathered into a flock, forming a V formation like geese or a flight of bombers and headed to the south-west ridge which September and Gwawrwen had clambered down. September saw that the sky in that direction was darkening.

"It's happened. The Malevolence has come," September said, staring at the blackening sky. It looked like a storm cloud growing on a summer's day but she knew it was the host of evil spirits pouring into the world.

"We must get back to Aeddon and Meilyr," Gwawrwen said.

Fear filled September. The horror that she had thought she had seen the last of on Gwlad was here, now, and she had no way to stop it.

"What can the dragons do?" she asked. Gwawrwen

shrugged and reached out to touch Adamant. September too, placed her hand on the unicorn's horn.

<The dragons have their fiery breath and their determination to protect the Earth. They can destroy the Evil.>

<But not defeat it,> September thought.

The unicorn lowered its head. <You are correct, but they can slow the spread of hate across the world.>

<They'll call more to help them, won't they?> September thought, thinking of the twenty or so dragons flying into battle with billions of spirits.

<More?>

<More dragons, from Ireland, Scotland, further away, China even?> Gwawrwen said.

The unicorn shook its heavy head slowly. <No, there are no more dragons anywhere in the world. Those that you saw are the last.>

September's breath caught in her throat. "No!" She exclaimed out loud.

<They have declined for centuries as men sought them out and destroyed them first with their swords and spears and recently with their powerful, fire-spitting weapons.>

Gwawrwen looked at September with eyes wide open with fear. "Then it is you, September. You must find the way. You must find magic as the dragon said."

September sighed, "But how? I still don't know what to do."

<You must learn from the people who use magic. We do not understand how your men and women manipulate the forces of the universe. Find the people who wield your magic.>

September looked at Gwawrwen, "You? You said people called you a sorceress?"

Gwawrwen shook her head, "They did but they were wrong. I have a skill with herbs and fungi, but I just make salves and medicines and spices that make food more tasty. I do not recite spells."

September's head jerked left and right, and up, looking around the valley as if she expected a magician to spring into sight. "Where are they then?"

"Not round here," Gwawrwen said, "Not any more. Perhaps amongst the learned men in London there are some who still practise the skills told of old."

September stared at her. "You mean the Royal Society? But they're scientists or at least trying to be."

"What is a scientist?" Gwawrwen said.

"They're ..." September wasn't sure how to explain. What made a scientist a scientist? She remembered Edward Tyson in London talking about dissecting a porpoise – and a mermaid. Perhaps the fellows of the Royal Society weren't unfamiliar with magical matters after all.

"Perhaps I do need to return to London," she said. "In any case, they will need warning of what is coming."

"But before you go, take me back to Aeddon and Meilyr. I must know that they are safe," Gwawrwen said.

"Yes, of course." She looked up to the ridge where the dragons had disappeared into the growing darkness. She didn't look forward to retracing their steps up the steep path. "Do we have to climb out of the valley first?"

<Do we?> Gwawrwen asked of Adamant.

<We will allow you to move from here,> the unicorn said, *<and know that we provide some protection to you and your companions that have visited and touched us.>*

<Aeddon has your protection?> Gwawrwen asked, her face lighting up.

<Yes, some. We cannot make him invincible to the Malevolence's attacks at this distance but his fondness for us will hide him from the spirits.>

<Thank you,> Gwawrwen said and September could hear the relief in her voice.

<Know also that you and your friends are welcome to find safety with us here. We can resist the hate of the spirits for some time yet.>

September hoped that the unicorn's confidence was justified. She wrapped Gwawrwen into her arms. <Thank you,> she thought, <I will find the answer and come back.>

<We have faith in you, September.>

September withdrew her hand from the unicorn's horn and immediately felt a sadness at the loss of the contact with the gentle creature. She visualised the dark room in Meilyr's cottage. The grass and trees and the unicorns disappeared behind cascades of indigo light.

Chapter 13

I go back to the Abbey to try to save my Master

September and Gwawrwen disappeared from my sight in a column of violet light that illuminated Meilyr's cottage. It was the third time I had seen the young woman perform her magic but at such close proximity the light hurt my eyes and the rush of wind all but bowled me over. Even Meilyr staggered and had to grip the table. His eyes were wide and staring as if he didn't believe that the two women had gone.

"That was Symudiad?" Meilyr finally gasped.

"That's what she calls it," I replied, "It is powerful magic."

"It certainly is, my boy," Meilyr added, still staring at the empty space where September and Gwawrwen had stood. "I hope the unicorns can answer their questions. I do not like this talk of malevolence and evil emerging from this thing that Ezekiel has called up."

I too shivered at the thought of the disasters that September had foretold. Surely my Master, bad-tempered and foolish though he was, could not be a servant of such evil. I wondered whether he still survived trapped within the shining egg, perhaps imprisoned by the demons that were once the cheeky putti.

"I must do as Gwawrwen suggested and keep watch on the Abbey," I said, overcoming my fears that pressed me to stay in Meilyr's cosy and secure cottage.

"It is a dangerous task with those demons loose," Meilyr said.

"But I must see what has become of Ezekiel."

"Then take care, boy. Keep out of sight of those creatures and come back here at the first impression of danger. Here, take my jerkin. You said the Cold Fire made the air and ground freeze." He took off his leather jacket and passed it to me. I put it on. Although it hung loosely I wrapped it tight around me and felt protected by it.

"Thank you, Meilyr. I will do as you say."

"I will visit my neighbours and warn them too. It may be that the church will provide more protection than their shacks."

I nodded and made my way to the door. I opened it a little and placed my face to the crack. The village street was deserted and quiet. Even at this distance there was a glow in the sky from the direction of the Abbey. I pulled the door open a little more and slipped out. I looked up. Thick, dark clouds filled the sky, moving swiftly in a circle centred over the Abbey. They glowed with the reflected light like a mistimed, exceptionally bright, white sunset. Thankfully there was no sign of the demons in the air.

I made my way down the steep street, keeping to the side so that if the demons or any of the spirits that September described appeared, I could take refuge in the cottages. Down below was the river, flowing as normal except that I could see ice spreading out from the far shore across the surface, as sometimes happened in the coldest of winters. I saw the bridge too, clear and empty. I had to cross it to approach the Abbey but knew that once I left the safety of the village I would be exposed to view. Nevertheless, I crouched down and half ran, half crept, along the track to the bridge and then keeping my head below the walls at the side of the bridge, crossed the river.

I paused before leaving the minimal protection that the parapet of the bridge provided and looked towards the Abbey. It was completely lost in the sphere of light that was too bright to look at directly. The cold in the air penetrated me and I shivered despite Meilyr's jacket. There was frost forming on my eyebrows from the cold wind that blew and snow fell from the clouds above that swirled around the Abbey.

The demons were still not in evidence so I left my refuge and walked along the track towards the ball of light. I say walked but it was more of a creep, hunched over as if expecting an attack from above at any moment. The cold grew in intensity with every step. My hands gripping the edge of the leather coat around me became numb, as did the toes in my worn shoes. I had to turn my head away from my objective as the light burned through my eyelids. I stumbled on, half blind, my ears filled with the icy gale that buffeted me. Beneath my feet, the surface changed from rough gravel to cobbles. I had entered the outer gate of the Abbey. I peered through slit eyes. The light was all around me but the wind had calmed and there was silence. But the cold, oh, the cold. The air froze in my lungs, and the shards of ice hurt every time I breathed. My head felt numb as if my brain itself was freezing solid. I knew I couldn't remain for long, but I had to find my Master.

Knowing my way from my years living there, I stumbled forward, with my eyes tight closed. I crossed the courtyard and came to the main entrance to the house. I entered, surprised that despite the all-encompassing Cold Fire the Abbey remained, apparently intact. I made my way along the corridor and into the kitchen and then approached the steps down to my Master's workshop. I descended into his domain, one careful step at a time. At the bottom I took a few trembling steps. My knees hit something and I stumbled. I put my hand out to steady myself and felt cloth turned hard. I opened my eyes a tiny fraction, scared at being blinded by the brilliant light. Through my eyelashes I saw a figure kneeling at my feet – my Master. I crouched down, reaching out to touch his shoulders. My hands nearly froze to him. His body was an immoveable block, his hair and beard as rigid as icicles.

Involuntarily, I flinched and my hands brushed his head. There was a loud sharp noise as frozen snow cracking and sliding from a roof. Ezekiel's frozen head fell to the floor and shattered into a thousand shards of flesh turned to ice. Then the rest of his body crumbled into a heap of fragments.

I leapt backwards and let out a cry of pure horror. I turned and ran, up the stairs to the kitchen, careering into table, doorjamb, the walls of the hallway until I was out of the Abbey and running towards the gate, my eyes squeezed shut. As I reached the gateway I heard screams behind me. The demons had become aware of my presence. I ran, ran as fast as I have ever run, back along the track to the bridge.

With the light dimming beyond my eyelids, I at last opened them. My vision was filled with spots of light, but I could just make out my path and the bridge ahead. The three demons came into view, flying over me but, for some reason I could not discern, they failed to see me. Perhaps I was hidden in the snow that was falling. I reached the bridge and ran across it though my lungs were ready to burst, and on up the street to the village.

I reached the first wooden house. Meilyr was there at the door, sacks draped over his shoulders to replace the jacket he had given me.

"Aeddon, here!" he called. I ran to him, "Are you pursued?" The demons had flown elsewhere, so I stopped and stood panting, my inside burning while my skin and flesh remained frozen.

"I don't think so," I gasped. Meilyr grabbed me and dragged me inside the dark hovel.

"You're frozen, boy," he said and hugged me to him. His body began to warm me and take the numbness from my limbs. I began to shiver. "How far did you get?" he asked.

My teeth chattered but I muttered. "Right into the Abbey. It is still there amidst the Cold Fire."

"Was there any trace of Soulbury?"

I nodded shakily but in the dark Meilyr probably couldn't see my gesture. I spoke. "My Master is … is dead."

He didn't appear surprised by my news. "You found his body?"

I began to sob. "It must have been the cold that killed him. He was frozen, a solid block. When I touched him, his body cr…crumbled into chunks of ice."

"Oh, Aeddon!" Meilyr hugged me tighter. "You did your best. You went back for him, putting your own life in danger. Those demons have been out again, scaring the villagers out of the little wits they possess. I've got them all to go up to the church. We must join them."

"I need to watch the Abbey for Gwawrwen and September," I said, my voice still shaky. Meilyr released me and opened the door to peer out.

"You can do that from the church tower. Come boy." He stepped out onto the street and I followed him. We hurried up the hill looking to the sky, warily, for signs of the demons. There were none.

We reached the small grey stone church with its slate roof and squat square tower. The door to the church was closed to us. Meilyr thumped on the heavy oak.

"Let us in, it is me, Meilyr and Aeddon."

An iron bolt was withdrawn and the door opened just wide enough to let us through. It had been some years since I attended a church service, Sunday was an ordinary working day for Ezekiel, but I had never seen the church so full. Every pew was occupied. The whole village was taking refuge there.

"Have you seen those devil creatures?" an old man asked.

"No. I don't know where they've got to," Meilyr answered. He took my hand and we pushed through the throng to the west end where the old stone font stood. There was an opening in the thick wall and steps that lead up the tower. We climbed the narrow steps that wound in a tight spiral up to the floor above the nave. We emerged into a square room about three paces across. A single rope hung from the centre of the ceiling. It was connected to the one bell used to call worshippers. Otherwise, the room appeared to be a storeroom with oak chests pushed against the walls. In the middle of each wall just above my head were window slits. I went to the south wall and climbed onto the chest that was there. I looked out. Despite the narrowness of the gaps and the thickness of the walls, by pressing my face to the stone I could look out and see the Abbey, or rather the shining ball that had taken its place. I squinted to protect my eyes from the light.

"Can you see?" Meilyr asked.

"Yes," I replied.

"What do you see?"

"The ball of Cold Fire and the storm clouds of ice and snow that circle above and around it."

"Not those demons?"

I shook my head slightly, "No." I heard Meilyr walk across the room and step onto the other chests, first on the north side, then the west, then he crossed the room to the eastern side of the tower.

"Ah, there they are," he said. A knot of fear formed in my chest but Meilyr spoke without emotion. "They sit on the roof of the nave like statues of the devil."

"Why?"

"Who knows. Perhaps they wait for us to emerge. I'll go to warn people not to leave." There was a thump as he stepped off the chest and then steps across the floor. I heard him puffing as he squeezed down the narrow stairs. I peered out of the window trying to watch without looking directly at the blinding light. A cold breeze irritated my eyes. They began to run with tears. Was it the chill or was it my sadness at the death of my Master, Ezekiel Soulbury, a victim of his own curiosity?

It did not seem long that I stood at that narrow slit before something took my attention. It was difficult to look at the bright globe but it seemed to me that the sphere of light was not as complete as it had been. I turned away to let my eyes recover and then looked again, squinting and holding up my hand to shade the brightness from my eyes. My premonition was correct. There was a speck of black amidst the white, a speck that became a streak like the opposite of lightning on a dark sky. It had the appearance of a crack forming in the white globe. As I watched, the shining ball did indeed seem to be splitting in two like an egg-shell. It was riven by a darkness that was as black as the light had been white. To my ears came a shrieking roar like nothing I have ever heard. Not even the roar of the dragon that took Ezekiel's horse came close to this scream which made the bones in my flesh quiver. Louder, more piercing than the demons' screech, it echoed in the tower. I tried to shout out but no sound would come from my lips. Nevertheless, I heard footsteps pounding up the stairs.

"What is that dreadful noise?" Meilyr shouted almost inaudibly over the din.

"The egg has cracked," I shouted as loudly as I could. "As September foretold."

"The sphere of light is broken?"

"Riven in two by darkness!" I cried. I pressed against the wall to watch. The crack had widened and the light was dying, replaced by the featureless blackness. Rather than being an absence of anything it seemed to have substance because it spread up into the sky like a smoke so dense and dark that it obliterated all else. It spread out, so instead of being a vertical column or pole of black it became an inverted cone rising and expanding.

Still the noise filled my ears, but now I realised it was not one sound, one creature, but many. It was a cacophony of numerous voices complaining and accusing. Though the words, if there were any, were too indistinct to interpret I felt the emotion of that horde. It was as September had forewarned us; it was hate. Even as I watched the spout of darkness grow and climb I felt that hate battering at me. Defeat, depression, dejection, the hate pressed on my heart, my mind and my soul.

"What is it?" Meilyr cried above the continuing noise.

"Darkness, the multitude of spirits of darkness, shouting their hate of all that is in the world that they come to destroy."

"Let me see." Meilyr clambered up beside me and elbowed me aside. To be truthful I was relieved to have that awful sight taken from my eyes.

He gasped. "We are lost. Nothing and no-one can withstand that barrage of evil." He continued to stare out of the slit as if enraptured by the horrible sight. "But wait, what is this?"

"What?" I cried and inserted my head between his body and the wall.

"Flying creatures," he said.

"Emerging from the darkness?" I said trying to peer out of the bottom of the window. At last I had a view of the sky.

"No, they come from the north. Dragons!"

"Where?" I shifted my viewpoint as much as I could until at last I saw them. They were circling around the expanding cloud of darkness. Ten, a dozen, more of them. Despite our distance from what had once been the site of the Abbey they looked huge, flapping their great feathered wings, their long necks stretched out in front of them. Gouts of fire emerged from their gaping mouths. As I watched, I saw the bursts of flame eat at the dark cloud. It looked as if a giant had taken mouthfuls from the black cone.

"They are fighting the evil!" I cried.

"They are!" Meilyr hooted with delight.

"I thought dragons themselves were evil," I said over the screams of the spirits and screeching roars of the dragons. "I have hated them since they killed my parents."

"I too," Meilyr replied, "I have cheered when there has been word of a dragon killed by a hunt, though that has been rare in recent years."

"But they are destroying the spirits of hate," I said watching the scene with awe in my heart. Some dragons were blasting their flames where the darkness rose from the site of the Abbey, others circled the rising column and others rose towards the expanding cloud which was stretching across the sky. Every exhaled breath of flame ate into the screaming multitude of spirits. And yet, and yet, the expanding cloud did not seem to decrease in extent or blackness. The dragons nibbled at the edges but appeared to avoid touching the darkness. I wondered if they feared it and my thoughts received confirmation when one dragon, in turning, dragged a wing through the ascending column of blackness. I saw its anguish as it arched its back in pain and stretched its long neck over to almost touch its tail. Its screams of agony could not be heard over the barrage of noise but I felt its torment. Its wings folded and it plummeted to the ground pursued by a plume of blackness that enveloped it before it hit the ground and consumed the creature.

"A dragon has died!" I cried, almost not believing what I saw.

Then there was another screeching from nearby and I caught a glimpse of the demons taking flight from the roof of the church where we hid, hastening to join the battle in the air. Smaller than the dragons they harried them like sparrows fighting off a hawk. Most of the dragons ignored them while continuing to belch balls of fire at the spirits of the darkness, but the demons attacked them tearing mouthfuls of flesh from their bellies and wings.

I saw one dragon turn on its tormentor and bat it away with a taloned foot, but another turning to pluck off the demon from its flank fell into the dark and never emerged. The demons, though just three in number, seemed invincible and immortal, for every time a dragon turned on them and tore them apart, or burned them to a crisp, or threw them into the ground, they reappeared from the smoke re-born. Nevertheless, the dragons continued to burn great gouges in the darkness.

Time went by and the noise of the battle remained. The dragons maintained their efforts against the darkness and the demons but slowly my euphoria died. Steadily but surely the dragons were losing. Despite their efforts, the darkness continued to grow unabated and the hateful cries of the spirits went on filling my ears. And their numbers were diminishing. No reinforcements arrived as one by one the dragons fell to the black cloud or the demons. When there were but five dragons still visible in the air they broke off their fight and fled from the scene, returning northwards.

"We are lost," Meilyr said, stepping down from the chest and sitting on it. He held his head in his hand. I too turned away from our viewpoint and sat beside him.

"What will become of us if even dragons are defeated?" I said. Meilyr merely shook his head and tears ran down his dark, hairy cheek.

"Surely, September will find a way," I said.

Meilyr looked up at the entrance to the stairway. "Where is she? Now, with this darkness settling over the world we need a saviour."

Chapter 14

September returns Gwawrwen to Llanllionio

September felt the flagged floor beneath her feet. A cacophony, chattering and screaming, greeted her arrival. She opened her eyes. It was dark, but she could just make out the familiar features of Meilyr's cottage. She released her grip on Gwawrwen and the woman staggered away from her, finding her balance. Gwawrwen covered her ears with her hands.

"What makes the noise? It's darker than night in here. Why? Is it not the same time of day as when we left the vale of the unicorns?"

"Yes," September replied over the ear-piercing row. "Symudiad takes no time. Is it darker than usual in here? The shutters are closed."

"Rarely is there so little light even at night to make the room so dark." Gwawrwen hurried to the window and flung back the shutters. There was barely any difference. She peered out through the glassless frame. "The sky is filled with black, it obscures the sun, and that noise fills me with a sense of dread."

September joined her and looked out. It was a sight she had seen before.

"It is the Malevolence. Billions of spirits that block out all light and the noise is their cries of hate. Listen carefully. You can hear each individual scream."

Gwawrwen shook her head. "I don't want to listen to hate. I want to put their cries out of my mind completely. Look what they are doing."

Together they watched patches of the black cloud descending. Trees that surrounded Meilyr's property crumbled into dust at the touch of the darkness. The spirits fell into the yard between the cottage and workshops, like a black snow. A chicken caught in the open, ran but was covered in the dust-like spirits and burst in an explosion of blood and flesh which in turn became dust.

"Is that the fate of all living things?" Gwawrwen said.

September nodded, horrified that these things should be happening on her own world, or close to her own world. "It is what the Malevolence does. It destroys all living matter. It will spread out across the Earth and destroy everything."

"What happened to the dragons? They came to fight it."

September shrugged. "It doesn't look as though they succeeded."

Gwawrwen turned to her. Her face was white and damp with tears. "We must do something, September."

"I must," September said striding towards the door. Her hand rested on the handle.

"Wait," Gwawrwen called, "What are you going to do?"

"I was sent here to stop the Malevolence coming into this world. I failed but now I must send it back," September said with a determination that she didn't feel.

"But you said you would return to London to find a magician."

"Yes, but the Malevolence is here now, destroying everything."

"What can you do?"

"Henshaw said I had the power within me. I must find it." She pulled the door open.

Gwawrwen rushed to her side. "The black cloud. Won't it harm you?"

"The unicorns said they would give us protection. You, me, Aeddon."

"I heard that but I'm afraid." Gwawrwen grabbed September's arm.

"So am I, but I have to try." September felt the fear in her growing. It was like an upwelling of icy water in her stomach. But she was pleased. It was fear that gave her control over the power of the Maengolauseren, the starstone, that she alone possessed. She stepped out into the yard with Gwawrwen hanging on to her. The smoky black spirits fell from above them but were deflected by some shield that protected them.

"The spirits aren't touching us," Gwawrwen said.

"It's as the unicorns said," September replied. She stretched her arm upwards towards the sky that was a dark as night; darker as there were no stars. She looked for the power within her. It didn't seem to be there but she hoped that it would come, nevertheless. Hope and fear, the strongest of the emotions in the armoury that she had wielded on Gwlad; powers which had ultimately overcome the Malevolence and her twin sister, Malice.

September stiffened her body, drew in a lungful of air and bellowed, "Ymadaelwch! Begone!" There was no explosion of violet light from her uplifted hand; no eruption of force to scatter the evil spirits and send them back to where they had come from. The blackness of the sky remained unbroken and the spirits continued to swirl around them like smuts of soot, still emitting their chorus of hate.

She pushed her hand higher into the sky and cried out again but all that happened was that Gwawrwen tightened her grip on her. A third time she shouted her command. No change. She lowered her arm and hung her head in dejection.

"It's no use," she sobbed, "I don't have the power I had."

"You do," Gwawrwen said shaking her, "I feel it in you, but you need a key to unleash it."

"A key that only a magician can give me."

Gwawrwen nodded. A gesture that September felt rather than saw because of the darkness that surrounded them.

"I know of none near here," Gwawrwen said.

"Then it is as we said when we were with the unicorns. I must return to London. Will you come with me?"

Gwawrwen hesitated as if considering. "No. I must find Aeddon and Meilyr and do what we can to help the people who live here."

"Where have they gone?"

"I'm not sure. Perhaps the church; that is always seen as a refuge in times of trouble. I will go there."

"We don't know how long the unicorns' protection will last," September worried for her companion.

"I know but I must find them and see what we can do for the villagers."

"Alright, I don't know how long it will take to find magic

but I'll be back with you as soon as I can."

Gwawrwen released her grip on September. "May you find the power that you need."

September closed her eyes and thought of the room she had left in Thomas Maslyn's house. She moved.

There was daylight again, September realised, as the violet light faded around her. She saw the higgledy-piggledy roofs from the lattice window of the bedroom she had spent the previous night in. There was a feeling of relief that the Malevolence had not yet spread to London, but she knew that it would not take long. The memory of the darkness surrounding her and Gwawrwen made her shiver but it also spurred her into action. She hurried from the bedroom and down the stairs to the parlour.

Sir Thomas Maslyn was sitting there as if frozen in a trance. He stirred as September approached and rose to his feet.

"Madam! You are recovered. Henshaw said that you were resting as you were sickening this morning."

September looked around but could see no sign of Henshaw.

"Where is Sir John?" Her voice trembled. She really wanted to pour out her fears and sense of failure to him. Had he really left her all alone, now when the Malevolence was loose in the world? The sense of being isolated, of having responsibility thrust on her returned as it had in her early days on Gwlad. But she had got through it there and become the powerful saviour that the Brains had hoped for. Presumably Henshaw and Cyfaill trusted her to get this universe out of the mess it was in. She knew that she wasn't going home until she was successful, or the Malevolence won. She took a deep breath and wiped the tears from her cheeks.

Maslyn stared at her as if uncertain, then jerked alert, "He has gone. He had business to attend to. I said I would watch over you my lady. Are you now recovered? Shall I call for some food and drink?"

September smiled at Henshaw's story to cover her absence. She wished she had been resting; so far, the day's activity had been disorientating and scary.

"I am well, thank you, Sir Thomas. I have a question for you."

"Please ask what you will, my lady."

"Do you know any magicians?"

"Magicians?" Maslyn looked bemused as if he had never been asked the question before.

September added some explanation. "Wizards, sorcerers, whatever you call them."

Maslyn shook his head. "No, my lady, England has no use for mages."

"But since I've been here, I mean, in your company, I have heard talk of alchemy and mermaids, dragons and unicorns. Aren't they magic?"

Maslyn shrugged as if in some agreement with what September said. "It is true that some have thought those creatures you mention to be magical as, indeed, so have been dolphins and elephants and ostriches, but philosophers know that they are all animals just like cattle and fishes. As for alchemy, some think its claims are indeed wizardry but most of us now consider it to be the game of charlatans seeking to hoodwink fools and imbeciles."

"But your own cousin is an alchemist."

Maslyn chuckled, "Poor Ezekiel. He has made a pauper of himself in his pointless quest for the philosopher's stone and gold."

"You write to him with news of the Royal Society."

"That is true, but I write in the hope of leading him to a more noble art, that of curiosity and philosophy."

September felt desolate. There was magic in this world, unlike her own, but it seemed the modern gentlemen denied it in favour of their new science.

"No magic at all?" she whispered.

"Oh, no doubt there are some who still try to emulate the magicians of the past," Maslyn said cheerily.

"So, you believe that there was magic?"

"Of course, my lady, how else could this world have come into being without the power of magic? How is that we find sea shells on mountain tops and gold buried in rock if they weren't put there by magic?"

Now it was September's turn to feel confused.

"So there used to be wizards and witches?"

"Yes, my lady, it is my belief that there were."

"But none left today?"

"None to my knowing, but others of the Fellows may have recorded their existence."

"Who should we speak to?" September felt a sudden eagerness to meet the other members of the Royal Society again.

"Well, Hooke, of course knows everything. Tyson is working on a mermaid so may have an interest in such matters. Newton has a precocious knowledge of the world but he won't be found in London."

"Where can we speak to Hooke?"

"He is often at Gresham College where the Society meets."

"Well, let's get there quickly. There is no time to waste."

Maslyn was galvanised into action. "I will get my man to call for a chair." He hurried from the room. September heard muffled cries and conversation. Moments later the door opened and Maslyn reappeared.

"Come my lady, your transport awaits."

He beckoned September to follow and they headed towards the door onto the street. On the pavement stood what looked like a tall box not unlike a coffin, with two long poles sticking through its sides and two scruffy men, one at each end. Maslyn opened the door at the front of the box and urged September to sit on the velvet covered seat. She settled herself warily but found the seat padded and soft. The door was closed on her and then there was a lurch and the box was lifted a few inches. It began to move forward carried by the bearers, swaying from side to side a little. Maslyn strode alongside.

"Is it far?" September asked.

"No more than two miles," Maslyn said, "It is close to the tavern where we met the gentlemen last evening."

"Of course," September said recalling the encounter which now seemed in an age gone by. Nevertheless, not yet a whole day had passed since her arrival in this place and already the hate-filled spirits of evil were loose and spreading across the world. She peered out of the window at the front of her box at the bit of sky she could see among the buildings. She half expected it to turn black at once but it didn't. Instead the streets continued their usual bustle, filled with carts carrying all sorts of goods and carriages conveying the well-off, but mainly there were pedestrians and other chairs. The irregular listing of the box and sudden stops and starts as the bearers negotiated the traffic made September feel rather uncomfortable. She wished she was hurrying along on her feet like Maslyn but apparently, that wasn't what ladies did.

Chapter 15

September visits the headquarters of the Royal Society of London

Seeing the City of London in daylight was a different experience to the journey of the previous night. The buildings, most of them just a few years old, seemed much more welcoming than they had in the dark. Not that she recognised much from the cart ride through the evening revellers. She did, though, recall the vast building site that was the new St. Paul's cathedral. They passed other new buildings rising from the devastation of the fire but then there came a change. The streets narrowed and old timber framed buildings leaned into the road. She recalled the alleyway in which she had arrived and the tavern which was anything but new. So this part was not burnt in the flames, she thought. I hope I can do something before it is destroyed by the spirits of the Malevolence.

They came to a building with high grey walls, where they stopped and her chair was lowered to the ground. Thomas Maslyn opened the door and took her hand.

"We are here, my lady, Gresham College."

She stepped onto the soiled pavement and looked up at the three-storey building. Maslyn took her arm and lead her under the pointed arch of the entrance. A man in a leather jerkin stood by the door. Maslyn enquired if Hooke was inside.

The doorman replied "Aye, Sir Thomas. Mr Hooke is in the Society's rooms. You and the lady may enter." He stepped towards the door and pulled it open.

Maslyn lead September through dark corridors and across a grassed courtyard. They re-entered the building and Maslyn tapped on an oak door. A gruff voice called something unintelligible. Maslyn pushed the door open and stood to the side to allow September to enter the room. It had high ceilings and large windows looking out onto the courtyard, but it was its contents that drew September's attention. There were tables covered in glassware and clay pots and jars. There were pieces of machinery, the purpose of which September could not guess, along with weighing scales, microscopes and telescopes. There were furnaces at the side of the room with flasks bubbling on them.

There was just one person in the room and September recognised the shrunken, curved-back figure of Robert Hooke. He looked up briefly as they crossed the room towards him then returned to examining the contraption of wires and weights that he was working on.

"My apologies for disturbing your endeavours, Mr. Hooke," Maslyn said, approaching Hooke tentatively.

Hooke looked up again, "Ah, Maslyn, to what do I owe this interruption? I have much to do as I am sure you aware."

"Yes, of course, Sir," Maslyn replied, bowing deeply, "I wish to introduce this lady, Miss Weekes. You may remember that she accompanied us to Mr Boyle's display last eve."

Hooke's eyes focussed on September, "Yes, of course I recall her. How can I assist you madam?"

September felt that she should engage Hooke in conversation before bringing up the subject of magic.

"Mr Boyle's experiments were interesting, weren't they?" she said, wondering if she sounded nervous.

Hooke shrugged. "They provided some entertainment, but nothing extraordinary. I have performed my own investigations into phosphorus."

"Oh, what urine did you use to make it?" September asked.

"That of my household, of course, my lady. What other source would you suggest?"

"You didn't think to use the pee of other animals?"

"London is full of animals; horses, dogs, rats that piss where they will. Only the human population will obey instructions to fill a bucket, hence I have not thought to utilise anything but human effusions." September thought he had a point but wanted to see what his reaction to Ezekiel Soulbury's experiment would be.

"You don't think unicorns' pee would be a suitable?"

Hooke let out a coarse laugh. "And why, pray, young woman, do you mention such creatures as unicorns?"

"Well, they're magical so perhaps the phosphorus you obtained from them would have magical qualities."

"Bah! Magic! The ramblings of the inmates of Bedlam."

"You don't believe in magic, Mr Hooke?"

"Believe? I believe what my eyes and instruments show me. No one believed that minuscule creatures existed in ordinary water until I focussed my microscope on them. No one could believe the complexity of God's insects till I drew what I saw through my lens. No one has revealed any truth in magic to me."

"But weren't there wizards and witches at one time?"

"Some may call themselves such, even now, but none since the great John Dee merited the title."

"John Dee?"

Maslyn stepped forward. "He was good queen Bess' magician, my lady."

"Queen Elizabeth? That's a while ago, isn't it?" September said.

"Dead some seventy years," Hooke growled.

"So there were magicians in the past?" September said, a little confused by Hooke's dismissal of magic.

Hooke drew himself to his full, if diminutive, height. "Deceivers and mountebanks the lot of them. Today we have natural philosophy, my lady, the product of full and proper curiosity in the wonders of natural knowledge."

September frowned. This was not the response she had expected. Hooke was not being at all helpful and time was passing. The Malevolence could be over London at any moment.

She faced Hooke again. He had returned to his machinery.

"But you mention John Dee as if you respect him."

Hooke sniffed. "A fine mathematician and seeker of the truth. He professed to finding some credence in the power of spells in times long before his life."

"Well, there we are."

"What evidence he found has been lost, madam."

September felt frustrated. "But if there have been no magicians since Dee, what about before him?"

Hooke waved his hand dismissively. "Tales, young lady."

"Perhaps John Dee thought there was some truth to them?" September said.

Hooke grunted and looked at Sir Thomas Maslyn. "Why Maslyn have you brought me this woman with her talk of magic that disturbs my work?"

Maslyn's face had turned white. "I am sorry Sir. She is a member of Sir John Henshaw's family and I have promised him that I would comply with her whims. She asked to speak to you."

"Well I have no more to say to her about magic," Hooke said turning away to remove a flask from a furnace.

September bit her lip. If she didn't get something from Hooke she didn't know where to go next.

"Mr Hooke," she said in as grown up a voice as she could imitate. "If I do not find out about the source of magic in this universe it is about to end."

Hooke placed the flask on the table and looked up at her. "What is about to end?"

"The world, time, life. Everything," she said.

Hooke's eyes narrowed. "What nonsense is this? Is the Earth about to stop in its passage around the Sun? Will the force of gravity cease to keep objects in their place?"

"I don't know about that but Evil has entered this universe and will shortly kill everyone and destroy all that there is."

"You sound like one of the doom-saying preachers calling down fire and brimstone on sinners," Hooke said.

"I'm not talking about religious stuff," September said, "It's happening now. Sir Thomas's cousin, Ezekiel Soulbury let it in."

Hooke looked at Maslyn. "What is the girl babbling about, Maslyn?"

Maslyn waved his arms in confusion. "I do not know, Sir. I do have a relative of that name."

September faced Maslyn. "You sent him a letter telling him about Boyle's experiments on phosphorus."

Maslyn nodded, "That is true, my lady."

"Ezekiel is or was an alchemist," she added.

"That is correct. He has spent his fortune in pursuing the arcane art."

"Well, he decided to follow the instructions you sent using unicorn urine."

Hooke glared at September. "How do you know this?"

"I was there, uh, before I came here."

"Ezekiel's home is in the north-west of Wales," Maslyn said with some incredulity in his voice.

"That's right," September said firmly, "Near where the unicorns live."

"Ah ..." Hooke held his hands together and tapped a finger against his lips. "So that is why you spoke of unicorns earlier."

"Yes, I wondered if you could guess what might happen?" September felt as if she was making progress at last.

"Unicorns are certainly creatures with some unique attributes," Hooke murmured.

"Like being able to defend themselves and their friends against evil and being able to speak to you through your mind."

"You have met them?" Hooke asked.

"Yes. They look like a white, woolly rhinoceros."

Hooke nodded in agreement.

"Um, there's something else," Maslyn said. Hooke and September looked at him. "Ezekiel once summoned a dragon."

"A dragon!" Hooke cried.

September nodded. "I know. I've seen them too."

Hooke glared at her. "You are quite an adventuress, my lady."

"Perhaps. But now try and tell me there isn't magic in the world."

Hooke's head shook so violently that his head may have fallen off if it wasn't fixed so firmly to his bent shoulders. "Unicorns, dragons, yes, they may have characteristics that some deem to be magical but you asked after magicians, lady. There are none, not one who reveals the skill to wield the powers of the universe in the manner that they claim."

"Not now perhaps but what about before John Dee?" September pushed.

"Tales, I said; myths and legends," Hooke resisted.

September replied in a calm, measured voice. "But perhaps

there is some truth in them."

Hooke sighed deeply and stood silently for a few breaths. September waited. Hooke looked at her.

"Perhaps," he said. "The greatest magician in works purporting to be history is Merlin, the magician of King Arthur."

"Merlin's real?" September said.

Hooke shook his head, "Not as told by Mallory. He merely re-wrote older tales." He looked at Maslyn. "Maslyn, you hail from Wales. You must know the stories handed down from generation to generation of kings, wizards, witches and druids?"

Maslyn nodded slowly. "Our estates are in the east, bordering England," he spoke as if this proximity to civilisation gave him respectability, then added, "but I did have the tales recited to me when I was a child."

Hooke was thoughtful. "Myrddin was the wizard on whom Mallory based Merlin, and there were others were there not?"

"That's right," Maslyn said, "Gwydion and Ceridwen …"

"These are real people?" September asked.

"They have a presence in the past," Hooke said, "Though what magic they actually performed I could not say."

"Theirs is a time long gone," Maslyn agreed.

"But there were some with skills that some consider magical who lived a mere four centuries or so ago," Hooke said.

"Who is it of which you speak?" Maslyn asked.

"The physicians of Myddfai," Hooke explained.

"Ah, yes," Maslyn said almost dancing in his excitement.

"Who are they?" September asked.

Maslyn answered her eagerly, "Three brothers who, legend says, were the outcome of the union of a farmer and a woman who lived beneath the surface of a lake. They became healers of great renown."

"But they were people of record," Hooke added, "There are books that preserve their remedies, and their place of residence is known."

September was doubtful, "A mother who lived underwater?"

"A mermaid perhaps," Maslyn said, "Tyson's investigations

show that they have human characteristics. Perhaps coitus between a man and a mermaid could be fruitful."

"Their descendants live on as healers in the same place," Hooke said.

"You said that there were no magicians today," September said.

"And I did not lie to you, my lady," Hooke said, "These masters of physic bring relief from ailments by prescribing concoctions made from the parts of plants, not by magic."

"Yet their line stretches back to the eldest of the original trio," Maslyn added

At last September felt a glimmer of hope. Gwawrwen had said she was known as a sorceress despite her herbal remedies not being touched by magic. These healers with their magical ancestry, however, might just point her to the source of her power. Their heritage crossed the centuries. She gasped. That thought had given her the clue to her problem. It didn't matter that the Malevolence was spreading across Wales at this very moment. She had been reminded already that she had within her the power of the Gwlyb Hoedl Gwyrthiol, the Elixir of Life, the freedom to live in all ages. She could go further back in the past to find the secrets of magic and then come back at any time she wished, to defeat the Malevolence.

"Where do I find these healers?" She asked, excitement making her heart beat faster. "Did you say the place was Myddfai?"

Maslyn answered, "That is correct, my lady. Myddfai in the county of Carmarthenshire in the south of the principality."

"I need a picture like you gave me of your cousin's home."

Hooke snorted. "You wish to see a representation of Myddfai painted on canvas?"

"A drawing will do."

Maslyn shook his head. "I know of no such example of the painter's or the draughtsman's art, my lady. It is most unusual for someone to record a panorama as seen by the eye."

"Hmm," mused Hooke, "I have no insight at all as to why you should require such an image, my lady, but would a representation of the form of the land in the area be of any application?"

September did not understand what he meant. The representation of the form of the land? Then it came to her. "Oh, you mean a map?"

"Mappa, yes," Hooke nodded. "I do believe the society received the recent edition of Mr Speed's 'Theatre of the Empire of Great Britaine'."

"I am certain you are correct, Sir," Maslyn said.

"What is that?" September asked.

Maslyn turned to her. "It is a bound set of all Mr John Speed's, er, maps, of the counties that make up the King's realm."

"Take the lady to the Society's library, Maslyn," Hooke said, waving his hand in dismissal, "and leave me to my tasks." He returned to concentrating on his instrument.

Sir Thomas Maslyn pointed to the exit. "Come my lady, perhaps Mr Hooke has provided the answer you require."

September followed Maslyn from Hooke's laboratory without another word from the hunched philosopher. They climbed a flight of stairs and entered another room, smaller, lower ceilinged with small windows. There were a few sets of shelves with books.

"This is the Royal Society's library," Maslyn said with pride. September thought it seemed rather a small library for such an important organisation. The books varied in size and thickness but each was bound in a hard leather cover. Maslyn searched the shelves till he found what was one of the larger volumes. He lifted it off the shelf and placed it on a table set against one of the windows.

"Here is Speed's exercise in cartography, my lady. Now let us see. We want the depiction of the county of Carmarthen." He turned the heavy covers and then the thick paper pages. "Ah, here we are."

September stood by his side and leaned forward. The title of the map said Caermarden. She wasn't familiar with maps of south Wales or anywhere but this didn't look much like any maps she had ever seen. There were little green hillocks to represent mountains, and branching rivers that looked like trees, but no roads. There were lots of place names some accompanied by little pictures of buildings. It didn't look at all like an accurate guide to the lay of the land at all.

"There is Myddfai," Maslyn said, "just south of Llanymthefry and north of the Black Mountain." September looked at where he pointed. Could she use this picture, she could hardly call it a map, as a guide to take her to the home of the fabled physicians? But, she reflected, she had travelled all around Gwlad with just the sketchiest of pictures in her head. She looked closely at the map, taking in the position of Myddfai, the towns and villages nearby, and the pattern of rivers. She had to give it try.

"Thank you, Sir Thomas. You have been most helpful, I must go now." She turned and strode towards the door.

Maslyn called to her. "My lady, where are you going? How to do you propose to travel to this far-off place?"

She didn't reply and stepped through the doorway. She closed the door behind her and stood with her eyes closed, visualising the map she had just studied. The image became overlaid with a picture of rolling hills, streams and rivers and a collection of small white-washed stone buildings.

Violet light descended around her, spinning like a whirlwind.

Chapter 16

I watch the coming of the black cloud

I took another look out of the narrow tower window. The black cloud was still spewing out of the site of the abbey but now I saw that some of it was descending. Descending towards us. I turned to Meilyr.

"The darkness of evil is falling upon us," I said, feeling fear grip my stomach.

"It is indeed like night," Meilyr said, misunderstanding me.

"No, Meilyr, the spirits are falling, like dust. They will cover the village. Who knows what will happen if they find their way into the tower?"

Meilyr leapt to his feet and looked out. "There's nothing to stop them. We must get down to the nave and warn people not to venture outside. We've seen what the black cloud can do to dragons."

We both ran to the stairway and pulled the door closed behind us. Even as I did so I heard the annoyed whine of the spirits entering the room through the window slits. We hurried down to the main part of the church. The villagers were standing in a huddle, their faces white with fear. They looked to us and each spoke at once.

"What has happened?"

"What is this noise?"

"We feel a great fear!"

"What danger are we in?"

Meilyr raised his arms to calm the people, although what he then said hardly made their fears subside. He raised his voice above the din of the spirits.

"A great evil has erupted from the Abbey, a dark cloud of hateful spirits. It is they that make the noise that fills our ears. They were attacked by dragons from the north ..."

"Dragons!" several people echoed.

"Yes, dragons, twenty or more. Though we may fear them

as our enemies they attacked the evil cloud."

"But the noise remains!" someone shouted.

"Yes," Meilyr continued, his voice becoming quieter, "The dragons failed."

"Showed their true natures and joined the evil no doubt," another villager said.

"No!" Meilyr shouted, "They died in their effort to stem the flow of the evil. We saw many of them fall, enveloped by the black cloud or harried by the demons we all saw before. The dragons were against the evil, but only a few survived and fled to safety."

"We are left, defenceless!" a woman cried.

I saw Meilyr pause before answering. "For now, we are safe in here," he said, "But the doors and windows must be kept closed. If you step out into the cloud you will surely die."

"We will die of hunger and thirst," a male voice cried, "we have no supplies in here."

Meilyr continued to try to reassure his friends and neighbours. "We must hope and pray that a saviour will come to our rescue and rid us of this evil cloud. Now I ask you to keep calm, rest, drive this maddening noise from your ears."

A few people heeded Meilyr's words and went to sit in the pews, hugging each other and covering their ears with their hands. Some remained to question us.

"Is this all Soulbury's doing? Has he brought evil and death on us all?" an elderly man said.

Meilyr turned to me. I couldn't absolve Ezekiel of all responsibility.

"My Master was indeed carrying out an experimentation at the time of the appearance of the cold fire, the great white orb, but he did not summon this evil or have any intention of doing so."

"He always was a fool," someone muttered.

"Meddling in things that should not be meddled in," another voice said.

A banging reverberated around the church. Something was thumping on the south door of the church.

"It is the evil trying to enter!" someone cried and they and others ran towards the chancel at the east end of the nave and fell to their knees at the altar, praying.

"That does not sound like the noise the black cloud makes," Meilyr said.

I shrugged, "I don't think so." The thudding of the door came again, sounding as if a person was hammering at it with their fists in order to be heard over the cacophony of the spirits.

"I think someone is trying to get in," I said.

"I think you're right, boy," Meilyr said. "Should we open the door and let them in?"

"And let the evil in? No, it must stay closed," a villager, a father of children, said.

The thumping came again.

"We must bring them to safety," Meilyr said and disregarding the villagers' protests he marched to the door. I followed him. "We must open it only sufficiently to let the person through whoever it may be, and close it immediately so as not to allow any of the evil smoke to enter."

I nodded and stood with Meilyr behind the door as he took hold of the key and handle. He twisted the key and the tumblers in the lock fell with a clunk. Then together we pulled the heavy door ajar. A person, I couldn't see who at that moment, slipped through the gap and we slammed the door shut immediately. Meilyr re-locked the door as I turned to see who had entered. I was surprised and delighted to see Gwawrwen. She saw me and we fell into each other's arms, greeting each other with tears of joy. The villagers who had hung back fearfully, now pressed close appealing for news about their homes and their livestock.

My own questions spilled out, running together. "Where is September? Did you meet the unicorns again? How did you get through the cloud?"

Gwawrwen pulled away from me. She looked very serious and glum.

"September has returned to London to speak to the eminent men. She has not been able to find the magic to defeat the evil, the Malevolence, as she names it. She hopes that the men she met at the Royal Society can help her."

"What do they know of magic?" I said.

"I couldn't say but we must hope that she is successful. I don't know how we can defeat this menace."

"The dragons can't," I said.

"You've seen the dragons! Tell me, tell me everything." The two of us and Meilyr moved to a pew and sat down. Some villagers clustered around us listening.

As quickly as I was able, I recounted all that had happened since she and September had left in the flash of blue light. Meilyr added some comments about our escape to the church, the eruption of the black cloud from the cold fire, and the desperate battle of the dragons.

"But how did you come through the darkness, unscathed?" I asked.

"It is the unicorns," Gwawrwen answered. "You and I and September touched them and heard their conversation so we have their protection. Their goodness keeps us safe from the evil spirits."

"So that is how I was able to get back to the Abbey without harm," I said. Gwawrwen nodded. "But Ezekiel also touched the unicorns and he is dead. I saw his frozen body crumble into shards of ice."

"The power of the unicorns has limitations," Gwawrwen said, "They cannot oppose this Malevolence alone, nor with the aid of the few dragons that are left. September must find magic."

The people around us made various noises of agreement or anguish. Suddenly, a young man ran to the door.

"No," Meilyr cried, leaping to his feet, "You cannot go outside!" The man was already turning the key.

"I must see my cow," he cried, turning the handle, "I should not have left her alone. If the sorceress can pass safely then so can I."

Gwawrwen and I ran to catch him, but he pulled the door open and stepped out of the church before we got there.

Gwawrwen and I fell on the door pushing it closed but through the crack we saw what happened. The screaming, black cloud flowed into the porch and settled on the man's head and shoulders. It clung to his chest and back and legs. He screamed in agony as his skin and flesh was torn from him turning to dust. His exposed organs burst like balloons forming flurries of red snow, then all that was left was a skeleton which collapsed to the ground disintegrating into powder. The spirits weren't satisfied though and poured towards the door, screeching their hate.

We pushed the door against the jamb just in time and Meilyr turned the key. I was shaking. I had seen dragons fall but I had not guessed what the spirits could do to other living creatures. The villagers cried and wailed, demanding to know what had happened to the young man. Meilyr faced them and with a sorrowful voice said that nothing could be done to help him. The villagers cried all the more, fearing for their own fates.

Gwawrwen took me in her arms. "We are safe, you and I," she said, but what you saw then happens to all the living when touched by the darkness. Trees are dust in moments and no animal can survive."

I looked at the door that held the spirits back. "That is wood that once was part of a living tree," I observed.

Gwawrwen nodded, "But it has been a door for centuries. I hope it will withstand the Malevolence for some time yet, along with the walls, the windows and the roof." I looked up to the wooden joists and the ceiling. How long would we and the villagers be safe in here?

"We've got to do something," I said. "We can't just wait for everyone to die or for September to return."

"You're right," Gwawrwen said, "but I do not know what we can do. Let me think and see if I can feel the wishes of the unicorns." She left me and went and stood under the tower, resting her hands on the ancient, stone font. She closed her eyes and seemed to stiffen as if unconscious.

"What is she doing?" Meilyr asked.

"Communicating with the unicorns," I replied, "Hoping that they can give us guidance."

"I hope someone can," Meilyr said, "I feel that the weight of evil resting on this place of worship will shortly crush it." I looked again at the ceiling wondering if Meilyr was right and that it would soon come crashing down on all of us.

Gwawrwen stood as still as a statue for some minutes till she stirred as if awaking. She straightened up and her eyes focussed on Meilyr and myself.

"The unicorns have a task for you and me," she said.

"Me too?" Meilyr said.

Gwawrwen shook her head. "No, Meilyr. Only Aeddon and I can venture out while the darkness hangs over us. You have not met the unicorns and do not have their protection. In any case I think your wisdom and guidance is needed here to preserve the people."

Meilyr nodded, understanding his responsibility for the village people.

"What are we to do?" I asked.

"Rescue the dragons," Gwawrwen said. I thought of the huge creatures we had seen soaring through the air emitting their fiery breath and wondered how the two of us could possibly help them.

"How?" I said.

"They have been overtaken by the deadly cloud and have taken refuge in a cave. Only with the unicorns' protection provided by you and me can they escape the fate of all living creatures touched by the dark spirits."

I thought of the dragons that I had seen fall under the smothering cloud and the brave fight they had put up.

"I see," I said, "We had better go to their aid. Do you know where they are?"

"The unicorns will guide me."

Meilyr drew himself to his full height. "I will see you out of the door." We moved towards the south door. Meilyr already had his hand on the key, when I became disturbed.

"Gwawrwen and I may be protected but when this door is opened the evil spirits will pour in."

Meilyr paused. "You are right. If we give them an opening, we are done for."

"Is there another exit? Gwawrwen asked.

Meilyr thought. "Of course there is. A small door from the rector's vestry. Come." He led us back to the nave and up towards the chancel before turning to the left. There was a small door in the side of the aisle, which he opened. Beyond the door was a small room used by the priest, when there was one, as a study, dressing room and for storing vestments. On the opposite side was another small door. Gwawrwen and I stepped into the vestry.

"Close the door, Meilyr," Gwawrwen said, "We will let ourselves out of the other and close it behind us. Perhaps the

Malevolence will not take advantage of the opening of a smaller door.

"May God go with you," Meilyr said and pulled the door closed.

Gwawrwen and I were alone. We crossed the room cluttered with a table, chairs, tall cupboards and chests. Gwawrwen pulled back the bolts that fastened the door and placed her hand on the latch.

"Are you ready, Aeddon? We must be quick."

I nodded and stood ready for the door to open. Gwawrwen pulled it open and I squeezed through, then stood behind it ready to shut it as Gwawrwen followed. I slammed the door into its place and hoped that the latch would hold.

Outside the noise of the spirits was even louder in my ears and as I turned away from the door I was almost overcome by the swirling darkness. Waves of the black spirits crashed against the walls and roof of the church but so far, the ancient stone and slate held firm. Despite their agitation the spirits ignored me and my companion. Gwawrwen grabbed my hand and tugged me away.

"Come," she said, "we must stay together else in this darkness and confusion we lose each other." I did not want to be alone amongst the baying spirits even with the knowledge that the unicorns were protecting me. I gripped Gwawrwen's hand tightly.

It was almost impossible to see our path but Gwawrwen led us up the hillside and out of the village. I soon realised that we were not following the path we had taken to the vale of the unicorns but some other route. I had no idea of where we were headed but Gwawrwen strode purposefully, obviously guided by the unicorns speaking in her head.

For what seemed an interminable and unmeasurable time we scrambled over rough ground, sometimes climbing, sometimes descending, never following a well-trodden path. All the time the darkness stretched across the sky and vortices of spirits descended to the ground around us like malign whirlwinds. There was no living thing left on the ground, not a blade of grass or branch of bush, no insects, no scurrying animals, no birds. The ground had been stripped to the bare rock.

At last, when I was beginning to tire, Gwawrwen stopped.

"The dragons are close," she said, "Can you not feel their presence?"

I stood still and became aware of a grumbling, ill temper in my head that was not my own.

"I think so," I said.

"They are below us I think," Gwawrwen said and began to scramble down a steep and treacherous slope. I followed, still keeping my grip on her hand. We reached the bottom of a narrow gully and in front of us, black on black, was the entrance to a cave. It would have been impossible to see except for the swirling clouds of spirits entering it. Then I heard a noise different to the screams of hate. It was a roar, not of lion or other beast but of a furnace burning fiercer than any Ezekiel had in his workspace. A blast of hot air and flame emerged from the cave which even at this distance singed my hair.

"They are inside," Gwawrwen said.

"I hope they know we are here," I said, "and don't burn us as well as the spirits."

"They know," was all Gwawrwen said. We stepped into the opening of the cave. It was broad and tall, big enough for a dragon. We groped our way along, the black cloud all around us but still, thankfully, oblivious of us. The cave bent this way and that but never narrowed as it burrowed into the mountain.

I felt disorientated and lost, hardly knowing which way was left or right or even up and down. Gwawrwen tugged me to the side and pulled me down against an outcrop of rock.

"Keep your head down," she commanded. I did as she said and only just in time. There was a huge roar and flames licked around the edges of the rock. The heat, I am sure would have burnt me to a cinder if I had not been behind the rock. It certainly charred the dark spirits. For a moment they were gone.

Gwawrwen leapt up and dragged me along. We rounded the bend in the cave and I immediately felt the presence of other creatures around me. We were in a large cavern but the five dragons, I could see the red glow in their five pairs of eyes, stood close together facing the entrance ready to repulse the next wave of spirits.

<GREETINGS, HUMAN FRIEND OF UNICORNS.>

The voice crashed into my head.

"Hello, Obsidian," Gwawrwen said, "The unicorns have guided us to your aid."

<IT IS STRANGE TIMES WHEN DRAGONS DEPEND ON PEOPLE FOR ASSISTANCE, BUT PLEASE STAND BEHIND US. WE MUST DEFEND OURSELVES.>

I reached out my hand to feel my way and touched the huge, scaly leg of the dragon. Its body was above me. I stumbled on until I my hands made contact with its long, leathery tail. At that moment, the dragons let out another blast of flame and the cave was illuminated. It was a vast cavern, many times the size of the Llanllionio church and it was filled by the five dragons. I wondered how they had squeezed through the passage we had just come along, but fear of contact with the black cloud must have given them the incentive to do so.

The flames guttered and the darkness returned although my eyes were filled with afterimages of the fiery light.

<NOW YOU ARE COME WE CAN ESCAPE FROM THIS PRISON,> the dragon said.

"The unicorns' protection will cover you if we can stay in contact," Gwawrwen said.

<CLIMB ON MY BACK, FEMALE. THE YOUNG MALE MAY RIDE ON GABBRO.>

"Did you hear that, Aeddon?" Gwawrwen said.

"Yes, but which dragon did he mean? I can't see anything,"

<HE MEANT ME.>

I felt a blast of hot, sulphurous breath on my face and became aware of a huge head of a dragon by my side.

<CLIMB ON MY NECK,> Gabbro said. I felt my way along the scale covered jaws behind the huge beak till I felt soft feathers. They were as long as my arm with shafts as thick as the branches of a tree.

<TAKE A FIRM GRIP,> the dragon instructed. I gripped a bunch of feathers in each hand and pulled myself up. It was like climbing a pine tree except that the feathers were not so rough. Although I could not see where I was climbing I felt when I reached the top of the creature's neck and sat astride it.

<ARE YOU SECURE?>

"Yes," I said, gripping feathers in both hands.

<THEN KEEP YOUR HEAD DOWN AS WE EXIT THE CAVE.>

I pressed myself down into the beast's neck as it started to move. It rocked from side to side as it strode forward on its two legs. Then we entered the tunnel and I felt through my hands and legs the dragon's body scraping against the rock as it squeezed its way along. The air was hot and stank of dragons' breath as the animals struggled to escape from their refuge.

It was only because the air was cooler that I knew for sure that we had left the cave. It was almost as dark outside under the cloud of evil as it had been in the mountain. The smoke-like spirits were all around but as before they seemed to ignore me and, I was relieved to note, Gabbro. The dragon took a few lumbering paces away from the cave mouth. Ahead, in the narrow gulley I could just make out the vast bulk of Obsidian and two other dragons.

The voice of the leading dragon boomed in my head. <THE EVIL IS BLIND TO US BUT WE MUST STAY IN CONTACT. NOW LET US LEAVE THIS PLACE.>

As the dragon's words faded in my head I was almost jerked from my seat as my steed stretched his wings and launched us into the spirit-filled air. With great lazy beats of his wings Gabbro gained height following Obsidian and two of the dragons. They flew so close together that their wings nearly collided but they endeavoured to keep their talons or the claws on the end of their wings touching the leading dragon. I twisted my head and in the murk could just make out the last dragon right above me, its talons each as big as my hand gripping the tip of Gabbro's tail.

I turned to look forward in hope of seeing some sign of our destination but for some minutes we flew through darkness. It was impossible to tell our speed as I could not see the ground but the wind buffeted me and Gabbro continue to catch the air in his beating wings. Then, as I peered ahead, I saw a light. It was a beacon of joy within the dark cloud of hate. Swiftly it grew till I could see that it was a shaft of sunlight piercing the black overcast sky.

<THERE IS OUR HOME> Obsidian called, <THE UNICORNS ARE HOLDING BACK THE HORDES OF EVIL, STILL.>

Now I could see that it was indeed the vale of the unicorns that was illuminated. The spirits of the Malevolence could not penetrate the barrier that the unicorns maintained from the ridge surrounding their home. I was filled with hope and a quiver of joyful excitement passed though my steed. I felt rather than saw our attendant dragon release its grip on Gabbro and soar up and over us, beating his wings with a greater urgency.

<NO, BASALT, DO NOT GO ON ALONE. YOU MUST REMAIN IN TOUCH WITH ME AND THE HUMAN.> Gabbro's words were too late. I watched, horrified as the spirits were drawn to the lone dragon like iron filings to a lodestone. The dragon let out one terrified puff of flame then a shriek of pain before he began to fall from the sky laden with the black scourge. Feathers, scales, gobbets of flesh, spurts of blood and guts burst from the doomed dragon turning to dust in the sir. I soon lost sight of Basalt in the gloom but I am sure there was nothing left of the creature before it reached the ground.

<DO NOT RELEASE YOUR GRIP ON ME, MY CHILDREN, UNTIL WE ARE IN THE UNICORNS' DOMAIN,> Obsidian instructed. The close formation of the three dragons flew on ahead of us.

Then we were in light. The evil was behind us and we flew over the craggy peaks that guarded the valley and down towards the green, lush meadows. Now I could see the white hair and skin of Gwawrwen as she clung to the neck of the leading dragon. The other two red-feathered creatures peeled off swooping down in a tight spiral to land beside the river. Obsidian and Gabbro made a more gentle descent, for my and Gwawrwen's sake, I think. We landed softly, close to the other two. Gabbro sank onto the grass and lowered his neck. I slid off and knelt in the soft pasture, shaking with relief that we had escaped the Malevolence and with grief for the death of the dragon.

"Thank you, Gabbro, for bringing me to safety," I said, placing my hand against the dragon's flank.

<THE GRATITUDE IS ALL MINE. WITHOUT YOU AND THE BENEFICENCE OF THE UNICORNS THE FATE OF ALL OF US WOUD BE THAT OF BASALT.> I could feel the strength of feeling in the dragon's thoughts.

A hand rested on my shoulder. I turned to see Gwawrwen looking at me with concern.

"Are you well, Aeddon? The evil spirits did not trouble you?"

"Oh, I am troubled," I said, "and so I think are the four remaining dragons by the death of Basalt."

"Of course. It is sad that he could not have patience and ignored the instructions of the dragon mother." Her words seemed to mask another concern.

"Something troubles you too Gwawrwen?" I said letting go of the soft feathers of the dragon.

"Yes. I expected the unicorns to be here to attend our arrival. Surely they must want to discuss the danger the world faces."

I agreed that the unicorns should have appeared as the dragons landed. I glanced up into the blue sky with the sun shining overhead while dark clouds ringed the valley

"Their power still holds so they must be here."

"Yes, but we must speak with them. Perhaps they are under the trees where we first met them. Come."

Gwawrwen strode off towards the copse by the river. I ran after her.

"Do you think they can do anything to defeat the evil?" I asked.

"I fear that this Malevolence is more powerful than even the unicorns. It is September that we must look to for salvation, but I have hope that the unicorns can continue to provide a haven for us and for others."

We reached the trees and hurried between them looking for the white beasts. We came upon them in the clearing but they were not standing awaiting our arrival. All three were lying on the ground, their legs tucked against their cylindrical bodies, and their heads bearing those distinctive horns resting in the grass. They were not creatures that should be lying on their flanks. I thought for a moment that they were indeed dead. Gwawrwen ran to the largest, Adamant, and knelt beside him. Then I saw that he was alive as his eyelids flickered and he tried to raise his head, but it sank onto the ground again. I too knelt and touched his horn.

"What is wrong?" Gwawrwen cried, her voice quavering, "Are you ill?"

<It is the evil, good lady.> The unicorn's words were faint in my mind. <It drains our energy. We cannot resist it for much longer. Soon the Malevolence will have dominion over the whole world.>

"No!" I cried and pressed my hands against the unicorn's side which rose and fell slowly with each feeble breath. "You mustn't die. You have to save us from the evil that I helped my Master bring into the world."

<That was foolishness not malicious intent. The alchemist cannot be blamed. We unwittingly aided him by providing the source of the Cold Fire.>

"You know everything," I blubbered, "You can find a way to save us all!"

<That is the task of the girl from beyond our universe. We hope she is successful but we fear that our time is diminishing.>

"There must be something we can do" Gwawrwen said, "Your energy is being sapped from you. We must find a way to reinforce your power."

"That's right!" I was eager to find any cause for hope. "You are a healer, Gwawrwen. Surely you have a remedy to strengthen the unicorns?"

Gwawrwen rocked back on her heels and looked at me. "I'm no sorceress, Aeddon."

"No, but you know how to wield the magic of plants." I glared at her, appealing to her.

<The boy is right,> Adamant thought, <you have knowledge and skills.>

Gwawrwen looked from me to the three prone unicorns.

"Perhaps ..." Gwawrwen said no more for several minutes. She did get up and go to the other two unicorns in turn. She knelt beside them, listening to their ragged breathing, feeling the pulse in their necks, looking into their clouded eyes. Finally, she stood up, faced me and spoke, though I think it was herself she was conversing with not me. "No single herb can possibly heal the wounds caused by the Malevolence and restore the strength of the unicorns, but if a number of different plants were taken then maybe their combined effects would do some good."

Her eyes focussed on me and she seemed to reach a decision. "Aeddon, I will need your assistance. There are certain plants that I need and I hope that they can be found in the unicorns' domain because we can certainly not search elsewhere."

"The evil destroys all plant and animal life that it touches," I said.

"Exactly, but we must work swiftly. I need a range of herbs and must then mix and unite them to produce a potion that may help restore the unicorns, or at least help them to hold on till September overcomes the Malevolence."

Chapter 17

I take flight with the dragon
to search for herbs

I hurried back through the trees to where the dragons were resting. I found the four of them sitting in the meadow by the river, their legs folded underneath them and their bodies resting on the grass. They looked like giant roosting chickens which I suppose is what they were. I am sure they were relishing the calm and safety after the battle with the evil cloud and their ordeal in the cave.

"Gwawrwen has a task for me," I said to all the dragons but Gabbro in particular. The male dragon hauled himself onto his two feet.

<I AM AT YOUR SERVICE, YOUNG HUMAN,> he said lowering his scaly head to me.

"The unicorns are ailing and we must find herbs to sustain them," I explained.

<WE KNOW,> Gabbro said and I remembered that they were in mental contact with the unicorns.

<THE EVIL IS DRAINING THE UNICORNS' POWERS," Obsidian said, <YOU MUST DO WHATEVER YOU CAN TO SUPPORT THEM.>

I clambered onto Gabbro's neck again. "We will," I said, "Gwawrwen has given me a list of herbs to collect. She thinks that they may be found at the margins of the valley and on the slopes. One is familiar to me but others are not."

<WE SHALL SEEK AND FIND WHAT YOU REQUIRE,> Gabbro said. Stretching out his huge wings he caught the air and we rose into the sky. We flew low and fast across the flat floodplain until we reached the margins of the valley and the ground started to rise. Bare rock appeared among the grass. I had pictures in my head of the herbs that Gwawrwen wanted me to look out for and I tried to match

them against the plants I saw below me.

"Slow down, please," I called, "I need time to look for the special plants."

<OF COURSE,> Gabbro said, slowing and circling lower in a wide, lazy glide.

"There!" I shouted and pointed to a rocky spot. A reddish stem and typical thistle flower heads had attracted my attention. "That is Ysgall Bendigaid I believe."

Gabbro descended gently to the hillside, gripping the outcrop in his talons to provide a secure landing. I slipped from his neck and ran to where I had seen the patch of plants. Though it was still early in the year the peculiar climate of the unicorn's vale ensured that some of the plants were already in flower. I plucked some flower heads and leaves as Gwawrwen instructed and stuffed them in her bag that she had loaned to me.

I resumed my seat on Gabbro's neck and we took off again. We flew higher up the mountainside. Above the ridge the sky was black with the Malevolence but still the evil spirits were being kept out of the valley. Nevertheless, the glowering cloud filled me with dread. It took all my willpower to look away and survey the ground.

The next plant I recognised was well known to me. It was Ffunel. Spindly-branched stems with narrow leaves and umbrella flower heads grew out of the cliffs. How could I reach the plant? There was no ledge wide enough or horizontal for a dragon to land and for me to dismount. I pointed out the plant I wanted to Gabbro and he found an answer. Flapping his wings in long, slow beats he hovered adjacent to the cliff face. The plant I indicated he took in his hooked beak. Large though his beak was he held the plant tenderly and gave it a gentle tug. The Ffunel came away from its thin soil and the dragon carried it away, flowers, stem and roots.

We turned away from the mountains. Gabbro twisted his head around so that I could grab the plant from his mouth. I was astonished at my own fearlessness in letting go of my grip on his feathers with one hand. I had quickly become accustomed to the joy of flight and the fear of falling from my seat seemed to have left me. I stuffed the Ffunel into the bag.

"That is enough of the rugged high places," I said. "But I am not sure where we will find Llysiau'r Hudol."

<IT DOES NOT GROW ON THE HARD GRANITE SLOPES?> Gabbro inquired as we circled over the valley.

"No. It prefers dry grassy hills," I replied wondering where in the vale conditions might suit the plant.

<AH. I KNOW WHERE WE COULD TRY.> Gabbro beat his wings and we turned down the valley. Beyond where we had met the unicorns, the valley widened for a time and there were low rounded hills between the meandering river and the steep, rugged mountains.

<PERHAPS HERE IS SUITABLE.> Gabbro swooped down and landed on one of the grass-covered hilltops. I dismounted and walked away from the dragon searching the ground for the plant I sought. There was an amazing variety of moorland plants but I soon picked out the small lilac blooms of Llysiau'r Hudol. I plucked a few stems from plants whose flowers had not yet opened and placed them gently with the other herbs in the bag. I returned to my steed and guide.

"That is all," I said as I clambered once more on his downy neck. "I hope Gwawrwen has found the other herbs she desired amongst the trees and on the meadows."

<WE SHALL RETURN AT ONCE SO THAT THE FEMALE CAN ASSIST THE UNICORNS.> With a single flexing of his legs Gabbro thrust us into the air and headed for the unicorns' home.

We landed as close to the trees as possible. I jumped from my perch and raced to where the unicorns lay. They had not moved and their once snow-white fur now appeared dulled. Gwawrwen was there, kneeling on the grass laying out plants. She looked up as I arrived and smiled tensely.

"Ah, Aeddon, good. Were you successful? The unicorns are ailing."

I opened the bag and pulled out the plants. "Yes, here is Llysiau'r Hudol, Ffunel and Ysgall Bendigaid. What effects do you expect them to have?"

Gwawrwen examined the fruits of my labour. "Very good, Aeddon. They should all combine to restore the unicorns somewhat. The Ffunel will stimulate their organs and the

Ysgall Bendigaid will overcome their weakness. The Llysiau'r Hudol is different. It will drive away the melancholia that besets the unicorns and strengthen their resolve against the malevolent spirits."

"Oh, that's good."

"But now Aeddon I need your help to prepare the herbs for the concoction, but I have no pots or utensils or even a fire to heat them on." Gwawrwen sat back on her heels and looked bereft.

"The dragons can surely provide us with fire," I said, "and perhaps there are stones in the river that are shaped for the purposes you have in mind."

Gwawrwen sighed and gave me a thin smile. "Of course, Aeddon. I am glad to have you with me."

"I'll go and look." I said and ran towards the river. It was quite wide at this point and the water trickled and gushed over rocks of many different sizes and shapes. I stepped into the flow and almost leapt out again as the water was as cold as ice. I took a deep breath and walked further out searching beneath the water for something, anything that might serve as cooking vessel. My heart beat quickened when I saw a rock that I thought might be suitable. I thrust my arms into the water and pulled up a large stone with a deep indentation in the top. It weighed me down as I returned to the bank and hurried back to Gwawrwen.

She was still on her knees but now had heaps of torn and crushed herbs laid out on leaves in front of her.

"Here," I said, "will this do?" I lowered the rock to the ground at her side. She examined it briefly.

"It's ideal, Aeddon." She piled the prepared herbs into the dimple and mixed them with a stick. "Now we just need a little water and heat."

"Let's take it to the dragons by the river," I said stooping to lift the stone again. I carried it, stumbling, to the edge of the wood and laid it down by the river bank. Gwawrwen scooped water from the river into the mixture. The dragons had all turned their necks to watch what we are doing.

"The mixture must be heated," I called to them. "Can you help?"

<OF COURSE, YOUNG MALE,> Obsidian said, raising

herself onto her legs and taking a few ungainly paces towards us. She lowered her great head until it was alongside the rock. <I THINK YOU SHOULD STAND ASIDE,> she said.

Gwawrwen and I realised that we were indeed standing rather close to a dragon about to flame. We retreated some yards.

Obsidian's nostrils flared as she breathed in then she opened her vast beak and blew out gently, or as gently as a giant dragon was capable of. A great flare of flame engulfed the rock and singed the grass around it. Steam rose and the rock glowed.

"I hope your concoction is not reduced to cinders," I said.

"So do I," Gwawrwen replied looking on with concern on her face.

The flames died and the mother dragon stepped back.

<THERE, I TRUST THAT IS SATISFACTORY.>

Gwawrwen and I took a few tentative paces forward. The scorched ground was still hot and the wisps of steam still rose from the improvised cauldron. I peered inside. The contents looked like a grey thick soup.

"I hope so too," Gwawrwen said. She took a wooden spoon from her bag and dipped it in the mixture. She drew it out and held it up to her nose. She sniffed and nodded.

"It may look unappetising but its odour suggests potency. Let's try it on the unicorns."

Gwawrwen headed back into the wood carefully holding the spoon so as not to spill the restorative infusion.

When we reached the three prone unicorns Adamant opened his eyes and endeavoured to raise his massive head weighed down with his horn. Emerallt too raised her eyelids but Rhuddem was motionless.

Adamant's thought came into my mind, <I fear Rhuddem has succumbed to the evil.>

Gwawrwen rushed to the female unicorn and knelt at her side. She felt for a pulse in the creature's neck and sobbed.

"It can't be too late to save her." She dipped a finger in the bowl of the spoon and rubbed the remedy over the unicorn's lips. There was no movement, not the slightest twitch of the muscles, of the unicorn. The body slumped lifeless, her fur a pale grey. Like Gwawrwen I felt a great sadness. To think that the noble creature had given up its life to protect us and the dragons from the hateful spirits. After the loss of the dragons, especially Basalt, it was almost too much to bear. I stood and Gwawrwen knelt in silent mourning for some moments.

<No medicine, magical or otherwise, can restore Rhuddem to life,> Adamant said, *<but your potion may help Emerallt and myself.>*

Adamant's words broke our solemn trance.

"Of course! How stupid of me to not come straight to your aid," Gwawrwen said gathering herself up and turning to the other female unicorn. The animal raised its head an inch from the ground and parted its lips. Gwawrwen held the spoon to the unicorn's mouth and tipped in some of the juice. A grey tongue flicked out and drew in the liquid. She swallowed. At once a white glow appeared in her cheeks, neck and chest which quickly spread across the whole creature's body.

"It's working!" I cried, full of joy. Gwawrwen went to Adamant and repeated the dose. He too quickly acquired a more healthy appearance of iridescent white. Minutes passed and muscles flexed in the legs of the male unicorn.

"Help me push him upright," Gwawrwen said. She moved to crouch behind the long back of the animal. I joined her and together we heaved at the weighty creature. With Adamant's own assistance we rolled him off his side. Now he hauled himself onto his legs and stood up. He snorted and shook himself.

<Thank you my friends,> he thought, *<let us do the same for Emerallt.>*

We soon had the other unicorn standing too. To my eyes, they looked as they had when I had first met them although they hung their heads so that their horns almost scraped against the ground.

<There is powerful magic, in your concoction,> Adamant said, *<It gives us strength and resolve to withstand the evil for a while longer.>*

"But Rhuddem is dead," Gwawrwen cried. The two unicorns plodded to the body of their fellow.

Adamant turned his huge head and looked on me and Gwawrwen with sad eyes. *<Her body is indeed lifeless, and*

we share your sorrow, but her spirit lives in us.>

"There are only two of you left," I said, a statement of the obvious and of no use.

<Two will be sufficient to keep this vale a place of safety until the girl can defeat the Malevolence.>

"Who knows what September is doing?" I said. At that moment, I saw a familiar violet glow appear between the trees.

Chapter 18

September arrives in Myddfai

She was standing in the middle of a dusty junction of three tracks. To her left and right were small cottages of stone and timber with wooden shutters covering window holes. Some appeared to be in disrepair but others were painted white and pink. She turned around and there was a low-roofed church standing on a slight rise in the middle of a graveyard.

Well, if this isn't Myddfai, I don't know where I am, September thought. She was alone but as she stood listening for sounds of activity she saw a man leave the church and walk down the path towards her. He was shorter than her and had a ring of curly white hair around his bald head. He was wearing black breeches and stockings, a black jacket and a white lace collar. When he looked up he seemed to show surprise as he took in her appearance.

"Good day, m'lady. You are a visitor to Myddfai?"

"Yes," September replied. She presumed that like the other people she had met he saw her as he expected to see her – a lady of the Stuart period. While her dress may not have caused surprise, her sudden arrival without an entourage or means of transport obviously did cause concern.

"You are alone? Surely you were accompanied on the journey from Llanymthefry?"

"I travel on my own." September decided to change the subject. "I'm here to meet one of the physicians of Myddfai."

The man bowed his head. "Many have come to Myddfai for that purpose. I am from that line although I am not gifted in the art of the herbal. I look after my parishioners' souls."

"You're the vicar?"

He bowed again, "The Reverend James Jones, at your service m'lady. Not as many come seeking the Myddfai remedies these days as they did in the centuries that have gone by."

"It is the knowledge that the physicians had that I am interested in."

"Ah, well I am not the one that can assist you, but you are lucky. My son David is boarding with us at present. He is endeavouring to follow the tradition although it could be that he is one of the last physicians of Myddfai. Come, let me show you the hospitality due to a visitor." Rev. Jones held out a hand to take September's arm and they set off together along one of the three lanes out of the small village.

As they walked, Rev. Jones commented on the weather, which was bright and sunny for the time of the year. September looked anxiously to the north. Although they were many miles from Maesycymer she fancied that the sky was darkening in that direction. Soon the Malevolence would be here and the calm of the countryside would be replaced by death and destruction. She had to find the secret of magic soon.

A few minutes of not too brisk walk brought them to the entrance to the grounds of a stone house somewhat larger, grander and more well-kept than the dwellings in the village. There were windows glazed with small oblongs of clear if uneven glass. September was lead into the hallway and then into a dark, wood-panelled drawing room. A house-maid came running and was sent off to fetch the son and refreshments. September was directed to sit on an upright settle next to the fireplace but no sooner had she done so than a young man came into the room, panting a little.

"You have a visitor, Father? A young lady. Ah ..." He saw September, halted and bowed. September noted a family likeness with the older man, a similar stockiness of build, height no greater than his father and curly hair though it was black and covered all of his head. He was wearing brown clothes of the same style as the Rev Jones although they appeared to be rather worn and dusty.

The Reverend grinned, "Yes, David. This is, uh ..."

"September."

He showed no surprise at her unusual name. "Ah, yes. She wishes to meet a physician of Myddfai."

David Jones bowed low. "M'lady September, I aspire to that title and I hope I can be of service to you. I am training in physic but my knowledge of the herbal is but poor at present."

"I must leave you to attend to business," Rev Jones said, "Myfanwy will be bringing food and drink. I hope you can provide the lady with what she needs, David." He left the room. The young man drew up a stool close to September and sat down looking up at her with an air that suggested he was unfamiliar with conversing with young women. She thought he looked like a puppy with his tongue hanging out.

"How may I assist you, m'lady? Is it a particular malady for which you require a remedy?"

"No. It's more general than that."

"Oh," David looked confused, "You see I know some of the cures such as will relieve pain or will increase the secretion of urine, or will reduce nervousness or …"

"It's none of those. I want to know about magic."

His mouth opened and he stared. "Magic?"

"Yes, I am told that the Physicians of Myddfai were known as famous magicians."

"I know nothing of magic, m'lady. I know which herbs to look out for and whether to pick the leaves or the flowers or perhaps the roots to make infusions and ointments and such like, but they are not magic."

September nodded. "I know that but I'm told that your ancestors did have magic."

"Ah, my ancestors. You mean the first Physicians of Myddfai, don't you?"

"I suppose so."

"The son of the Lady of the Lake, and his sons."

"That's it. I'm told she wasn't human, that she lived underwater."

"That is what the tale says. The Lady came out of the water to meet the young farmer. He fell in love and eventually she agreed to marry him on condition that he did not strike her. They lived happily and had three sons, the first was called Rhiwallon. But three times the husband unintentionally tapped her. She returned to the lake but later appeared to Rhiwallon and taught him her skills with herbs and healing. I and my father are descended from Rhiwallon."

September looked at the young man eagerly. "If the lady

really lived underwater she must be magical. Is that right, David?"

"Well, yes, m'lady."

"And if she taught your ancestor magic then she could teach me."

"But that was five hundred years ago!"

"That doesn't matter. Do you know where Rhiwallon lived with his mother and father?"

"Yes, it's called Esgair Laethdy. It's a short distance from here."

"Take me there, please, David." September stood up and held out her hand to the young man.

"But ..."

"Please. It's very important." September was not used to being bossy but it seemed that her manner was effective

David Jones sighed and stood up. Perhaps he was familiar with being told what to do. He took September's arm and led her from the room just as the maid arrived with a tray laden with food and drink.

"We're going out, Myfanwy," David said, "Please tell my father we'll be back soon."

David marched from the house, across the garden and out into the field beyond the hedge, leading September by her hand. They crossed a few fields containing sheep and cattle grazing on the spring grass. Overhead the sky remained blue with a few white clouds. Only the hills to the south and east looked dark. Nevertheless, September could feel the growing evil entering the world.

David however was oblivious of the impending doom. He chattered about his ancestors, the people who used to come to learn the wisdom of the physicians and his plans to become a surgeon as well as a herbalist. As they walked, he pointed out plants growing amongst the crops, pasture, and hedgerows, naming them and describing their use in remedies. September let him chatter. She thought it was a sign of youth rather than a display of his knowledge. Eventually they came to a ruined farmhouse. September could see that it had once been a considerable structure much added to. Now though there were gaps in the roof, shutters hung lopsidedly from windows and there were holes in some of the lath and plaster walls. The garden around the house was overgrown but September could see that there was a profusion of different plants which she guessed were part of the Physicians' collection.

David pointed. "This is it. As you can see no-one lives here now. The Physicians moved away as their fame spread and the farm fell into disuse."

September tried to imagine the farm occupied and busy. "But Rhiwallon lived here with his two brothers and father five hundred years ago?"

"So it is believed."

"Well, thank you, David. I hope your studies go well."

The young man looked crestfallen. "What do you mean? Is that it? You just wanted to see where the first Physicians lived?"

"That's right."

"But you asked about their magic. How can this derelict farm help you?"

"It's your ancestors I want to meet."

"But they are dead and gone these centuries past!"

"To you perhaps, but not to me. Thank you for your help, David."

The physician stared at her not understanding her words.

September held in her mind an image of a man with three sons, living in this place, centuries in the past.

"Take me then," she said.

Ribbons of violet light surrounded her, obscuring David and the ruined farmyard.

"September! What's happening?"

David Jones' cries faded as the violet light grew more intense. She felt dizzy and unsteady.

Chapter 19

September meets the first Physician of Myddfai

There was firm ground beneath her feet again and as the spinning lights faded September could see her surroundings. When she looked into the distance she saw that the line of hills was as it had been but nearby was very much changed. The farmhouse was greatly reduced in size but did appear to be in reasonable condition with a weather-tight roof and lime-washed walls. The ground near the house was dusty, hard-packed earth at which chickens pecked and a pile of logs was stacked against a wall. A young man in a simple mud-coloured tunic and trousers was scraping at a contraption which September recognised as a plough. When he saw her he reacted with surprise, standing up and turning to face her. September thought she could see a likeness with David Jones. The young man had curly black hair and was no taller than her but his body was thinner and there was a suggestion of well-used muscles under the rough clothes.

"Pardon, lady, I was unaware of your approach, although your sudden appearance makes me question the truth of my sight."

"I am really here," she said, "I'm September. And you are …?"

"Rhiwallon, lady."

"The oldest son."

"That is true. The oldest of three sons of my father."

"And of your mother."

He frowned. "Why do you mention my mother?"

"Because I would like to meet her."

Rhiwallon made a noise like a wounded dog, grabbed a broom from the ground and advanced towards September. She backed away holding up her hands to fend him off.

He shouted, "You are a stranger. Why do you ask of my mother? What falsehoods have you heard about my father and mother?"

September shook her head. Why was the young man so angry? Had she arrived later than she intended, after the Lady had left the family.

"None I hope," she said, "Your mother knows about magic, doesn't she?"

Rhiwallon froze, the broom handle raised in readiness to strike her.

"You talk of magic. Some people fear those that can weave spells. It can be dangerous to be labelled a witch."

"I don't want to hurt anyone," September said standing well out of range of the boy's broom, "I just want to speak to her."

"She's not here," Rhiwallon said. September wondered if she had arrived too late and his mother had already returned to the lake. "What do you know of my mother?" he asked

"That she came out of a lake. Your father fell in love with her and persuaded her to marry him."

"If you know that then you must know of the bargain she made."

"That if he hit her three times, she'd go away again."

"That's right. My father loved my mother and would never have hit her out of anger or lust."

"But he did hit her, didn't he?" She was right, the mysterious Lady had left her husband and sons.

Rhiwallon slumped. The broom dropped from his hands.

"Three times in public. They were nothing, on no occasion did he mean her harm."

"Nevertheless, the agreement was broken. She left?"

"A week since. While my brothers and I struggle to find food to put on the table my father lies in his bed, heartbroken." Rhiwallon glanced towards the house. "She took with her all the cattle and sheep and pigs that she brought to the marriage. Now we have nothing but a few chickens and land that must be sown."

"I understand your father's distress and why you are upset."

"What can you know?"

What did she know? She didn't know what it was like to lose a mother but in becoming the saviour of worlds and the tool of the Brains she had lost many things.

"I know the tale of your mother and father and I know your story, what you become and your descendants."

"You see the future?"

"I am from the future, well, your future."

Rhiwallon stared at her. "I don't understand. Why are you here?"

September stepped forward holding out her hands, a gesture she hoped he would respond to.

"As I said, to meet your mother. I am hoping that she has the knowledge which can help me save the world a few hundred years from now."

Rhiwallon shook his head. "I hear your words but they make no sense to me. Save the world from what?"

"A great evil, the Malevolence. It lurks outside the universe but has found a way in. It will destroy everything if I don't stop it. But I need magic."

"Hah! We thought we had a magical existence, the love of a wife and mother, food aplenty, a comfortable life. Now we have nothing, or at least nothing to live for."

"That may be your father's feeling but you have your life in front of you."

Rhiwallon shrugged. "What can I do?"

"Have you seen your mother since she left your home?"

"She returned to her people beneath the waters of the Llyn y Fan Fach. How could I see her?"

"She will appear to you. She has things to show and tell you."

"But the bargain …"

"Was with your father. It is over but you are her son. She still feels responsibility for you."

"You think so?"

"Take my hands. Show me the lake. We'll go there."

He at last took hold of her outstretched hands. "What do you mean?"

"Think of what it looks like and you will see."

He closed his eyes. A picture came into September's head of a ridge in an arc encircling a dark, almost circular lake at its foot. Ribbons of indigo light wrapped around the two of them.

Rhiwallon stumbled and fell against her. She was prepared for the moment of disorientation, and caught him. His body felt hard through the clothes. Her vision cleared and she saw the smooth dark surface of the lake ahead of her and the surrounding curve of the mountain, partly illuminated by the afternoon sun.

The young man regained his balance and stood up looking around, his eyes wide with wonder.

"You are indeed a witch. We are at the shore of Llyn y Fan Fach when a moment ago we were miles hence."

"I'm not a witch. Moving is the one skill I seem to have."

"Why have you brought me here?"

"This is where your mother lives, isn't it? She will come to you."

Rhiwallon looked doubtful. "So you say. I thought that once my father had lost her she would be lost to her sons too."

"No, she'll come. You'll see."

They stood side by side looking across the still waters unruffled even by a breeze. They waited for minutes then September noticed ripples some way out from the bank. The circles spread out but new ones formed closer to the shore. Something broke the surface, a head. Then she was striding out of the lake towards them. She was a tall, slim woman with black hair down to her waist, dressed in a white gown which, despite the water cascading from her, appeared to be dry. She stepped from the water on to the dry land but her feet were hidden in the folds of her dress.

"My son," she said in a soft, melodic voice.

"Mother!"

"You have a companion."

"Yes, she brought me here. She said you would come to speak to me, that you had things to tell me."

"Perhaps I have, Rhiwallon. It pained me to leave you when the bargain with your father was broken. I am still your Mother and have love for you and your brothers."

There was ecstatic happiness on Rhiwallon's face.

"You will come home?"

The lady shook her head. "No, that part of my life is over, but I will meet you here from time to time to speak with you.

Now, this young woman has travelled from afar to question me. Return to your home, Rhiwallon. Come again a week from now."

The man was sad but he turned away and trudged off along a track that lead away from the lake and the mountain.

The Lady of the Lake turned to look at September. "Thank you for bringing my son to me. I have much to teach him."

"You do. Can we talk now?"

"Certainly, but come with me to my home."

"Under the water?"

"Of course." The Lady held out her hand and it was September's turn to take it and be lead. The Lady guided her to the water's edge and carried on. September put a foot in the water expecting it to be cold. Instead she could feel nothing. It was as if the water was an illusion and not really there. Together they walked out into the lake each step taking them into deeper water. September looked down as the water rose up her legs to her waist and then up her chest. When the water reached her neck, she clamped her mouth shut although she could not feel it lapping under chin. Then the surface of the water was moving up her face. She saw the line pass her eyes although she did not feel it.

She felt she had to breathe but she kept her mouth clenched shut.

"You can take air normally," the Lady said at her side. Tentatively, September inhaled, half expecting the rush of water into her lungs but instead she felt the welcome flow of air. She relaxed although she didn't understand what was happening and breathed in fully. The surface of the water was above her and she could see it rippling and reflecting light just as if she was submerged in a swimming pool. Yet she still had no feeling of being immersed.

The Lady swam in a slow circle around her. Her dress had disappeared. Her arms and breasts were bare and her lower half resembled a dolphin. She remembered Edward Tyson's discussion of the similarity of a mermaid and a porpoise.

"You are a mermaid!" September exclaimed.

"That is one guise. To Rhiwallon and his father I was a woman but others called me a fairy or a witch. I can be many things."

"A shape-shifter?"

"That describes my nature."

"But you were a woman for years while you were married to Rhiwallon's father and you gave birth to three sons."

"I wanted to see what it was like to live on land in one body. I loved my husband but I came to regret leaving this life."

"So you made sure your bargain was broken."

The Lady sighed. "Yes, it was hard on him and my sons but I had to return."

"But you will help Rhiwallon?"

"I shall pass on my knowledge so he can heal his fellows and feel satisfaction in his life."

They had been walking and swimming deeper into the lake until they came to what looked to September like a house without walls or roof. In a shallow depression in the lake bed was a couch and chairs, table and cupboards. All the furniture had a spongy appearance as if it had been grown that way. The Lady swam into the submarine home and settled onto the couch with her tail just hanging off the end. She indicated one of the chairs. September sat down and felt herself suspended as if resting on a soft balloon. It moulded to her body and was extremely comfortable.

"Welcome to my home," the Lady said, "My people are going about their own business but will return soon. I sense you have a great burden which you seek to lift from your shoulders."

September sighed and rested her head back. She felt a bit as if she was on a psychiatrist's couch.

"Yes, I have a responsibility which couldn't be bigger really."

"To save the world from evil."

"You know?"

"I can guess and I can feel your power and your anxiety."

"I was supposed to stop the Malevolence getting into the world, but I failed and it's here. Not now, in about five hundred years' time. I have to stop it, drive it back, but I don't know how. I need magic but I don't have the power." It all poured out in a torrent. Her chest throbbed and she sobbed.

"My girl, you have immense power. I can feel it now, within you."

September looked at the Lady through tear-bleared eyes. It seemed strange that only her cheeks were damp while she was apparently under the water of the lake.

"I can move through space and time, from one universe to another but that's all. Before, on the other world where I fought the Malevolence I had all sorts of powers which I could use by just feeling an emotion, but here, like in my own universe, I don't have anything else. Here where there are dragons and unicorns, and mermaids, there seems to be lots of magic. I think I need magic to defeat the Malevolence."

The Lady laughed. "Magic! Humans always go on about magic. Some want it, some seek it, some pretend to have it."

"But it exists, doesn't it?" September felt desperate. Was the Lady going to solve her problem or not.

"Yes and no," the Lady said.

"What do you mean?"

"There is I suppose, for want of a better word, magic, in the nature of all things. Dragons fly, breathe fire which I suppose you will say is magical but is just the nature of dragons. Unicorns exude peace and goodness and communicate by thought – that's unicorns for you. Mermaids, well we change our form or give men the illusion of the form they wish to see. That's us. Humans think that making patterns in the air with bits of stick, or cooking up potions, or mouthing strange words and phrases will have some miraculous effect. It won't, it's not in human nature."

"There are no real magicians?"

"No, only those who aspire to be or pretend to have the skills."

September sighed. "So how am I supposed to defeat the Malevolence."

The Lady frowned. "You said your task was to stop this evil entering the world. Why did you fail?"

"I was too late. By the time I had discovered that the Malevolence was using Ezekiel Soulbury to open a gateway into this universe, it was already through."

"How can you be late? You told me this happens five

hundred years from now. You came from that time. You said you can travel anywhere in time and space."

"Yes, but ..." September stopped speaking. How could she be so dense? The Brains had brought her into the universe to deal with the Malevolence. They'd left her to it with little guidance, but Cyfaill and Henshaw knew that she had the power given to her by the Gwlyb Hoedl Gwyrthiol. The Lady was right she could be anywhere, anywhen. She needn't be late for anything.

"All I have to do is stop Soulbury from making Cold Fire," she said.

"Now I don't know what you mean," the Lady said.

"No, you've done it. You've told me what I need to do. Now I know where and how it happens I can go to the correct time and stop it."

"Meddling with time could be dangerous. Don't be too hasty," the Lady warned.

September nodded. "Yes, I know, I've done it before. I know that in one reality, the one I left behind, the Malevolence broke through. Perhaps I can't stop the world being destroyed on that timeline. But if I can prevent the void opening earlier then a new reality will open up for this universe, in which everyone lives. The Evil's victory will be small."

"Now you're speaking of your nature, girl. One which understands the difficulties of interfering with time. It is beyond me."

September sat up on the squashy seat, feeling eager and alert. "No, you're right. It is complex and I must get it sorted in my head before I do anything stupid. But I can do it. I can defeat the Malevolence, again." She pushed herself off the cushion-like chair and stood up on the sandy lakebed.

"I must get back to people I left to face the evil."

The Lady flicked a fin and drifted off her couch. She floated upright in front of September.

"You don't have to hurry. Stay and meet my family and friends."

"No, I know a few hours here wouldn't matter but I can't put it off now. I have to go."

"I understand. Good luck with your task."

"Thanks. You'll teach Rhiwallon well. He and his descendants will become famous physicians."

"Thank you for bringing him to meet me."

September closed her eyes and summoned up an image of the unicorns' vale sometime after she had left Gwawrwen. Violet light descended from the surface of the water above her. She saw the Lady waving as her view was obscured.

Chapter 20

September returns to the vale of the unicorns

The birthmark on her hip burned and her skin prickled. It signalled that the Malevolence was near, but not here. September opened her eyes to see the oak trees of the unicorn's home. The evil spirits had not entered the vale then. She heard a cry and then saw Aeddon running towards her.

"September, September! Is the evil defeated?" He skidded to a halt in front of her. Behind came Gwawrwen and two unicorns.

"No, not yet, but it can be, I'm certain. I'm glad you are still safe."

"We are, but the unicorns have struggled to keep the dark cloud at bay. One has died."

Sadness filled September. A unicorn gone. She must act to stop any more deaths of these fine, loving creatures. But she was torn. How could she stop the Malevolence and protect all these beings? What should she do first?

Gwawrwen embraced her. "You have found the answer to your questions then, September? Do you have magic?"

"Yes and no," and she found herself recalling the Lady of the Lake giving the same enigmatic answer. "There are things I must do but first I need to speak with you, the unicorns and the dragons. Where are they?"

"Just outside the wood," Gwawrwen said, "Come, let us meet with them." She led September, Aeddon and the unicorns out of the group of trees. September saw the four, huge, red bird-like creatures sitting in the meadow.

"Four? Where are the others?" September asked.

"Dead," Aeddon replied, "They were killed by the evil."

There was lead in September's stomach. So many of the fierce, magnificent creatures taken by the Malevolence. How could she make up for their sacrifice?

The dragons saw them arriving and heaved themselves onto their taloned feet. The four dragons, two unicorns and three people formed a circle. Now that she was out in the open country September looked up to the ridge surrounding the valley. The dark cloud that filled the sky beyond the valley filled her with terror. That was what she had to defeat. She had to end this timeline.

<HAS THE CHILD FROM BEYOND LEARNED HOW TO DEFEAT THE EVIL CLOUD?> The female dragon's voice battered against September's brain

"I have an idea." September answered looking at the leading dragon.

<YOU HAVE MAGIC?>

"Sort of. I had it all along but didn't realise it. It's not what I thought was needed to defeat the Malevolence."

<WE DO NOT UNDERSTAND. WHAT IS IT YOU MUST DO?>

"I must go back and stop Soulbury, the alchemist, making Cold Fire."

"Ezekiel is dead. Frozen." Aeddon said, "I saw his body before the spirits came."

"He's dead now, but I must go back in time and stop him making the special phosphorus."

"Back in time?" Aeddon muttered.

<You risk confusing the timeline of the universe by changing what has already occurred,> Adamant's thought came to September like a gentle breeze.

"I know, and that's why I am wondering what to do. If I leave you here while changing the path of time in the past you, this you, will be trapped here and can only succumb to the Malevolence."

<We will be in a dead branch of time that will wither.>

"And die. Yes, all of you, including the spirits of the Malevolence." September was grateful that Adamant understood what she was beginning to plan.

<The fate of all creatures is to die.>

"But if I leave you here you will weaken and fall to the black cloud. I don't want you to experience that fate."

<ENOUGH OF OUR FELLOWS HAVE ALREADY MET THEIR END IN THE EVIL SMOKE.>

"And many people too," Gwawrwen added.

"I know, and I am sorry for every one that has died." September wasn't sure whether she could possibly comprehend the number of deaths that had already occurred. <BUT IF WE MUST DIE TO SAVE THE GREATER NUMBER THEN THAT IS A FATE WE MUST ACCEPT.> Obsidian said and the other three dragons bellowed their agreement.

"There must be something I can do to save you as well as going back to stop the Malevolence breaking through," September said. There was an idea in her head that she was struggling to grasp hold of. It was all about time.

"The unicorns and dragons are so few," Aeddon said, his face downcast. "Their numbers were diminishing before the evil cloud appeared."

Gwawrwen nodded. "People have threatened them and encroached on their lands."

"That's it!" September brightened. "The unicorns and dragons need to be somewhere that isn't overrun by people."

"What do you mean?" Gwawrwen asked and Aeddon looked confused as well.

"The past, before people were everywhere. I can take the unicorns and dragons back to a time when they won't be bothered and can live their lives."

<And replenish our numbers,> Adamant thought, <I think that is a good plan, September.>

Obsidian nodded her great head. <AWAY FROM PEOPLE WITH SWORDS AND GUNS? A PLACE WHERE WILD CREATURES ROAM THAT WE CAN HUNT FOR FOOD? YES, I THINK THAT IS AN EXCELLENT IDEA.>

Gwawrwen frowned. "What about us, September? Will you take us back to help you stop Ezekiel?"

"I don't think I can do that," September said, shaking her head. "You will be there too. I don't think it's a good idea to meet yourselves."

Gwawrwen raised a hand to her face. "I hadn't thought of that. Just think the shock our earlier selves would have to meet us as we are now."

"Will we stay here and die?" Aeddon said, his voice trembling.

"I think the only answer is to take you back with the unicorns and dragons," September said.

"How far back do you think we need to go?" Gwawrwen asked.

September shrugged, "I'm not sure. Five or six thousand years. That's before civilisations grew up around the world but otherwise things were pretty much like they are now."

"Do you mean when Adam and Eve were still in Paradise?" Aeddon said, his eyes wide.

"Um?" September wasn't sure how to answer. Did the people, at this time, still believe what they read in the Bible?

Gwawrwen spoke before September could reply. "I think September is suggesting that there is more to the world than we read in the Bible, Aeddon."

Aeddon looked doubtful. "But the priest of the church in Llanllionio reads stories from the Bible about the devil and evil monsters and the terrible things that can happen to sinners. Is that not what is happening now?"

September hadn't studied religion. "I don't think the Bible mentions the Malevolence," she said uncertainly.

Gwawrwen nodded. "September is right. This destruction was not foretold in Christian texts nor in any others. Not even Ezekiel's friends in the Royal Society, who have studied truths unknown to past generations, will have knowledge of the Malevolence."

<The stories humans tell themselves are for purposes other than an explanation of the truths of the universe> Adamant said. Aeddon was thoughtful.

<LET US GO THEN, CHILD. WE ARE EAGER TO SEE OUR NEW HOME, AND HUNGRY.> The other three dragons roared their agreement. The noise made September, Aeddon and Gwawrwen cover their ears until the echoes bouncing off the valley sides had ceased.

"I need a marker," September said. "A point in the past I can latch on to take you all there. If we go back to the same place, this valley, is there something I can use?"

The two unicorns faced each other, their horns touching. They didn't move for a few minutes. At last Adamant faced September.

<This valley was formed by ice that retreated. There is a

large boulder in the shape of an acorn at the bottom of the water fall. It fell when the dam holding the water at the top of the valley collapsed as the ice melted.>

"I know that rock," Aeddon cried, "We passed it when we descended from the ridge. It's huge! I can't believe it ever moved."

<Yes, young man, it did move. Its fall created the waterfall and the initial torrent made a noise that is remembered to this day.>

"Only by you unicorns," Gwawrwen commented. "Do you really remember everything that has happened?"

<Yes, friend of unicorns. Our lives are long and we recall all that has occurred.>

September had been thinking. "I remember seeing that boulder too and if you remember it falling I can fix on that moment. Let me see it."

September's head was filled with the roar and sight of falling water and rock. It obscured her view of the head of the valley except for the massive grey boulder that at first toppled at the top and then fell the thousand or so feet to the valley floor. Aeddon and Gwawrwen cried out as they too received the image from Adamant.

<THAT IS THE TIME WE ARE MOVING TO?> Obsidian asked.

"It's the only time long ago that I can be sure of getting all of you to," September said.

<THERE WILL BE DANGERS, CREATURES THAT NO LONGER EXIST THAT COULD HARM UNICORNS.>

"I suppose that's right," September said.

<TAKE ME FIRST.> Obsidian said, <I CAN CHECK THE VALLEY FOR THE OTHERS AND PROVIDE PROTECTION WHEN THEY ARRIVE.>

"That's a good idea," September said, eager to be making a start on the project. "Shall we leave."

<CLIMB ON MY NECK. IT WOULD BE SAFEST IF WE TRAVELLED ACROSS THE AGES IN FLIGHT.> The mother dragon lowered her head to the ground. September walked towards her wondering how she was to get on board.

"Use her feathers to climb up," Aeddon said. "They're very

strong, but comfortable to sit on."

"Thanks," September said taking a handful of the red feathers in her hands and hauling herself up. Soon she was sitting astride and the dragon reared up on its legs and extended its wings.

"I'll be back for the rest of you as soon as we've gone," September called out. Obsidian swept her wings downwards and the dragon lifted off the ground with September clutching at the feathers. She did not feel at all secure even though her legs gripped the dragon's long, sturdy neck.

They gained height and the dragon circled over the river, keeping as far as possible from the black wall of evil that rose from the ridge to the top of the sky. September focussed on the image that Adamant had given her.

The air beat against September's face. "Are you ready, Obsidian?" she said through her pursed lips. "Moving in time may disturb you. I don't want you to fall when we go back."

<I CAN FLY WHEN I AM ASLEEP AND I CAN FLY WHEN I AM SPITTING FIRE AT MY ENEMIES,> the dragon roared in reply <I DO NOT THINK A PASSAGE THROUGH TIME WILL DISORIENT ME.>

"Okay then. Here we go," September stiffened her grip on the dragon and closed her eyes. She thought of the moment the boulder fell.

They moved.

September's head span. Dizziness and nausea made her retch. Was it the time jump that had made her ill? She opened her eyes. No, it wasn't the change in time. They were falling through the air, spinning, the air rushing past them.

"Obsidian!" September cried though her words were whipped away. She clung on to the dragon's neck. Glancing down, the ground seemed close and approaching fast.

<WHAT IS IT CHILD?> The dragon straightened her wings, the spiralling descent became a dive then they were soaring up into the sky above the vale. September saw the great lake of water trapped between the two peaks and the earthen dam beginning to crack. Water streamed through and a huge boulder in its midst rocked. The sky all around was clear of the black evil.

"Are you alright, Obsidian?" September called.

<FORGIVE ME CHILD. I WAS MISTAKEN. A JOURNEY THROUGH TIME IS NOT AS EASY AS I THOUGHT. YOU MUST WARN THE OTHERS, PARTICULARLY MY SON AND DAUGHTERS, TO TAKE CARE.>

A shadow passed over September and she looked up. It was a black bird; a big black bird. She suddenly realised how big it was; not as large as the dragon but its body was as long as September herself and its wingspan four times that. There wasn't just one of them either. Six of the gigantic birds were circling around Obsidian, squawking loudly. One after another they swooped on the dragon, raking it with their talons.

"What are they?" September asked.

<1 HAVE NEVER SEEN SUCH CREATURES BEFORE. GO AND BRING MY OFFSPRING. I CAN HANDLE THESE OVERGROWN SPARROWS. I DOUBT THAT THEY HAVE EXPERIENCED FLAME BEFORE.>

September ducked as another of the black birds soared over her and Obsidian banked to keep her safe.

"Okay, I'm going." Now she had to think of returning on her own, leaving Obsidian alone in the prehistoric world. She imagined herself back with unicorns and the others. Violet light enveloped her.

September found herself sitting on her bottom on the grass. Her vision cleared and she looked up into the huge face of Adamant. She looked around. Aeddon and Gwawrwen were looking up into the sky.

<*You are back already, my child,*> the unicorn said. <*You found it as I described?*>

"Yes, but there are giant birds attacking Obsidian," September got to her feet. Gwawrwen and Aeddon looked at her in astonishment.

Aeddon pointed to the sky, "But we saw you up there, a moment ago."

"That's time travel," September said brushing herself down, "I can come back at the same moment I left. Now I need to get the other dragons there to help Obsidian."

Gwawrwen frowned, "These giant birds? I know of no such creatures."

"It's thousands of years ago," September reminded her, "I expect they became extinct quickly and left no trace here." She hastened to the three remaining dragons that were watching.

<YOU WISH TO TAKE ALL THREE OF US AT ONCE TO JOIN OUR MOTHER?> Gabbro said.

"I want to try it," September said, "I've never tried moving in time with more than one person, er, or dragon, but if you stay close together and I think of all of you at once I hope it will work."

The male dragon lowered its head, <WELL, LET US GO. I WANT TO SEE THESE OVERSIZE BLACK BIRDS AND SINGE THEIR WINGS TO TEACH THEM A LESSON.>

September clambered onto his neck and they launched into the sky along with the other two dragons. They climbed high into the sky then formed into a close formation. They glided with Gabbro's wingtip touching his fellows on either side. September closed her eyes and thought of all of them moving to join Obsidian.

She was ready for the sickening feeling in her stomach on this occasion as the dragon plummeted. It was only a moment before Gabbro recovered from the temporal transition but they had fallen a few hundred feet in that time. He soared back up into the sky over the valley, the other two dragons not far from them. A short distance away September saw Obsidian being harassed by the six black birds that seemed tiny in comparison to the huge dragon. She also saw the rock at the top of the cliff toppling over the edge.

"I'm going back," she said.

<FAREWELL ...> was all she heard as she was wrapped in violet light once more.

This time she was on her back on the grass. She looked up. Two human and two unicorn faces looked down at her.

Aeddon lowered his hand to her. She grabbed it and pulled herself up.

"Is it the turn of the unicorns now, September?" he said.

"Yes, I suppose so," she replied, shaking her head to rid herself of the dizziness. How many more times would she have to do this? Each time-swap left her feeling a little faint.

"Wait, September," Gwawrwen said, "If you take the unicorns we will be left with no protection from the Malevolence. Will we be taken by the evil?"

September had an image of her friends being drawn into the darkness and turned to dust.

"No, I won't let that happen," she said.

"Then what are we to do?" Aeddon said.

<The humans must come with us and start a new life in the past,> Adamant thought.

"Live in the past!" Aeddon cried.

"Adamant is right," Gwawrwen said, "September says that this time will soon end and our lives with it. If we wish to live we must go with the dragons and unicorns."

<And the others.>

"The others?" Aeddon said, his face screwed up with confusion.

<The others of your sort who still survive in the building of stone.>

"The church!" Gwawrwen exclaimed.

"Meilyr and the villagers of Llanllionio," Aeddon cried, "How could I forget them."

"We must save them," Gwawrwen said.

September had been listening to the conversation and was wondering how many more people and creatures she would be expected to convey to the past. Would she have to save all the creatures of the vale?

"And what of the rest of the people of this world?" Aeddon asked, his voice trembling.

September shook her head, "I don't know. I think that once I have stopped the Malevolence from entering this universe, this time loop will wither and the evil spirits that make up the black cloud will fade away. Everyone left in this world will simply cease to be and their lives will carry on in the new timeline."

"But not the people of Llanllionio?" Gwawrwen said.

<They have already met the Malevolence. Unless they are removed from this existence they will fall to the evil,> the unicorn announced.

"I think that's right," September nodded.

"We must take them with us," Aeddon said, folding his arms as if to emphasise the decision.

"I suppose so," September said.

<You must return to the village, and transfer the humans to the past before returning finally for us,> Adamant thought.

September couldn't disagree with the noble animal. "Okay, take my hand Aeddon, Gwawrwen. Give me a picture of the church."

Chapter 21

September meets the people of Llanllionio

It was dark; almost as dark as the realm of the Malevolence beyond the universe. September's birthmark burned as if it was on fire and the cacophony of hate that surrounded her added to the dizziness she felt from the time jumps. The cloud of evil spirits was so dense that she could not see her companions or the church.

"We must be outside the church," Gwawrwen said from September's right.

"I couldn't put us inside because of all the people in the space," September said.

Aeddon spoke with a tremulous voice from her left, "This evil presence scares me. I wonder how much longer the unicorns can save us from them."

"You're right Aeddon," Gwawrwen said, "Protecting us draws on the strength my potion gave them. We must take the people away quickly. Now where is the entrance?"

September reached out her hand and was surprised when she touched a hard surface. Was it stone? No, it was wood; wood with iron.

"I think it is here," she said, "Your mind picture brought us right to it."

September felt Gwawrwen's hand on hers then reaching further to the door.

"Yes, September," Gwawrwen said; there was obvious relief in her voice. "It is the door to the vestry. It is unlocked."

September heard the heavy latch lift and the creak as the door opened. The three of them rushed through the crack. September stood in the room still unable to see a thing as there was no light, but the noise of the spirits was slightly reduced by the thick walls of the church. The door slammed shut.

"This way," Aeddon said from nearby. September reached out and found the cloth of his jacket. She grabbed it and followed him across the small room, bumping against a table. Her arms brushed the doorpost as they entered the church.

Shouts and cries pounded her ears. Flailing fists and swinging feet battered her head and shoulders and legs. She felt herself being pushed down to the floor under the weight of people pressing against her, air driven from her lungs

"Stop! It's us!" Aeddon's voice cried out. "It's me, Aeddon."

The beating stopped. September found that she could breathe again and she could stand up. Even better, she could see. A few candles burned around the nave casting a dim yellow light, but nevertheless allowing her to see the group of people clustered around the three of them. The faces were pale, a look of terror on each. September understood why. Even here in the body of the church the noise of the spirits outside hurt her ears. The windows were dark with the evil cloud. There were ominous creaks from the roof above their heads.

Meilyr pushed to the front of the group. "I'm sorry boy, Gwawrwen, September. The people are scared. They thought you belonged to the evil that assaults us."

"We've come to take you away," Gwawrwen said, pushing her white hair away from her face and straightening the clothes that had been tugged at.

"You are still under the protection of the unicorns?" Meilyr asked.

"Yes, but their power weakens," Gwawrwen replied. Meilyr looked anxious.

"Then how are we to escape this evil. Even these stone walls and slate roof cannot protect us for much longer. You can hear the timbers protesting at the weight of the black cloud that presses upon them."

"We're going to take you all a long way away from the Malevolence," Aeddon said.

Meilyr was confused. "But isn't it spreading across the land. Did you not say that it would soon cover the whole world?"

"A long way in time," Gwawrwen said. Meilyr looked even more bemused. "September can take us all to a time before all this began."

"Before that fool, Ezekiel meddled with what he did not understand?"

"No, a lot longer ago than that," Gwawrwen said. Meilyr looked from her to September.

"To avoid meeting yourselves and your ancestors I must take you back to a time before this area was inhabited," September said.

"Thousands of years, she says," Aeddon added, "When the world had just begun."

"It's not quite like that," September said, "but it is thousands of years. You will be alone and will have to look after yourselves."

"We've always done that, haven't we?" Meilyr turned to the villagers who had been listening with open mouths and wide eyes.

"There will be no civilisation or anything," September explained, "and no metal tools unless you know how to make them yourselves."

"We have all sorts of skills amongst us here," Meilyr said, "farmers, woodsmen, carpenters, even a stonemason and farrier. And me of course."

"You'll need everyone," September said, realising something of the hardships the people would face. She looked at each one of them gazing at her, each of them scarcely understanding the conversation they were having. Did they realise that their lives were about to change for ever?

"Well, let's go. The sooner we are away from this menace, the better," Meilyr said. He paused. "Are we going to travel as you do, by Symudiad?"

"Yes. If we all join hands and form a circle I think I can do it."

If it was possible, Meilyr's weather-beaten face turned whiter. "I'll just get everyone prepared then."

He turned again to address the concerned crowd and explained what was going to happen. There were some complaints about leaving their homes, crops and livestock until Meilyr pointed out that they had already been destroyed and the country turned into a barren wasteland. He added that if people wanted to wait till the church collapsed and the spirits fell on them then they were free to do so. There was a rush as people hurried to pick up the few items that they had brought with them. They returned to the foursome with a look of expectation on their faces.

September looked around the group of twenty to thirty people of all ages. Could she really transport all of them to the distant past in one group? She had to try.

Meilyr organised them into a raggedy circle and persuaded them all to link their hands.

"You must keep hold of the people on each side of you," September said. "You will see blue light and then what you see here will disappear. It feels strange but everything should be fine where we're going."

There were lots of worried looks and firmer grips taken of neighbours' hands. September took hold of Gwawrwen's and Aeddon's hands

"Right. We're going," she said. She closed her eyes and thought of the vale of the unicorns as it was in the past. She thought of the acorn boulder resting at the top of the ridge and the four dragons in the sky.

Bands of violet light descended as if from a merry-go-round, spinning around the group, faster and faster. The candle-lit church disappeared beyond the light. The roar of the evil spirits faded. She held on to the image of Cwm Dreigiau after the ice age as her head itself seemed to spin. The floor went from beneath her feet.

She was sprawling on rough ground. Her grip on Gwawrwen's and Aeddon's hands broke. When she came to rest on her back she opened her eyes. There was blue sky above with four red dragons circling high above. She turned her head and saw the top of the valley a mile or so away. The huge boulder was toppling, starting to fall. The dam, of which it was part, began to break up, fountains of water spurted out. She rolled over, got to her feet and looked around. The people were doing the same while staring at their surroundings and shivering. September noticed too that the air was chill.

Aeddon was at her side. "Where is the river?"

September looked. The familiar gently babbling stream that watered the valley of the unicorns was not visible. She shrugged.

"No river has yet flowed in this vale," Gwawrwen said. "The water has been held back. Look."

She pointed to the head of the valley. The boulder was falling, crashing into the mountainside, pieces of rock the size of paving slabs sheering off and flying off into the air. The air was filled with the noise of falling rock and the rupturing dam. The dam was crumbling, water pouring through and over the edge of the ridge.

"The waterfall is beginning," Aeddon cried.

"Yes, and it's going to flood where we are," Meilyr said. "We've got to get to higher ground. Come on." He urged the people to follow him and set off at a run towards a part of the valley floor that looked a little higher.

How could I be so stupid, September thought. I chose this time because the falling boulder provide a landmark in time but I hadn't thought what would happen when the dam burst and released the lake it had held back. She too began to run after the village people.

Some, while running, had looked up into the sky. They saw the dragons, shouted with fear and pointed.

"Don't worry about them," Gwawrwen shouted, "They are our friends and allies." Their fear of the dragons outweighed by the terror of the falling waters, the people ran on. September glanced over her shoulder and saw water mixed with earth and rock cascading down the sheer side of the mountain, around and over the boulder now sitting at the bottom. A wave of water spread out across the valley floor unconstrained by any water course. She turned back and ran faster, catching the villagers who fled the flood.

They reached the small rise, puffing and panting. Older members of the group collapsed to the rocky ground while others looked at the scene. The roar of the waterfall was deafening even at the distance of a couple of miles and the cliff was obscured by spray from the falling water. The flood was rushing past their refuge scouring a path through the valley floor.

"Is this really Cwm Dreigiau?" Aeddon asked, turning around to look at the whole valley.

"Of course it is," Gwawrwen replied, "Don't you recognise the ridge and there now is the waterfall with the acorn rock at its foot."

Aeddon shrugged. "Yes, I suppose it is, but it looks so different. Where are the trees?"

September could understand Aeddon's confusion. As he had observed, the valley was almost treeless except for a few small, scattered pine trees that she did not recognise.

"They haven't grown yet, lad," Meilyr said between breaths, "This is new land only recently released from the grip of the ice. The plants we are familiar with haven't had time to become established yet."

"You understand?" September said, surprised that Meilyr seemed to know about ice-ages.

"Aye, lady. I travelled in my youth across Britain and Scotland and across the North Sea I saw places where snow and ice linger still, where great glaciers grind their path to the ocean. I saw places such as this where new life was taking hold."

Aeddon knelt and examined the ground at his feet. "Even the grass is different."

"Most of what covers the land isn't even grass, my boy. It's moss and similar plants. But the grasses will come."

The people had begun to recover from their escape from the Malevolence and the flood. The complaints were beginning.

"How are we to survive?"

"What can we eat?"

"It's cold. How do we get warm?"

September looked at them and at the valley. The water was now forming a broad river bordered by land covered in patchy green. She thought she saw some movement in the distance.

"There are things to eat out there. Look," she said, pointing, "The dragons have their prey."

In the sky the four dragons were wheeling and swooping on the giant birds that had been harrying them. The hunters had become the hunted. September watched as the largest dragon,

Obsidian, turning sharply in mid-air, directed a blast of fire at one of the feathered creatures. The bird flared for a moment then began to fall. Obsidian dived after it and plucked it from the sky. The dragon flew down to the ground a few hundred yards from where the humans watched from their hill. September noted how all the people looked on with hungry eyes as the dragon tore the bird apart with its beak and swallowed the pieces in single gulps. Above, the other dragons made their kills while the remaining birds fled.

September broke off from watching the dragons' feeding time, remembering that her task was not yet done. "I'll go and fetch the unicorns, then I can see if there is anything more I can do," she said.

Gwawrwen smiled. "Do that. I long to see them safe."

September nodded and thought of her destination.

Chapter 22

September returns to the unicorns

The two unicorns were standing under the oak trees, trembling. September approached them and placed her right hand on the male's horn.

"Are you alright?" she asked.

The unicorn's thoughts came to her faintly. *<We live still. I am glad you were not away long, traveller through time and space.>*

September had taken care not to arrive before she had left with Gwawrwen and Aeddon nor before she had rescued the villagers from the church. It meant that it was just a few minutes since she had left the unicorns. Their weakness troubled her.

"Gwawrwen's potion isn't working?" she asked.

<Oh, it works, friend, but the evil grows stronger by the moment and keeping even this small area protected becomes increasingly more difficult.>

"It's time I took you to join the others then, but I think life will be difficult in the past. I hadn't realised how different this place would be just after the ice had gone."

<I hope we can provide the people with some assistance, the dragons too. Emerallt and I are ready.>

The smaller unicorn came to September's side, nuzzling against her thigh. September placed her left hand on her horn.

She thought of the valley as she had just left it, with the new river flowing through it and the people clustered on the low hilltop. Blue light engulfed her and the two unicorns.

September steadied herself with her grip on the two horns and opened her eyes. She sighed with relief that she had brought the two unicorns exactly where she had aimed for. They were on level ground between the flood waters and the side of the valley just a few hundred yards from the low hill that was the refuge of the people.

The head of Adamant moved slowly as the unicorn took in the panorama.

<As you said, young lady, it is very different to the home we have left to the evil. Nevertheless, we will survive, all of us, dragons, unicorns and people.>

"I hope so," September said, feeling responsible for the hardships that lay ahead.

<Rescuing us from the spirits of hate was one thing. Now you must embark on your more important task – defeating the Malevolence and ensuring it does not invade this world in what is now our future.>

September nodded. "Yes, I should go but I will return to see how you are getting on." She released the unicorns' horns and stood with her arms folded across her body. Where and when should she go to oppose the Malevolence? When was the crucial moment when the evil gained entry? She recalled her first meeting with Aeddon and Gwawrwen on the morning that Ezekiel Soulbury had made phosphorus and had been consumed by the Cold Fire. She wrapped herself in light.

She stood on grass beside a stone wall. It was a grey morning but with clear sky to the east where the sun was rising over the hills. She recognised the abbey and its surroundings. It was peaceful. There was no-one about, not even any animals moving or birds flying. She turned to face the entrance to the abbey. There were cries and the sound of feet running. Three figures emerged from the gateway, a young boy, a woman with white hair and a girl of similar appearance in a school skirt and blazer. She recognised herself running after Aeddon and Gwawrwen. She shrank back against the wall not wanting to be seen, least of all by her earlier (if that was the correct term) self. The three ran away from the abbey towards the river. As they did so, the solid walls of stone merged into a white glow that spread from within the ruins. She felt a blast of cold that made her shiver. Overhead, dark clouds formed with lightning flashing within them.

She remembered this moment of her first meeting with Aeddon and Gwawrwen, when the Cold Fire was expanding.

She watched the three figures stop and huddle together to talk, glancing back at the abbey that was now engulfed in the dazzling white dome. She heard a screech and looked up. Three dark bird-like creatures emerged from the whiteness. It was the demons attacking the three. She recalled the fight. Now she knew that it was already too late to stop the Malevolence making an entry into the universe. She needed to be earlier. She thought of a moment in time.

The scene was just about the same as her previous arrival, if a little dimmer as the sun had not risen above the hills. This time she did not hesitate but strode into the abbey grounds and towards the main door into the house. She lifted the latch and entered the hallway. The air inside retained some heat still, but all was quiet. September wasn't sure where to go but then she heard whispering ahead. She crept forward towards the sound and came to a stone staircase down into a basement. Sitting at the bottom were Aeddon and Gwawrwen. They were intent in watching what was happening in the subterranean room.

September hurried down the stairs, pushed between the boy and the women and entered the laboratory. Behind her she heard surprised shouts; ahead, beyond the furnace stood the bearded figure of the alchemist, Ezekiel Soulbury. She hadn't seen him before but needed no description to recognise him. He was holding a clay flask in one hand and digging into it with a rod held in his other.

"No!" September cried, "Don't release the Cold Fire." Soulbury looked up, his eyes unfocussed. His hand stopped poking.

"What?" he said.

There was fluttering overhead. It was the three putti. Aeddon had described them to her. They hovered above Soulbury's head, their white feathered wings beating rapidly. They glared at her and hissed like angry swans. September circled the furnace and approached the mystic.

"You mustn't bring the phosphorus out into the air," she said.

"Why not?" Soulbury said, resuming his scooping.

"Because you'll let the evil in," September cried and

reached for his wrist. The putti screamed and flew at September battering at her with their short arms, fat feet and wings. They pushed September away. Aeddon and Gwawrwen stood up and each took a step forwards. September warded off the creatures with one arm and reached out with the other but Soulbury turned away and withdrew the spatula from the flask.

Time seemed to stop. Aeddon and Gwawrwen halted mid-step, the alchemist froze, his eyes wide open and staring at the globule on the end of his rod. September too found her limbs immobile. Only the putti remained in motion, wings flapping as they hung in the air.

The pea-sized piece of phosphorus glowed a brilliant white, a whiteness that drove the darkness and shadows from the whole room. The light grew as she stared at it engulfing Soulbury's fingers, hand, wrist.

"Cold Fire!" Ezekiel exclaimed.

"Does it not feel hot?" Gwawrwen cried and edged forward.

Ezekiel remained like a statue, his eyes fixed on the torch that he held.

"No heat," he muttered, "but cold. It feels colder than the hardest frost. It draws heat from me. My hand is numb. I cannot feel it."

Aeddon started to move towards his master.

"No, get out. It's too late to do anything," September shouted. She ran away from the alchemist whose whole arm was now enclosed in a white globe as bright, but whiter than the sun. She pushed Aeddon and Gwawrwen, stumbling up the stairs. She stopped at the bottom, turned and looked at the growing ball of cold fire feeling its heat-sucking coldness. The putti circled, basking in the freezing light.

She was too late again. Earlier still she must be to prevent events leading to the coming of the Malevolence. She closed her eyes, thought and moved.

She was still standing on the threshold of Soulbury's laboratory but now it was dark. There was just a glimmer of light from two candles and the merest glow from the furnace. In the shadows, she could see a cloaked figure pouring liquid from skins into large ceramic flasks. September breathed out. She'd got here before he had started the process to extract the phosphorus from the unicorns' urine.

Soulbury paused in pouring and looked up. "Who's there? Boy?" He peered through the gloom. "Gwawrwen?"

September stepped forward. "No, I'm not Gwawrwen."

He stared at her. "No, I see you are not. You share her features but you have fewer years. Who are you? What are you doing in my home?"

"It doesn't matter who I am but I'm here to warn you."

"Warn me! Of what?"

"Don't do this experiment. Don't try to get phosphorus from the unicorns' pee."

"Why indeed not!"

"It's dangerous."

Soulbury let out a roar. "Of course it's dangerous. Many a time a vessel has exploded with the force of one of the King's cannon. Danger is part of the exploration of the natural world as much for an alchemist at his furnace as an explorer of the Americas or a navigator of the seven seas."

"No, it's more than that," September said trying to speak calmly and sensibly, "If you purify the phosphorus you will let a great evil enter the world."

Soulbury snorted. "What nonsense. That sounds like the claptrap of the papists. They think that experimentalists like me are trying to see the mind of God and promise all kinds of dire retributions."

"This is real," September said becoming frustrated. "Outside the universe, the Malevolence waits for a chance to enter to destroy the world and everything there is."

"Malevolence? What insanity is this? Have you escaped from Bedlam, girl? You are a girl are you not?"

"Yes, I'm a girl and I've seen what the Malevolence can do to this world and others."

"The hallucinations of a mad-woman."

There was a succession of loud thuds. September almost jumped thinking that some fiendish monster was behind her. She turned to look but it was only Aeddon burdened with logs some of which he had dropped coming down the stairs.

"Who is this?" Aeddon said, eyes wide with wonder.

"Oh, some girl that appeared from nowhere muttering nonsense about evil and commanding me to refrain from extracting the Phosphorus from the unicorns' piss." Soulbury returned to pouring the noxious fluid. Aeddon put the firewood down.

"I'm September," she said, "and I'm trying to tell him that what he's doing will destroy the world and everything in it."

"Surely, it can't be that dangerous," Aeddon said. "My master has called on some perilous forces before as I know to my own detriment, but destroy the world? It can't be."

"It's true I tell you!" September cried.

"Oh, get her out of my way," Soulbury moaned.

Aeddon moved towards September. He reached out to take her arm. September shrugged him off.

"I'm not going till I'm sure I've stopped you," she said.

"Get rid of her, I said," Soulbury bawled. There was a fluttering of wings and a high-pitched screeching. The three putti appeared from the stairway. They flew at September, circled her, slapping at her with their arms and legs. September held up her arms to protect her face and fend them off but they pushed at her. She took a step away from where the alchemist worked.

"That's right, my servants," Soulbury said, "Take her away, away from here entirely."

September continued to back away from the onslaught of the three child-like fiends. They pressed closer and closer, their limbs battering her and their wings smothering her. The claw-like nails of their fingers and toes raked at her. She crouched down, covering her head with her arms as the blows came at her like hailstones. It was no use staying here. She had to get to safety. She moved.

Chapter 23

September finds herself in darkness

It was dark. Darker than dark; light wasn't just absent, it had never existed here. She knew this place or rather no-place. Between universes, a place that only had time and space because she occupied it. Not that it was empty. It was filled by the nameless spirits of hate that constituted the Malevolence; senseless, formless entities that only desired to turn everything to darkness. Their screaming presence filled her brain. She had been here before and knew that whatever powers she had were insufficient to hold back the destructive hordes beyond the worlds where people lived.

There was something different here though. There were other beings with her. The putti. They were invisible in the darkness and like the spirits, lacked bodies, but they were there. Their arms and legs and wings beat at her still. What damage could they do her? They were incapable of inflicting physical hurt on her but as she floated in the void she quickly realised the danger she was in. The incessant virtual battering and the soundless caterwauling of the putti, added to the silent screams of the spirits, insinuated into her mind. She found herself crumbling, little bits of her consciousness breaking off and fading into the dimensionless emptiness. Memories of home, family, friends, school, her experiences as the bearer of the Maengolauseren, flaked off like dead skin. She knew that she was losing something but not what it was she had lost. This was what the putti were doing, wearing her away until she was a nothing: no character, no history, just another lost soul.

She realised that her determination to get away from the putti had brought her here. She had not chosen a destination in any of the universes she knew and so she had come to this limbo outside space and time. She had to get back to the world she had left, a time before Soulbury became obsessed with Cold Fire. She needed peace and rest, somewhere, somewhen, where she could recover and draw back the lost bits of herself. Her sense of identity continued to fragment; she was shrinking, dissolving. Where could she go? She was losing the ability to think of a real time and place as her memories departed. She just wanted to feel safe. An image passed through her mind, a place of refuge, somewhere that she wished to be, although where or when it was she wasn't certain. She took herself there.

She tumbled across rough rock. This wasn't the peaceful idyll that she had visualised. She put out an arm and stopped rolling. She sat up, looked around, confused. Where was she if not at her destination?

To her left, a stream gurgled as it flowed over and around rocks before pouring over an edge and fell, to where? Beyond the water, the mountains rose to craggy peaks as they did on her right. Ahead, a valley was lit up by bright sunlight in a blue sky with a scattering of cotton-wool clouds. Down below was lush pasture and woodland. There, indeed, was the place of peace that she had imagined. There was a fragment of a memory of this place left in her disrupted mind.

September picked herself up. She was unsteady on her legs, her head fuzzy as if not part of her and despite the warmth of the sun she felt shivery. She stumbled to the edge looking for a route down, not quite sure what she was looking for. There appeared to be a path, scuffed by feet human and otherwise, snaking down between rocks to the side of the roaring waterfall. She followed it, stumbling and reaching out to steady herself, zig-zagging down. Now she could see down to the pool at the bottom of the waterfall and beside it, a huge boulder shaped like an acorn. For some forgotten reason, it gave her comfort.

Slowly she negotiated the path down to the valley floor and then followed the stream towards an oak wood. As she reached the first trees, three heavy creatures emerged to greet her. Their white fur and proud horns on the end of the broad snouts gave her a tingle of remembrance. The leading creature came forward and lowered its head to her. September wrapped her arms around its horn knowing that it was the thing to do although not understanding why.

A voice spoke in her head. *<Child, you are injured. Your mind is fractured.>*

"You know me?"

<Of course, bearer of the Maengolauseren. You are a friend of unicorns, a saviour of universes.>

"I am? I don't remember."

<Your memories have been torn from you. You have barely survived your ordeal in the darkness.>

"Ordeal? I ..." She didn't know what she meant to say.

<Rest. We will gather your memories for you and restore you to health.>

The unicorn lowered its huge head still more. Her legs crumpled and she subsided onto the grass. Through half open, sleepy eyes she saw the other two unicorns approach and rest their horns against her body. She slept and dreamed.

Images, one after another, faces, objects, places. At first they meant nothing, were as strange as dreams often are. Then she began to recognise things, people, events. Mother, father, sisters and brother; the starstone resting in her hand; her exploits on Gwlad; the discovery and realisation that she was, or had become, someone special; the Cemegwr or Brains; her mission.

September opened her eyes. She was lying on the grass beneath the trees. Sunlight filtered through the leaves, filling her vision with dappled green. At the periphery of her sight were three massive, white faces with vicious-appearing horns, but she knew, remembered again, that they were harmless, gentle, peaceful creatures - the unicorns.

She sat up, discovering that she felt well and complete.

"Thank you," she said, "I didn't understand what had happened to me."

<Your mind was almost lost to the evil,> Adamant said in her head.

She held her head in her hands as if checking that it was still in place. "But you restored my memories?"

<They were dispersed, and barely held to you by the thread of your character, but between us we were able to draw them from the beyond, before they were dissipated by the spirits of hate.>

"So, I'm complete again?" She wasn't sure. She felt well and she believed herself to be whole but how could you tell if an area of your memory was missing?

<So we believe.>

September got to her feet still resting her hand on the unicorn's horn. "Then I must get on with my task. I have to stop Ezekiel obtaining phosphorus."

<That's correct, child.>

September bit her lip. "But nothing I've tried works. I've gone back and back from the time when the Cold Fire ignited, but I keep getting stopped. The putti get in the way and prevent me from doing anything to disturb Ezekiel's experiment."

<The putti are the servants of the Malevolence. Their task is to see that the barrier between this world and the beyond is broken down.>

"Aeddon seemed to accept them as irritating pets of his master."

<That is what they appeared to be while they bided their time, until Ezekiel Soulbury would do their mischief.>

"Where did they come from? How did they get here?"

<Ah, that was a result of another of Ezekiel Soulbury's investigations.>

"He summoned the putti, like the dragon that Aeddon and Gwawrwen told me about?"

<That is correct.>

September frowned. The unicorn seemed to know everything that had happened, but how? When was she? This couldn't be after the coming of the Malevolence, because there was no black cloud and, in any case, here there were three unicorns and she had taken the two that survived along with the dragons and the people into the past.

"When are we? Are we at a time before Soulbury, Aeddon, and Gwawrwen come to ask for your pee?" she asked.

<We are in the now. The event you refer to is at another now.>

"You mean it's in the future? But you seem to know everything that's happened and is going to happen. You know that the Malevolence is trying to invade the world and you know the part that Ezekiel played, is going to play."

September felt her head spinning. Her jumps forwards and backwards in time had left her confused.

<There are many things we have memory of.>

"You remember the future as well as the past?"

<There is only now and the memories of other nows.>

September held her head in her hands. The unicorns seemed a little like the Brains, Cyfaill, Henshaw and the Cemegwr, who apparently knew everything but had limited influence over events. She was the one who could hop around doing things. Except she didn't seem to be able to do what she needed to do here.

"Why did you let Ezekiel have your pee if you knew it would lead to the Malevolence getting in?"

<It was in our memory as having been. If it had not occurred, you would not be here.>

The frustration almost made her scream at the unicorn. "That's true enough, because if there had been no danger of the Malevolence breaking through, the Brains wouldn't have brought me here." If everything that had happened must happen, then how could she stop it. She sighed deeply. "What can I do to help if it's all going to happen as I've seen it happen?"

The unicorn rubbed its horn against her side. Presumably it was meant as a gesture of reassurance.

<Because those nows that you have witnessed are not the only nows that we recall.>

"What do you mean?"

<We have experienced nows where this world is lost to the Malevolence, where the dragons and the people and ourselves fall to the evil, but in other nows you took them and us to a now where we yet survive.>

"You see both?"

<We see all the nows of this world.>

A lightbulb lit in September's head. "Are you Brains?"

<No, child, though we know of them. They roam the Omniverse, we are merely creatures of this universe, though perhaps they had a role in our creation.>

September felt that she was beginning to see the picture, complicated though it was.

"I'm back to where I was. I was trying to change the future

by stopping Ezekiel Soulbury making Cold Fire and then turning what happened afterwards into a loop of time which will wither and fade."

<That is correct.>

"But I haven't been able to stop him because the putti interfered."

<Their purpose is to ensure that the alchemist opens the world to the Malevolence.>

"So it is the putti that are the problem. I must stop Ezekiel summoning them."

<You have your answer to the problem.>

"But when did they appear?"

<When the dragon was summoned.>

"Aeddon mentioned that. Didn't the dragon kill his parents?"

<That is so.>

"If I stop Ezekiel summoning the dragon I can prevent the putti coming and save Aeddon's mother and father!" September felt a burst of joy. She could actually do something good.

<Yes, child. That would be most satisfactory.>

"I know where to go, but when?"

<We have a memory of the event. Open your mind and I will share it with you. Prepare yourself to move.>

September stood still, hand on Adamant's horn, eyes closed, breathing gently, mind receptive. She felt the huge animal next to her, making soft noises as it breathed. She saw the walls of Abaty Maesycymer, the sun high in the clear blue sky. She smelled the perfume from flowers in the meadow beside the river, and heard the birds singing. Her hand no longer touched the hard horn, her feet no longer rested on the grass.

Chapter 24

September travels to Abaty Maesycymer

She opened her eyes and saw the scene that the unicorn had given her. The open gates of the Abbey were ahead of her. She passed through them and paused, looking around. The place was a little less ruinous than she remembered. The roof of the house and stables had fewer holes, the cobbled yard was less rutted and weed grown. There appeared to be curtains at the small windows, and clean linens hung from a washing line. September walked towards the oak door. It opened as she approached and a middle-aged woman stepped out, examining her.

"And who might you be?" she said.

"I need to speak to Ezekiel Soulbury," September replied.

"The Master is a busy gentleman and in any case, he doesn't pause in his work to speak to urchins or vagrants."

September realised that the woman was not seeing her as a lady as the men in London had, or even as a clean, young woman as Aeddon and Gwawrwen had done. This woman imagined she was seeing a grubby child. September did not know how she could change the woman's perception. Who was she? September recalled what Aeddon had told her. His mother and father worked for Soulbury and had been present when the dragon came.

"I am a friend of Aeddon," she said, hoping that would be a sufficient identifier.

The woman just looked disgusted. "Not of my Aeddon. I have never seen you before, child. Be gone." She stepped back and slammed the door. September stood there stunned for a few moments. She had not anticipated that she would be prevented from even approaching the alchemist. She stepped away from the door and began to walk around the house. The ruined abbey came into view. A man was digging the soil in front of the wall. He stooped to lift a turnip. Was he Aeddon's father?

"Excuse me. Can you tell me where I can find Ezekiel Soulbury?" she asked. The man paused in his work and looked up at her. At least his expression wasn't one of disgust like the woman, who was presumably his wife.

"And why do you wish to meet the Master?" he asked in a gentle voice.

"I have some information for him."

"Ah, well, I doubt that he will wish to listen. His mind is on his work, but you will find him in the sanctuary of the Abbey church," he pointed through the broken walls. "Take care though before you disturb him. He is engaged on some great work, or so he says."

September thanked him. He smiled at her as she climbed over the low ragged wall and entered the church. No roof remained at all, nor glass in the windows, and much of the stone from walls had gone, no doubt to be used in the building of the house and other structures. The floor was rough where some stones had been levered out while others remained. To her right was the east end of the church, where the walls seemed to be more complete and rose in a semi-circle around a stone altar. This must be the sanctuary that the gardener had referred to because there was Ezekiel Soulbury. He was using the altar as a workbench with its top surface covered with various objects and utensils. Beside it sat a brazier which smoked and gave off heat that made the air above ripple. Soulbury was leant over the altar peering into a book.

September approached, finding her footing across the rough floor. As she neared, she examined the objects in front of the alchemist. There were jars stuffed with materials, jugs of liquid, vessels for mixing and heating, and three small sculptures. At first September thought they were birds but as she got closer she saw that they were models of the putti. They looked like innocent cherubs with their childish bodies, chubby faces and feathered wings. They appeared to be made of clay.

Soulbury looked up from his reading and noticed her standing a few feet from the altar.

"Who, may I ask, are you?" he said in a strong and authoritative voice.

September examined him. She had seen little of him in the future when his clothes were old and worn, his beard and hair grey and straggly and body hunched and thin. Now though he appeared almost a young man. He stood tall and straight, with his dark hair and beard trimmed neatly. He wore a heavy cloak in a rust-brown velvet.

"I am September," she announced as boldly as she could manage.

"I do not know you, yet you resemble someone I do know," he said.

"We have not met yet," she replied, "although I have met your cousin, Thomas Maslyn."

Soulbury's eyes widened. "Where did you make the acquaintance of my cousin?"

"In London, with the members of the Royal Society."

The alchemist looked confused. "But Thomas still resides in Flintshire with his father, when he is not at Oxford. I had not heard that he has made the acquaintance of any of the philosophers that meet under the auspices of the Royal Society of London."

September winced. She had forgotten that this was eight years earlier and that the people in London she had met would also be eight years younger. Young Thomas Maslyn was yet to make a name for himself in the city or to start his correspondence with his cousin about the Society's meetings.

"Ah, it was a brief meeting. Perhaps he was just visiting," September flustered. Ezekiel shrugged as if it was not a matter that interested him.

"Why are you here girl, interrupting my work?" he muttered.

"To tell you to stop," she said.

"Stop! Why on earth should I do that and why should I listen to the words of a young maid?"

"Because I know that what you are doing is dangerous."

Soulbury snorted. "Danger, of course there is danger. A spark may enter my eye; I may cut a finger when chopping the ingredients of the recipe." He looked up, "a stone may fall on my head."

"No, your experiments are dangerous. You don't know the power that will be released." September felt exasperated that the man wasn't listening to her.

"Power you say? There is power in what I do?" His eyes sparkled, excited by the thought.

"Dark powers, evil."

He waved her away. "Nonsense. With this concoction, I merely intend to give animation to this lifeless clay." He indicated the three model putti and the bowl of multi-coloured mixture that stood beside them.

"How will you do that?" September asked, intrigued despite her fears.

Soulbury pointed to a sheet of dark and ragged parchment that lay on the altar to his side. "This document details how to give life to a golem. I discovered it amongst some ancient scrolls that came into my possession."

"Why do you want to do it?" September asked. She wondered what a golem was. The only Gollum she knew of was in the Lord of the Rings, films she had sort of watched with her brother. She didn't think that Gollum was made of clay, nor did he resemble a sweet cherub.

"Curiosity, child. To see if it can be done, and if it can, then the animated creatures, the putti, will be my servants. I always have need for workers eager to do my bidding."

"How do you know that they will obey you?"

"Because I will be their Master, the one who gives them life."

"Ah, I don't think it works like that," September said biting her lip. The putti had seemed to follow no instructions, just the urges of the Malevolence.

"I shall prove it to you. Stand aside and observe." He lifted the bowl and tipped the contents over the three clay models. The oily mixture ran over their heads and bodies and wings. Soulbury reached to the brazier and grasped a poker that had been buried in the heart of the fire.

"Wait! Does anyone know what you are doing?" September cried.

Soulbury paused with the poker half drawn from the flames. "Why should I inform anyone else of my intentions? This is my secret endeavour." He pulled the poker out and brandished its glowing tip in front of him."

"Ezekiel! What are you doing?" The female shout came from behind September. She turned and saw Gwawrwen hurrying up through the nave. She looked little different to how September recalled her from the future.

"Oh, heaven forbid!" the alchemist cried, "Am I not to be left alone when engaged in my work. What do you think I am doing woman? Summoning a dragon?"

Gwawrwen stopped some distance from the altar. "Who is this girl?"

"How am I supposed to know?" Ezekiel cried, "I almost thought she was you when she first appeared, but she is not." He looked down at his manuscript and began reading aloud in a language that September did not understand. He touched the red-hot poker to the first of the models. Multi-coloured smoke erupted quickly obscuring the altar, the model putti and Ezekiel Soulbury from view.

"No, Ezekiel!" Gwawrwen cried and September realised what she must do. She moved.

Her feet slipped on loose gravel and she swayed. September opened her eyes and gasped. She was where she intended to be but had not properly prepared herself for materialising on a ledge close to the top of a sheer cliff. She steadied herself and glanced down into the sunlit valley of the unicorns before turning to examine her surroundings. The ledge was thankfully a few metres wide and she stepped away from the edge. Most of the space was taken up by a huge red dragon that lowered its head to look at her. Wisps of smoke emerged from the nostrils at the top of a curved black beak the size of her head. The sulphurous fumes made September wheeze and cough.

<WHAT IS THIS CREATURE THAT HAS APPEARED BEFORE ME?> The words rang inside September's head. She saw the fiery red eyes on either side of the huge leathery head examining her.

"Obsidian?" September said hoping that she had located the mother of the dragons.

<THAT IS MY NAME. WHO IS IT THAT SPEAKS?> The dragon cocked its head to one side.

"I am September. We haven't met yet, but we will. I need your help to prevent a great evil happening."

<YOU HAVE THE APPEARANCE OF THE PEOPLE WHO OCCUPY THE VALLEYS AND HILLS OF OUR LAND AND WHO KEEP THE ANIMALS THAT ARE OUR PREY, YET YOU DO NOT SEEM LIKE THEM. YOU HAVE THE BEARING OF THE HIGHER BEINGS.>

"Yes, the Brains. We discussed all this before. I'm September."

<BEFORE?>

September was muddled again. "No later, perhaps in a different time-loop if I can stop Ezekiel now."

<YOUR SPEECH MAKES NO SENSE, CHILD.>

"Look, it's simple. One of the people you mentioned is about to make a big mistake that will let the evil from beyond come in a few years' time. We need to stop him now and you are the only being that can do it."

Although time didn't matter September was impatient and frustrated that she had to explain things to the dragon all over again.

<THE EVIL WILL DESTROY THE WHOLE WORLD AND EVERY LIVING THING IN IT?>

"That's right."

<BUT WE CANNOT DESTROY EVIL.>

"No, but you can save everything by preventing the servants of the evil coming to open the world to it."

<THESE SERVANTS?>

"They're called putti. I think you could destroy them."

The dragon pondered for a few moments before September sensed her response

<WELL, CLIMB ON MY NECK CHILD AND TAKE ME TO THIS FOOLISH ONE WHO THREATENS OUR EXISTENCE.>

The dragon lowered its head to the surface of the ledge and September clambered up the crimson feathers. She sat astride.

"When we're in the air, I will take you there and show you what needs to be done."

<AS YOU WISH, CHILD.> The dragon spread its wings and leapt from the ledge. They plummeted down the cliff

face gaining speed and lift with September clinging on in terror. With the ground approaching ever faster Obsidian pulled out of the dive and soared across the floor of the valley. She gained height, circling.
<NOW, CHILD. I AM READY.>
September thought of the scene at the abbey that she had just left. They moved.

They were circling a few hundred feet above the ruins of the Abbey. September could see the whole scene. Smoke was rising from the sanctuary, obscuring Ezekiel and the altar. Gwawrwen was looking up and cowering. Two people were in the kitchen garden just outside the walls of the abbey. Their white faces showed they were looking up at the appearance of the dragon.
September looked back at the smoke. Rising from it were three figures. They had pale bodies with wings as white as a swan's. The putti had been given life.
"There they are," September shouted, "The babies with wings. They are the servants of the Evil."
<I SEE THEM AND SENSE THEIR CONNECTION TO THE EVIL BEYOND.>
"They must be destroyed."
<I WILL SCORCH THEM WITH MY FLAME.>
"Good. I'm going to leave you and see what I can do down there."
<FAREWELL THEN CHILD.>
September took one more glance at the ground and imagined herself there. Violet light enveloped her.

She staggered, regaining her balance on her feet and looked around. The altar and Ezekiel were hidden behind smoke but the three putti were emerging from it. High above, the dragon had begun its dive. September turned and ran away from the altar, stumbling over the rough stones.
Gwawrwen was cowering by the stump of a pillar but staring up into the sky and muttering, "He's done it, he really has summoned a dragon."
September arrived at full pelt, wrapped her arms around Gwawrwen's waist and carried her, staggering to the opening

in the wall of the nave. Aeddon's mother and father were there, frozen to the spot with their eyes fixed on the dragon.

September bundled Gwawrwen onwards. "Come on," she shouted, "Get inside." She risked a glance up into the sky. Obsidian had pulled out of her dive and with flame flaring from her open beak she bore down on the three Putti fluttered around the plume of smoke. The flames caught one of the putti and it ignited instantly. Within the ball of flame September could see the outline of the creature writhing in agony. The dragon swooped on along the length of the nave, pulled up, twisted and clawed for height.

The flaming putti guttered and a charred object fell to the ground within the abbey. The two others seemed to become aware of their plight and flapped their wings in agitation. They had barely begun to gain height when the dragon was on them again, flame belching from its beak.

"Go on, get in the house." September pushed Gwawrwen and Aeddon's parents towards the house. They stumbled towards it, their eyes still fixed on the dragon. Certain that they were moving to safety, September turned and headed back into the ruins of the abbey. She was in time to see another fireball engulf the second putti as the third, and last, sought to escape. Once again, the dragon beat its huge wings to gain height for a final attack.

The charred form of the second putti fell to the floor of the abbey in front of September. She bent to look at it. Completely covered in black soot it nevertheless looked like the clay model Soulbury had had on the altar. She held her hand near it and felt the heat of the dragon's breath still radiating from it. Nearby there was a loose stone from the floor of the abbey. September heaved it up with both hands, stood up straight and dropped the stone on the putti. It shattered into a thousand pieces.

The roar of a gale caused her to look up. Obsidian swooped across the nave just above the walls and caught the last putti in its flame as the small creature fled across the ruins of the monastic buildings. For a third time, a ball of fire as bright as the sun surrounded the being and it fell to the ground black and lifeless. September ran to see where it landed. She scrambled over the fallen walls and found the dark, clay model lying in grass which it had singed. She found another hefty stone and smashed it down on the dead putti again and again until it was an unrecognisable pile of shards.

Now she only had to find the remains of the first. She returned to the nave, scanning the ground for the blackened object. It stood out against the pale grey limestone from which the Abbey had been built. It lay close the altar. September approached it with her stone clasped in her hand. She brought it down fast on the model and it cracked into many pieces.

"My putti!" Ezekiel cried, emerging from the thinning cloud of smoke over the altar. "You have destroyed them."

"They were evil!" September shouted back. The sound of huge beating wings came from above her. She looked up to see Obsidian descending slowly, her scaly legs hanging down and massive talons stretched wide. She was about to clasp Ezekiel. They closed on his shoulders and as the man screamed the dragon rose into the air with him dangling from her claws.

September leapt up. "No," she screamed, "Don't kill him."

The dragon hovered, her wings gripping the air. Ezekiel hung ten metres above the ground.

<WHY SHOULD I NOT KILL HIM? HE THREATENED TO BRING EVIL INTO THE WORLD.> The dragon's complaint thundered in September's head.

"He didn't know what he was doing," September appealed.

<IGNORANCE IS NO DEFENCE. HIS KIND HAVE LITTLE LOVE FOR US AND WOULD SEE US EXTINCT.>

"I know, I know, but they don't understand. Please let him go. Killing him is not the answer."

The dragon hovered for a few moments longer then slowly sank to the ground. When Ezekiel's feet touched the floor of the Abbey, the dragon released him. He slumped to the ground and September ran to him. The dragon flew a short way down the nave and landed on her two feet.

<YOU SEEM TO HAVE WISDOM, CHILD, DESPITE YOUR LACK OF YEARS. IF YOU HAVE CONTACT WITH THE BEYOND THEN WE DRAGONS AND OTHER CREATURES SHOULD LISTEN TO YOU.>

September knelt at Ezekiel's side. He groaned and began to sit up.

"Ow, my shoulders," he said reaching stiffly to rub each in turn. September examined him. The thick velvet that covered where the dragon had gripped him was not marked in any way.

"I don't think Obsidian has damaged you," September said, amazed to find that Ezekiel was largely unharmed. She turned to look at the dragon which was preening itself. "Thank you," she called.

<THE SERVANTS OF THE EVIL ARE NO MORE?>

"I think so. Your flames killed them and I've smashed up what remained. I don't think they can serve the Malevolence in the future."

<THIS FOOLISH ONE WILL NOT TRY AGAIN?>

"I'll make sure of that, but I'll need you and the unicorns, humans and all the other creatures to be on their guard to make sure that nothing like this can happen again."

<WE WILL MEET TO DISCUSS THIS. NOW CHILD, I MUST EAT TO REPLENISH MY FIRE AND ENERGY.>

"Thank you. We will meet again."

The dragon extended its wings which stretched across the ruined nave. It took off, circled for height over the abbey and then headed towards the mountains.

Gwawrwen and Aeddon's parents came running from the house.

"The dragon? Has it gone?" Aeddon's mother asked, looking anxiously into the sky.

"Is the Master safe?" her husband enquired.

"What happened there?" Gwawrwen said, approaching September, "and who are you?"

September sighed. How much could she explain? Had she completed her task? Was this universe now safe from the Malevolence? Perhaps it was, so long as Ezekiel could be persuaded that his dabbling in the black arts of alchemy must stop. She realised too that humans must cooperate with dragons, unicorns, mermaids and whatever other intelligent creatures existed in this universe, to protect their world from the evil. When she had arrived, she had thought this world was much like her own, albeit it was in her past, but she understood now that this universe was very different and its future in this timeline was unclear to her.

"I don't know what to say," she said. She was still working out how to explain what the appearance of the dragon meant when a small boy ran into the abbey shouting.

"Mama, Papa. There's a dragon!"

He ran up to his mother and leapt into her arms.

"It's alright, Aeddon, it's gone now. We are well."

Aeddon's father laid a hand on the boy's head and also reassured him. The boy let go of his mother and looked around at Ezekiel, Gwawrwen and September.

"Who is the lady dressed in glowing blue?" he said. The others looked at September wondering what he meant. She guessed that Aeddon was seeing her in a different form to the urchin seen by his mother and father, or the poor young woman seen by Gwawrwen and Soulbury. He seemed to see her in her guise as the bearer of the starstone, the Cludydd o Maengolauseren, the saviour of the world of Gwlad, the role that had given her the power to move in space and time. The boy had special sight.

"What are you, indeed?" Ezekiel Soulbury said, and the others also looked at September.

"Are you some sorceress?" Gwawrwen asked

"I will try to explain," September said, not knowing how to start. "I'm not from this place. I don't belong here but I do know that what you were trying to do, Ezekiel Soulbury, was very dangerous."

"You said that," Soulbury growled.

"Yes, but you don't know how dangerous, not just to you but to everyone and everything in the world."

"But the putti were mere children," Soulbury muttered.

Gwawrwen looked mystified. "I thought you were summoning a dragon."

"Why would I do that?" Soulbury said as if the thought had never crossed his mind.

"How should I know?" Gwawrwen replied. "What were these putti creatures?"

"Servants of evil," September said quickly. "Believe me I know."

Gwawrwen looked doubtful but Soulbury shifted

nervously. "I didn't think the tale could be true," he said in a whisper.

"What tale?" They all said at once.

Soulbury nodded to the altar. "The manuscript I was following is an ancient copy of an even older document which seems to tell of the great powers beyond the world. The putti were part of it. I found them mentioned in other writings, so I thought I would see if they would give me control over the powers of this universe."

"Oh, you are a fool," Gwawrwen said, "What proof did you have that these servants would answer your commands?" She slapped his shoulder.

Soulbury shrank from the woman's attack.

"This manuscript?" September said. She was wondering. "You said it was a copy, but old. How old?"

Soulbury shrugged. "It is impossible to say. It has been copied many times I think. The original writing could have been done thousands of years ago, when the world was young."

"Where did you get it?" Gwawrwen asked."

"It was found not far from here. In a cave in Cwm Dreigiau."

"Valley of Dragons," September said, "The home of the unicorns."

Ezekiel nodded uneasily.

"You stole a document from the unicorns," Gwawrwen exclaimed.

"Not me, I bought it from Twm Bach who bought it from the man who found it. But it wasn't the unicorns'," Soulbury said, hurt by the accusation, "They do not write. It was written by a human."

"Who?" September asked.

Soulbury shifted from foot to foot and screwed up his face. "The name is unclear. In some places it appears to be Adam, the ancestor of all men, but in others it is rendered more like the name of the child here."

They all looked at the small boy.

"Aeddon!" Gwawrwen said.

September began to realise what had happened. "Where is the manuscript? Do you still have it?" she asked.

Soulbury looked bereft, "Alas it is gone, consumed in the fire that engulfed the altar when I gave the putti life."

"And that was the only copy?" September asked, hoping for a particular answer.

"Alas, yes, to my knowledge," Soulbury said.

September breathed easily again. "Good. You don't want to know what that manuscript said. It's good that it's gone, but I think I need to speak to someone. Gwawrwen come with me."

The white-haired woman frowned but followed September from the Abbey until they were out of sight and hearing of the other people.

"You must watch Ezekiel and make sure he doesn't try to repeat his experiments." September said.

"But he says the manuscript is destroyed," the woman replied.

"I hope that's true, but if he tries again to make putti come to life or ever talks about Cold Fire he must not be allowed to carry out his experiments. Do you get me?"

"I don't understand. What is this Cold Fire?"

"I can't explain, but if Ezekiel ever mentions trying to make it you must stop him."

Gwawrwen examined September as if looking for evidence that what she said was correct.

At last she spoke. "I don't know what is going on but I trust you. Perhaps it is because we look alike, maybe we are even related. I feel you are telling the truth and wish to protect us from evil. I will stay by Ezekiel's side and ensure his dabblings are without danger."

"Good. I trust you too, Gwawrwen. Now I must go and make sure nothing comes of this."

"Go? Where?"

September thought of a time and a place. "Not where, when." She was engulfed in blue light.

Chapter 25

September joins the people, dragons and unicorns where she left them

Noise pounded her ears: water falling, crashing on to rock, stone falling onto stone, the roar of dragons, and through it all the cries of people. September covered her ears with her hands and opened her eyes. Above, dragons wheeled in the sky; in front of her the great rock was falling from the ridge in a huge cascade of water. The rock landed at the base of the cliff with a deafening crash and September felt the ground beneath her feet tremble. The great acorn-shaped rock stood there with the water falling on and around it, shrouded in a cloud of water droplets. She realised that the water wasn't following a defined river course but was spreading out across the valley floor to where she was standing amid scrubby moss and thin soil that barely covered the rock beneath. She turned to look down the valley and saw the people she had brought here standing on the patch of slightly higher ground. She was relieved that they were safe from the waters that were steadily spreading across the valley. The two unicorns stood a short distance away, their white hides standing out against the dark rock of the valley and the mountains beyond. Many of the people were looking at them. September began to walk towards them, breaking into a run as water began to lap at her feet.

She puffed up the gentle rise to reach the group of people standing on the top of the hill. Many of them seemed stunned by their new surroundings, staring with wide, unblinking eyes at the waterfall and the steadily spreading flood, the bare rock of the valley sides and the huge and terrifying creatures that circled above them. Many of the people had their arms wrapped around their bodies, were slapping themselves or hopping from one foot to the other. They were cold.

September noted that the temperature was indeed lower than it had been on her visits to this valley in the future. The ice age had ended but the world, or this part of it, had barely warmed up.

September looked around for Aeddon, Gwawrwen and Meilyr and found them huddled together at the edge of the group of people looking down at the unicorns who were slowly making their way across the valley to join them.

"September! You are with us," Gwawrwen said, smiling broadly, "You have brought the unicorns to us."

For September, a lot seemed to have happened since she had done that task but she remembered that she had brought the dragons, the people and the unicorns to this place in the same seconds that the rock fell beside the waterfall and had returned now at the same moment in time. For the people, hardly any time had passed at all.

"Dragons!" someone cried out, "They've come to eat us all!" Others took up the cry and cowered in fear.

"No," September said, "The dragons are your friends. They will not attack you."

"That is what they have done throughout history," an old man said, "They take cattle, sheep and people if they can."

"But they were our allies in the battle with the dark evil," Aeddon said.

"Hmph," the man growled, "for what good it did us. You've brought us to this God forsaken place. If the cold or the floods don't kill us, then we will starve. What is there to eat here?" he pointed across the barren floor of the valley.

"The people are complaining with some justification," Meilyr said, "Even if the dragons do not see us as a meal, we need shelter, warmth and food ourselves."

September did not know what to do but she felt a presence and turned to see the two unicorns climbing the hill to join them. Most of the people stepped back, watching the unicorns with a mixture of awe and fear.

<Child, this place is not yet the peaceful paradise that we made it,> Adamant said in her mind. September shook her head. <The people have good reason to fear for their futures. Settling in this time will be a difficult struggle, but we will help them, as will the dragons.>

"The dragons?" Meilyr said showing that he, like the rest of the people were hearing the unicorn's words.

<Yes, we have given them instructions.>

September looked up and saw the four dragons flying away across the mountains to the south.

<They will return,> Adamant continued, *<This is and always will be their home, as it is ours, but you should move to a more clement area with adequate supplies of food and the materials that you need. For now though, we will see to your needs here. Some of you are feeling the cold. Come and press yourselves to our bodies. We will warm you.>*

Some children did not need to be instructed by the adults but rushed forward and pressed themselves against Adamant's and Emerallt's neck and flanks. A few of the older people came forward too and pushed against the sturdy, white creatures.

Gwawrwen spoke. "We are alone here, aren't we, except for the dragons and unicorns? No other people inhabit this land at this time?" September nodded.

"It is we who must provide for ourselves," Meilyr said, "The unicorn is correct. We must find a place that is more suitable for us than this cold valley."

"That will take time," Gwawrwen said.

"Yes, so we must find shelter for the moment," Meilyr said.

<There are caves in the cliffs,> Adamant said. *<The dragons will roost on the high ledges as is their custom. The caves will provide you with shelter.>*

"There, that's a start," said Meilyr, "Then we will need fuel and food and we can start to plan our move."

"Look!" Aeddon exclaimed, pointing into the southern sky, "A dragon returns."

The dragon flew towards them, starting another panic amongst the villagers. As the dragon approached, September could see that it carried something in its talons. It was not one of the birds the dragons themselves had eaten, but a four-legged beast. It was huge.

The dragon descended to the hilltop into the space vacated by the frightened people. It released the creature, which fell, lifeless, to the ground. It was a cow-like animal twice the size

of any bull that September had ever seen. Obsidian, for it was
her, settled beside her prey, folding her great wings to her side.

<YOU WILL NEED FOOD AS YOU BEGIN YOUR
NEW LIFE IN THIS TIME,> the dragon thought.

Gwawrwen stepped forward and addressed the dragon.
"Thank you, Obsidian, we are grateful. We have very little to
help us set up home here so the gift of food is much
appreciated."

<THERE ARE OTHER ANIMALS IN THIS VALLEY
THAT SEEK TO EAT THESE PLANT EATERS. THEY
MAY SEE YOU AS TASTY MORSELS, AS INDEED MY
FELLOWS HAVE DONE, PREVIOUSLY.>

"Thank you," Gwawrwen repeated, "we shall watch out for
these predators and appreciate your protection. I hope that
people and dragons will not be enemies here."

"Well, we have food," Meilyr said, "I can skin it and make
use of the hide. Luckily, I have my knife," He tapped the
blade at his waist, "but we need fire to cook the meat."

"The trees are few, but perhaps they will provide sufficient
wood for fuel," Aeddon said.

"Gather a group of the people to go and collect firewood,"
Gwawrwen said.

"I don't think that will be necessary,' September said
pointing into the sky.

The other three dragons had reappeared in the distance also
bearing burdens. As they drew near September and the others
could see that they carried bushes and trees in their claws,
apparently torn from the ground. They dropped their burdens
alongside the dead animal, forming a bonfire-like heap. The
three younger dragons flew up into the sky

"That is a goodly pile of firewood," Meilyr said, "but
lighting the fire could be a problem."

"Perhaps someone has a flint with them," Gwawrwen said,
"or perhaps we could request a flame from the dragons? They
seem keen to help us."

Meilyr chuckled, "That is indeed a welcome change."

<IF FIRE IS WHAT YOU DESIRE, I CAN OBLIGE.>
Obsidian said. The dragon waddled towards the heap of
trunks and branches. She opened her beak and a roaring
flame emerged. Some of the people turned and ran away, but

the dragon's target was just the firewood. The flames touched it and instantly a roaring fire ignited.

The dragon unfolded her wings and beat the air. The wind fanned the flames and the dragon soared up into the sky. She circled and came to hover, facing September and the others. <WE WILL KEEP YOU SUPPLIED WITH KINDLING AND MEAT. NOW WE WILL SEEK OUR OWN FOOD AND RETURN TO OUR PLACE OF REST.> The dragon climbed up into the sky and re-joined her children.

"There," September said, "I told you the dragons were your friends." The people ran to warm themselves at the great bonfire.

Meilyr drew his knife from his belt. "I hope there are more knives between us. Butchering this animal could be a lengthy and tiring task. Couldn't the dragon have brought a smaller animal?"

"I don't think the dragon considered this large," Gwawrwen said surveying the mound of flesh covered in thick brown fur. "but quarry like this will provide us with skins to keep us warm. You will have to start tanning hides again, Meilyr."

While Meilyr and a couple of other men with knives began hacking their way into the dead animal and the rest of the people continued to warm themselves at the fire, September approached Aeddon.

"I think I have made your lives difficult bringing you to this time," she said.

"But we are alive," the boy said with a broad smile on his face, "You didn't leave us to be consumed by the Evil. I think it will be exciting here as we find ways to look after ourselves."

"I wouldn't know where to start," September said, "and I don't think people I know back home would have much idea either. You've got to grow your own food, make clothes and tools. How do you even make metal?"

Aeddon looked around at the former villagers of Llanllionio. "I think we've got people who can do those things. There wasn't much we needed that we couldn't make ourselves. Meilyr knows lots of skills, but ..." He gazed off into the distance, thinking.

"What is it Aeddon?" September asked.

Aeddon came back down to earth. "I will have to learn how to make parchment or paper. I'm not sure if anyone in Llanllionio knew how to do that."

"Why do you need paper?" September said then realised that it was a silly question.

"We will need to preserve what we know for our descendants. I intend to write an account of how we came to be here."

"Ah, yes," September remembered why she had returned to this time. "I'm not sure you should do that, Aeddon."

"Why not? People in years to come will want to know how we came to be friends with dragons and unicorns and how you carried us from a world destroyed by the dark evil."

"Brought about by Ezekiel Soulbury's experiments."

"Yes, of course, I must record Ezekiel's role in the story," Aeddon said eagerly.

"But think about it, Aeddon. If you write about the putti and Cold Fire and the Malevolence, then someone in the future, perhaps Ezekiel himself, may be tempted to try out some of the ideas and allow the evil into the world."

Aeddon pondered. "Do you really think the words that I write could have such a result?"

"I don't think, I know, Aeddon. You must not mention Cold Fire in your writing. In fact, I do not think it will be wise to say that you and the people from Llanllionio, and the dragons and unicorns, came from the future. People who read it may be worried and think that the evil was about to come and destroy everything."

"Ah, yes, I understand, September. But what shall I write? Ezekiel trained me in writing so that I could record all that he did." The boy appeared sad, as if his whole reason for existence had been taken away. September considered and then answered.

"You must do what you said, and write down all the skills and knowledge that your descendants will need. You can even add some of Ezekiel's chemical experiments. Make it a sort of encyclopaedia."

"Yes! That's it. Oh, I must see if Meilyr has any idea how to make vellum or paper."

"But remember," September warned, "No mention of Cold Fire."

"No, no, definitely, not at all." Aeddon hurried off to find Meilyr.

Gwawrwen approached September, and glanced at the departing Aeddon.

"The boy seems engaged on an urgent task," she said.

"I think he's found his life's work," September said.

Gwawrwen chuckled. "You've given us all a lifetime of work. A different life to the one we have experienced till now."

September shrugged. "I'm sorry. It seemed the only way to save you from the Malevolence."

"Oh, don't think I'm not grateful. I, all of us, are, or will be one day, I'm sure. It will be a different life: on our own, finding and making all that we need, but living in harmony with dragons and unicorns."

"And other creatures."

"Yes, of course. The lives of people to come will be very different."

"Perhaps." September wasn't sure how the universe would differ in this new timeline.

"Will you stay with us, September?"

"No, my task is done. I think it's time … ha! I think I should return to my own time and place."

"That is a pity. We seem to have hardly begun to know each other yet we share our looks and I feel a connection with you. I would love to hear how you came to be what you are."

"That would take a lot of telling and I'm not sure I know how to explain all that's gone on. I don't know why things have happened the way they have, to bring you and me together. It was Ezekiel that let the Malevolence into the world but your presence seems to have been important."

"Well, I was present when he summoned the dragon that killed Aeddon's parents and I did lead him to the unicorns, so I suppose I am responsible in some respects. You have opened my eyes, September. My task from now on must be to ensure that people and dragons and unicorns live harmoniously and that never again is there opportunity for the evil to come into the world."

September sighed and hugged Gwawrwen. "That sounds like a very important life's work. Good luck." She released the other woman and stepped back. "Now I think I must go. There is one more place I must visit." She summoned up an image in her mind and was wrapped in the whirling indigo light.

Chapter 26

September goes back to London

The dark, stinking alley was as she remembered it, which was as it should be since she had used her memory of it to bring her here. Smoke from the chimneys of the huddled together buildings rose and mixed to form a cloud that obscured the night sky. The only moon to be seen was hanging from the wall of the inn at the end of the passageway. She was back at the place where she had first come to this world, but, she hoped, a few minutes earlier.

"Henshaw, are you there?" she called.

A figure emerged out of the shadows, taking form from nothing; a gentleman in long coat and breeches.

"My Lady. Welcome." He doffed his feathered-hat and bowed. The silver buckles on his shoes glinted despite the lack of light.

"You know who I am?" September said, "I wanted to meet you and this was the only place I could think of, but I haven't arrived yet have I?"

"No, my lady," Henshaw replaced his hat and smiled at her apparently unfazed by her comment, "and the answer to your first question is yes, September Weekes, I know who you are."

"You know what has happened?"

Henshaw nodded slightly. "You were, ah, will be, summoned to keep the Malevolence at bay. You have been successful. I congratulate you."

"I'm not sure if I have done what was needed. I seem to have tied knots in the timeline of this universe."

"Time can indeed be thought of as a piece of string which can be twisted into various loops and loose ends."

"But the world that the Malevolence entered and destroyed. That is gone?"

"Yes, September. The putti are destroyed, Soulbury himself did not summon a dragon, Aeddon's parents were not killed.

You have set the world on a different path. One in which Soulbury does not make Cold Fire. The former timeline in which the Malevolence came has withered and faded away. The evil's victory was short-lived."

"But what about the people and the unicorns and dragons I rescued?" September was worried that they too had disappeared.

"Ah, that is interesting. You have introduced a time loop into this universe's existence. The creatures you saved and took back in time, survived and became the ancestors of those that live in the present. Except for the unicorns of course. They do not age, or die except under exceptional circumstances."

"But if the future that I took them from no longer happens how do they get into the past?" September's head hurt with the paradoxes.

"The only answer to that my lady is that it was you. You were there, you are the thread that binds all these instants of time, these nows, together."

"That's how Adamant referred to time – nows."

"The unicorn is wise and knowledgeable."

"So, Adamant and Emerallt lived through all the thousands of years?"

"Yes, and had children of whom Rhuddem is one."

September remembered the unicorn that had not survived the Malevolence. She felt tears in her eyes. "Rhuddem who died saving us all."

"Many died, unicorn, dragons, people, other creatures, but the world survived thanks to you, September."

"But will they? I've learned that people kill the dragons, hunt the unicorns and even mermaids are captured so that scientists can dissect them."

"That may have been what you were told in that other time, but come with me. There are things that you should see." He held out his hands to her to take hold of. "There's no need to travel by cart this time," he added. They were surrounded by a tornado of violet light.

The whirling lights made her feel sick, which was strange considering the number of times she had moved in this fashion. Perhaps it was because this time they weren't moving to a place that she had visualised. September began to feel some sympathy for the people she had transported.

Henshaw held her in his arms as the lights faded and she regained her sense of balance. She looked around. They were in the shadows beneath branches in a field or park. The many trees surrounding them were hung with lanterns which illuminated the whole area.

"Where are we?" she asked.

"St James' Park. We've just moved across the city. It's the same time."

Here, with no buildings close by, the air was a little fresher. The sky was dark but filled with stars. September saw that they were not alone in the park. There were people strolling in ones and twos, some on horseback and in sedan chairs, and – she blinked and looked again, yes, her eyes had not deceived her – there was a unicorn surrounded by a group of people, adults and children. Some were stroking the white fur on its flanks while two or three rested their hands on the proud horn and the end of its broad snout.

"Is that really …?" September said, almost unbelieving.

"Yes," Henshaw replied, "That's Saffir, one of a pair of unicorns that live in London. I expect his mate, Opal, is around here somewhere."

"Unicorns in London?"

"You haven't seen it all yet. Come on."

They walked along a gravel path through the park. Many people seemed to be going in the same direction. Up ahead the lights were bigger, more numerous and brighter. September was eager to find out where Henshaw was taking her and where all these people were headed. She quickened their pace until they reached a junction with other paths where people were milling around, chatting to each other and buying sweet chestnuts and drinks from vendors. Henshaw didn't stop though. He led September on till they drew up behind a group of men. They were walking slowly because in the middle was a short, hunched figure with a walking stick who September recognised even from the rear. Henshaw and September caught up with the group. The small, bent man looked up and September's guess was confirmed.

"Ah, Henshaw, Good evening," Robert Hooke said. He

waved his stick ahead of him, "You are here for the entertainment?"

Henshaw bowed and nodded, "Indeed. Good evening Mr Hooke, Sir Robert, gentlemen."

September also recognised the taller figure of Sir Robert Boyle accompanying Hooke. She smiled and did a small curtsey.

"Who is this charming young woman?" Boyle asked.

"Er, my niece, Sir Robert. Down from the country for a few days," Henshaw replied, "I said I would bring her to the evening's events."

"Ah yes," Hooke said. "We shall not stay long. Boyle has promised to show me his sample of the Phosphorus that he has made, and darkness apparently contributes to the spectacle. But do not let my slow progress delay your enjoyment of the evening."

Henshaw bowed again, "It is a pleasure to see you gentlemen." He took September's arm and they continued along the path.

"Boyle's phosphorus is where the Cold Fire came from," September said, suddenly feeling worried that perhaps the Malevolence had not been defeated.

"Boyle's experimenting was not the problem," Henshaw replied, "It was Soulbury's interpretation of the recipe coupled with the proximity of the putti that allowed the Malevolence to enter the universe. That will not occur in this timeline since you destroyed the putti."

September felt a weight fall away from her and hurried alongside Henshaw, eager to see what had drawn the gentlemen of the Royal Society, along with the crowds, to this park at night. They had not gone much further when through the throng she could see that they were beside a lake. They stopped on the bank beside many other people.

"There," Henshaw said pointing out over the water. September looked. There was an island in the centre of the lake, a low flat island devoid of trees but what was standing there made her gasp. It was a dragon. It stood with its wings folded against its side and its head lifted up. As September watched it opened its beak and a blast of flame emerged, lighting up the whole lake and its surroundings.

In the light, September saw that there were people in boats on the water and amongst them were other creatures in the water. They were mermaids and mermen. They swam and dived and leapt into the air, the water streaming off their smooth dolphin-like tails. Both the men and the women were naked but had long hair that being wet draped over their chests. They appeared unconcerned by the cold air which had the humans wrapped in woollen coats. A few of the mercreatures rested with their arms on the sides of the boats talking to the people inside.

"Is this really happening?" September said, blinking to make sure that she was seeing clearly.

"Yes, and it's all thanks to you." Henshaw placed a friendly arm around her shoulder. "You see, by taking the people, unicorns and dragons back in time you made them live together or rather you made the humans familiar with the other creatures and at the very least tolerate their presence in the world. The timeline turned out a little different this time round."

"Oh, that's great." September felt a mixture of happiness and embarrassment that Henshaw and the Brains should think she had done so much. "I've hopped back and forth so much I almost forget which timeline I'm in. What is it like for people when their timeline changes?"

Henshaw waved his hands in dismissal. "You may find these time-jumps and different universes confusing but for people fixed in time and place they are meaningless. They have no experience of other timelines."

September nodded, understanding that she was unique in experiencing the different times. She looked around at the people and creatures enjoying the evening. "This one seems to have worked out peaceful and happy."

"It's not a complete utopia. You didn't achieve that impossibility. The humans are still burning too much wood and coal and spreading across all the lands in growing numbers. That's causing a certain amount of friction with dragons and other creatures as they compete for space. Of course, the Malevolence is still there in the beyond waiting to take advantage of any opportunity to destroy this and every other universe."

September sighed. "Hmm. I think someone said we can win the battles but the war will never be over."

Henshaw chortled. "That's the Omniverse for you. You could say that the struggle between the Brains, the Malevolence and the inhabitants of the universes is its reason for existence."

"I gather that means I'm not going to be left alone to get on with my life?" September looked at the crowds on the bank and on the lake, humans and merpeople, dragon and unicorn, and wondered what it would be like to be normal again without the worry of when and if the Malevolence was going to come and destroy it all.

"You're rather special September, and there are things for you to do."

September sighed again, a tired sigh, "I'd like to go home for a rest. Do you think you Brains will allow me to do that instead of sending me off to prevent another disaster?"

Henshaw chortled, "Of course. When we have need of you we can find you at any point in your timeline."

"That's what worries me. I can be plucked out of my life at any time or place." September had another look around the merry crowd

"But you can be returned to the moment you left," Henshaw said. "Come, let us find a spot, a little less exposed, for your departure."

He took September's arm again and lead her from the crowd around the lake into a small copse of trees. September looked at the Brain who masqueraded as a seventeenth century gentleman.

"This world is certainly a lot more different to my home than I thought."

"It certainly is."

"I suppose there are other Earths with other differences?"

"There are an uncountable number, my Lady, as well as innumerable other universes but every single one threatened by the Malevolence."

"Then it's a good job I can hop between times and you are not limited by time," September said not sure she felt as light-hearted as she sounded.

"Your assistance is greatly appreciated, September."

Henshaw bowed low.

She closed her eyes as the familiar lurch of Symudiad came over her.

She was falling, she reached out with her hand and grabbed cold porcelain. Her eyes opened. Her surroundings were familiar – the girls' loos at school. She rested both hands on the washbasin and looked in the mirror. She seemed no different – white hair, round face, fat body, although not as gross as she had once been. She felt exhausted but she didn't look any more tired than when she had come into the lavatory before she had been whisked away to 1680 London. She looked behind her. Neither Cyfaill or any other being was there.

She went into a cubicle and sat on the loo for a few minutes. The events of the past two days (was that all it was?) seemed like a blur, a vague half-forgotten memory. Breathing calmly, she recalled Gwawrwen, Aeddon, Adamant, Obsidian, Robert Boyle and the Lady of the Lake. She was pleased to have those memories of people and fantastic creatures. They were elsewhere and elsewhen. Other matters were of concern now. She was back in her own time now, it was her own life she had to take charge of. She stepped out of the cubicle and took one more look in the mirror, just checking that she was simply September Weekes, schoolgirl. Then she pulled the door open and walked back along the corridor to the row of seats outside the deputy head's office.

Her mother looked up. "At last, September. You were such a long time I was wondering if you were alright. You don't feel ill do you?"

September smiled and sat down beside her. "No mother. I'm fine."

Epilogue

I had a dream

I had a dream last night. I dreamed that my Master, Ezekiel, had made Cold Fire and that his servants, the putti had become demons. I awoke all of a sweat fearing that my dream was true and that I was the boy again who had experienced such happenings. So much time has passed now that that memory has become like a dream where the sequence of events become confused and details are vague and inconsistent. Yet, I know they were true and that we were brought here by the sorceress September and yes, I know that those events that recurred in my dream, though they lie in my past are in fact from the future, a future which September assured us would no longer happen. My head aches with the mere thought of it.

It is a future that will occur long after my lifetime. I near the end of my time on Earth and will follow most of the people who came here with me into death's rest soon. The future and this world belong to our sons and daughters now, and indeed the young dragons and unicorns and merpeople that we share this land and seas with.

I am content because I have ended the work I have spent my life on, my great encyclopaedia of the knowledge possessed by humans, unicorns, dragons and mercreatures. Perhaps such a work is never fully finished as there is always new knowledge to add, but I am tired and have no desire to do so myself. Now I hope that my descendants will read it and extend it as they see fit. Perhaps one day soon we will have iron in sufficient quantity and quality to build a printing machine, though I fear one of our children will have to reinvent that apparatus since neither I nor Meilyr or any other of our companions had that skill.

I will just go and rest on the bank of the estuary and gaze out to sea or at the mountains, which ever takes my fancy.

Perhaps some of the villagers of Llanllionio Newydd will come and chat, perhaps a mermaid or merman will rise from the waters to converse, or I may hope that a unicorn will come down from the peaks or a dragon emerge from the clouds to pass the time of day.

Perhaps I will doze and dream of September, the twin in appearance of Gwawrwen, and I will awaken happy but still confused as to who or what she was, or is. She told me not to write about Cold Fire and I have not, although it still troubles my sleep. I have warned of the dangers of dabbling in the powers beyond our world, the putti being a manifestation of that evil. None of us who came from the future have ever mentioned the source of the evil or the part played by Ezekiel to the children. I hope that will keep their descendants safe in the time to come and that the Malevolence shall never enter the world.

The End

Historical Note

In our universe, it really was in 1680 that phosphorus and its strange properties were revealed to the world. Phosphorus had been discovered by a secretive alchemist, Hennig Brandt, in Hamburg around 1669. The news reached Sir Robert Boyle in London and with his assistant, Ambrose Godfrey, he set about making it – from urine supplied by his, or rather his sister's, household in Pall Mall. He reported on phosphorus in the *Philosophical Transactions of the Royal Society of London* and demonstrated its light-giving properties to guests although possibly not on the scale that September witnessed. Godfrey actually went into business preparing phosphorus for sale to other interested chemists using the resources of the capital's population. It was some time before other sources of the element were discovered. Other experimenters tried to copy Boyle's method but, like Ezekiel Soulbury, were not always successful. They suspected Boyle had a secret ingredient or method, but he didn't.

Robert Hooke was the leading member of the Royal Society in 1680 and prepared demonstrations for the regular meetings of the fellows at Gresham College. As well as his scientific work, he was a partner of Sir Christopher Wren in the rebuilding of London following the Great Fire of 1666. The other gentlemen mentioned, except for Thomas Maslyn, are historical figures and were Fellows of the Royal Society. Edward Tyson did indeed write about his dissection of a porpoise in the *Transactions* showing that it was more like a land mammal than a fish.

The map that September used to get to Myddfai is in the collection of maps, *The Theatre of the Empire of Great Britain* by John Speed, which is still in print. The Physicians of Myddfai were famous in Wales until the eighteenth century for their healing remedies using plants. They claimed to be descendants of the first physicians who were the sons of the farmer and the Lady of the Lake. A gravestone in

Myddfai church records David Jones, surgeon, as one of the last physicians. Myddfai is in Carmarthenshire, just a few miles from the LLyn y Fan Fach, from which the lady of the lake emerged to marry the young farmer although the legend does not suggest she was a shape-changing mermaid.

Abaty Maesycymer is based on Cymer Abbey near Dolgellau in north-west Wales but Llanllionio is a fictional village although there would have been places like it in the seventeenth century. Cwm Dreigiau, The Valley of Dragons and home of the unicorns doesn't exist and neither, sadly, do the dragons or unicorns – at least not in our universe.

Sources

The Shocking History of Phosphorus,
John Emsley pub. Macmillan 2000

Britain's Tudor Maps County by County,
John Speed pub. Batsford 1988

Welsh Herbal Medicine,
David Hoffmann pub. Abercastle Publications 1978

Philosophical Transactions of the Royal Society,
available on-line at
http://rstl.royalsocietypublishing.org/content/by/year

Myddfai Community Hall and Visitor Centre
http://www.myddfai.org/the-physicians-of-myddfai/

Acknowledgements

As usual the publication of a new novel is the work of more than one person. I would like to thank Peter of Elsewhen Press for making the decision to publish and doing all the work of preparing the manuscript for publication that I don't understand at all. I would also like to express my thanks and wonder to Alison for the stunning cover. Bryony did a marvellous job of copyediting, correcting my grammatical and typing errors and sorting out the, thankfully fairly minor, plot-holes and continuity errors. Also thanks to Sofia for the proofreading. Finally, I have to thank my wife, Alison, for encouraging me to keep writing and for all her support.

The inspiration for any story comes from a variety of sources. In this case the initial idea arose from seeing an old painting in an exhibition at the Museum of the History of Science in Oxford. It showed an alchemist in his laboratory with putti flying around him. The Museum has an amazing collection of artefacts including Robert Hooke's original microscopes, astrolabes, pocket sundials, and enough brass instruments to keep any steam-punk fan happy. I commend the Museum to readers and thank the curators and volunteers for their efforts. I also want to thank the volunteers at Myddfai Community Centre for their assistance during and after a visit. I also need to thank the authors of the books in my list of sources for helping me build the background to the story.

Lastly, I thank you the reader for getting this far. I hope you enjoyed the story.

Peter R Ellis

Elsewhen Press
an independent publisher specialising in Speculative Fiction

Visit the Elsewhen Press website at elsewhen.co.uk for the latest information on all of our titles, authors and events; to read our blog; find out where to buy our books and ebooks; or to place an order.

Sign up for the Elsewhen Press InFlight Newsletter at elsewhen.co.uk/newsletter

Evil Above the Stars by Peter R. Ellis

Peter R. Ellis' thrilling fantasy series, *Evil Above the Stars*, appeals to fantasy and science fiction readers of all ages, especially fans of JRR Tolkien and Stephen Donaldson. Were the ideas embodied in alchemy ever right? What realities were the basis of Celtic mythology? Visit bit.ly/EvilAbove

Volume 1: Seventh Child

September Weekes discovers a stone that takes her to *Gwlad*, where she is hailed as the one with the power to defend them against the evil known as the Malevolence. September meets the leader and bearers of metals linked to the seven 'planets' that give them special powers to resist the elemental manifestations of the Malevolence. She returns home, but a fortnight later, is drawn back to find that two years have passed and there have been more attacks. She must help defend *Gwlad* against the Malevolence.

ISBN: 9781908168702 (epub, kindle) / ISBN: 9781908168603 (256pp paperback)

Volume 2: The Power of Seven

September with the Council of *Gwlad* must plan the defence of the Land. The time of the next Conjunction will soon be at hand. The planets, the Sun and the Moon will all be together in the sky. At that point the protection of the heavenly bodies will be at its weakest and *Gwlad* will be more dependent than ever on September. But now it seems that she must defeat Malice, the guiding force behind the Malevolence, if she is to save the Land and all its people. Will she be strong enough; and, if not, to whom can she turn for help?

ISBN: 9781908168719 (epub, kindle) / ISBN: 9781908168610 (288pp paperback)

Volume 3: Unity of Seven

September is back home and it is still the night of her birthday, despite having spent over three months in *Gwlad* battling the Malevolence. Back to facing the bullies at school she worries about the people of *Gwlad*. She must discover a way to return to the universe of *Gwlad* and the answer seems to lie in her family history. The five *Cludydds* before September and her mother were her ancestors. The clues take her on a journey in time and space which reveals that while in great danger she is also the key to the survival of all the universes. September must overcome her own fears, accept an extraordinary future and, once again, face the evil above the stars.

ISBN: 9781908168917 (epub, kindle) / ISBN: 9781908168818 (256pp paperback)

And now, September Weekes returns...

Cold Fire

September thought she was getting used to transporting, but this time it was different. As far as she could tell, her appearance hadn't changed, she was still even wearing her school uniform. But in a London of 1680, others saw her as a lady of considerable social standing. She had been brought here to stop something happening that would give the Malevolence an opportunity to enter the universe. But she didn't know what. Her first stop would be a tavern, to meet Robert Hooke, and then off to see Sir Robert Boyle demonstrate to the Royal Society the results of his investigations of the phosphorus and its cold fire.

ISBN: 9781911409168 (epub, kindle) / ISBN: 9781911409069 (256pp paperback)

Existence is
Elsewhen
Twenty stories from twenty great authors
including
John Gribbin
Peter R. Ellis
Rhys Hughes
Christopher Nuttall
Douglas Thompson

The title *Existence is Elsewhen* paraphrases the last sentence of André Breton's 1924 *Manifesto of Surrealism*, perfectly summing up the intent behind this anthology of stories from a wonderful collection of authors. Different worlds... different times. It's what Elsewhen Press has been about since we launched our first title in 2011.

Here, we present twenty science fiction stories for you to enjoy. We are delighted that headlining this collection is the fantastic **John Gribbin,** with a worrying vision of medical research in the near future. Future global healthcare is the theme of **J A Christy's** story; while the ultimate in spare part surgery is where **Dave Weaver** takes us. **Edwin Hayward's** search for a renewable protein source turns out to be digital; and **Tanya Reimer's** story with characters we think we know gives us pause for thought about another food we take for granted. Evolution is examined too, with **Andy McKell's** chilling tale of what states could become if genetics are used to drive policy. Similarly, **Robin Moran's** story explores the societal impact of an undesirable evolutionary trend; while **Douglas Thompson** provides a truly surreal warning of an impending disaster that will reverse evolution, with dire consequences.

On a lighter note, we have satire from **Steve Harrison** discovering who really owns the Earth (and why); and **Ira Nayman,** who uses the surreal alternative realities of his *Transdimensional Authority* series as the setting for a detective story mash-up of Agatha Christie and Dashiel Hammett. Pursuing the crime-solving theme, **Peter Wolfe** explores life, and death, on a space station; while **Stefan Jackson** follows a police investigation into some bizarre cold-blooded murders in a cyberpunk future. Going into the past, albeit an 1831 set in the alternate Britain of his *Royal Sorceress* series, **Christopher Nuttall** reports on an investigation into a girl with strange powers.

Strange powers in the present-day is the theme for **Tej Turner,** who tells a poignant tale of how extra-sensory perception makes it easier for a husband to bear his dying wife's last few days. Difficult decisions are the theme of **Chloe Skye's** heart-rending story exploring personal sacrifice. Relationships aren't always so close, as **Susan Oke's** tale demonstrates, when sibling rivalry is taken to the limit. Relationships are the backdrop to **Peter R. Ellis's** story where a spectacular mid-winter event on a newly- colonised distant planet involves a Madonna and Child. Coming right back to Earth and in what feels like an almost imminent future, **Siobhan McVeigh** tells a cautionary tale for anyone thinking of using technology to deflect the blame for their actions. Building on the remarkable setting of Pera from her *LiGa* series, and developing Pera's legendary *Book of Shadow*, **Sanem Ozdural** spins the creation myth of the first light tree in a lyrical and poetic song. Also exploring language, the master of fantastika and absurdism, **Rhys Hughes,** extrapolates the way in which language changes over time, with an entertaining result.

ISBN: 9781908168955 (epub, kindle) / ISBN: 9781908168856 (320pp paperback)
Visit bit.ly/ExistenceIsElsewhen

THE SYMPHONY OF THE CURSED TRILOGY
REBECCA HALL
INSTRUMENT OF PEACE

Raised in the world-leading Academy of magic rather than by his absentee parents, Mitch has come to see it as his home. He's spent more time with his friends than his family and the opinion of his maths teacher matters far more than that of his parents. His peaceful life is shattered when a devastating earthquake strikes and almost claims his little brother's life. But this earthquake is no natural phenomenon, it's a result of the ongoing war between Heaven and Hell. To protect the Academy, one of the teachers makes an ill-advised contract with a fallen angel, unwittingly bringing down The Twisted Curse on staff and students.

Even as they struggle to rebuild the school, things begin to go wrong. The curse starts small, with truancy, incomplete assignments, and negligent teachers over-reacting to minor transgressions, but it isn't long before the bad behaviour escalates to vandalism, rioting and attempted murder. As they succumb to the influence of the curse, Mitch's friends drift away and his girlfriend cheats on him. When the first death comes, Mitch unites with the only other students who, like him, appear to be immune to the curse; together they are determined to find the cause of the problem and stop it.

INSTRUMENT OF WAR

The Angels are coming.

The Host wants to know what the Academy was trying to hide and why the Fallen agreed to it. They want the Instrument of War, the one thing that can tip the Eternity War in their favour and put an end to the stalemate. Any impact on the Academy staff, students or buildings is just collateral damage.

Mitch would like to forget that the last year ever happened, but that doesn't seem likely with Little Red Riding Hood now teaching Teratology. The vampire isn't quite as terrifying as he first thought, but she's not the only monster at the Academy. The Fallen are spying on everyone, the new Principal is an angel and there's an enchanting exchange student with Faerie blood.

Angry and nervous of the angels surrounding him, Mitch tries to put the pieces together. He knows that Hayley is the Archangel Gabriel. He knows that she can determine the course of the Eternity War. He also knows that the Fallen will do anything to hide Gabriel from the Host – even allowing an innocent girl to be kidnapped.

INSTRUMENT OF CHAOS

The long hidden heart of the Twisted Curse had been found, concealed in a realm that no angel can enter, where magic runs wild and time is just another direction. The Twisted Curse is the key to ending the Eternity War and it can only be broken by someone willing to traverse the depths of Faerie.

Unfortunately, Mitch has other things on his mind. For reasons that currently escape him he's going to university, making regular trips to the Netherworld and hunting down a demon. The Academy might have prepared him for university but Netherworlds and demons were inexplicably left off the curriculum, not to mention curse breaking.

And then the Angels return, and this time they're hunting his best friend.

Visit bit.ly/SymphonyCursed

About the author

Peter R. Ellis would like to say he's been a writer all his life but it is only since retiring as a teacher in 2010 that he has been able to devote enough time to writing to call it a career. Brought up in Cardiff, he studied Chemical Physics at the University of Kent at Canterbury, then taught chemistry (and a bit of physics) in Norwich, the Isle of Wight and Thames Valley. His first experience of publishing was in writing educational materials, which he has continued to do since retiring. Of his fictional writing, *Evil Above the Stars* was his first published speculative fiction series, in which we were introduced to September Weekes.

Peter has been a fan of science fiction and fantasy since he was young, has an (almost) complete collection of classic SF by Asimov, Ballard, Clarke, Heinlein and Niven, among others, while also enjoying fantasy by Tolkien, Donaldson and Ursula Le Guin. Of more recent authors Iain M Banks, Alastair Reynolds and China Mieville have his greatest respect. His Welsh upbringing also engendered a love of the language (even though he can't speak it) and of Welsh mythology like the *Mabinogion*. All these strands come together in the *Evil Above the Stars* series and now *the September Weekes novels*. He lives in Herefordshire with his wife, Alison, who is a great supporter.